SWEET TOOTH

HELEN JULIET

Sweet Tooth

1

—————

HANS

"I'm going to be sick," Hans Jager bellowed over the howling wind.

The thing about twin sisters in Hans's experience, however, was that typically they laughed when you said stuff like that.

In fact, Greta cackled. There was definitely glee there. Hans could tell, even at a hundred miles an hour. Dastardly glee.

"What was that?" she yelled through her helmet's visor. She revved the engine of her Suzuki Bandit as Hans held on to her waist for dear life. "Go faster?"

Hans shut his mouth for fear of antagonising her any more as the motorbike picked up speed. Daylight was fading rapidly away as they raced further and further from London. The winter sun was slipping behind the fog-soaked pine trees that lined the edges of the motorway. If the roar of the engine hadn't been so loud, Hans would have sworn he'd heard a wolf baying.

"Get a fucking grip," he grumbled to himself.

But try as he might, he'd never been a daredevil like his

sister. He was more the big, teddy bear type rather than the 'let's jump off this mountain for fun' type. Honestly, if they hadn't been born within minutes of each other, Hans might have questioned they were related at all.

"Greta," he said in a warning tone. "I'd like to get home in one piece."

"Liar," she shot back tonelessly. "You don't want to go home at all."

There was no arguing with that.

Hans sighed, resting his head on his crazy sister's shoulder, allowing her to hurtle them along the M4 towards the town of Gingerbread in Gloucestershire for the first time in ten years.

Merry fucking Christmas.

The thing was – the thing that Hans resented most in that very moment – was that he actually adored Christmas. It was magical, and he wasn't afraid to admit that to anyone. People just seemed *nicer* at Christmas. They remembered you existed. Sometimes there were presents. There were always loads of parties to drop in on, so he never felt lonely. And no matter how long it was since you'd seen one another, Christmas was always the time to pick up exactly where you'd left off, no hard feelings.

Unless you happened to be going back to Gingerbread. In which case, there would be no picking up of anything of the sort and plenty of hard feelings, Hans was certain.

Nothing good came from his home town. Well…maybe one thing.

One person.

Hans didn't want to think about that now, though. He ground his teeth as the two of them pelted down the motorway past snow-coated fields. Flocks of sheep were dotted around, protected from the cold by their thick, woolly coats. It was such a familiar vista, and yet Hans deliberately hadn't seen livestock in person since he'd moved to London. The sight gave him a rush of familiarity yet strangeness. Painful nostalgia. He assumed it would be the first of many times he'd feel that way over the next twenty-four hours.

For the hundredth time, he asked himself *why* he'd agreed to set foot back in this awful place. He was only going to get hurt, Greta was only going to get angry, and nothing would ever change.

But…something *had* changed. Their father had begged his children to come home for the first time in a decade. It was the first communication outside of generic Christmas and birthday cards they'd heard from him in years. It was enough of a Christmas miracle that Hans had agreed to get on his sister's bloody bike and risk his life to go see their old man.

After all, it seemed like this might be the last chance they'd ever get to visit him.

Hans shook his head. They didn't know anything until they talked more with their dad. He'd been very vague with the details of his medical condition, other than it would be a good idea to meet up. That didn't exactly sound like good news, but until they knew anything for sure, there wasn't much point in speculating.

Hans could only hope that as they had been willingly invited back home, their step-mother would actually *allow* Hans and Greta to see their dad and speak to him properly. Part of him dared to hope that if they were ever going to reconnect with their dad, there was no better time than the season of goodwill.

Mercifully, Greta took the turn-off from the motorway, and soon A-roads were giving way to winding country lanes, forcing her to slow down and save the contents of Hans's stomach. He breathed deeply as the cold air whipped past them, blinking as he took in a vista that was looking more and more like he remembered from his youth.

There was no denying that the Cotswolds was one of the most beautiful places in the whole of the United Kingdom. Stretching across six counties, it was a unique part of the country, made up of picturesque tiny villages, rushing streams and rivers, and hills upon hills that gave it its unmistakable landscape. As apprehensive as Hans was to be coming back after all this time, he couldn't deny the way his heart panged from the beauty.

There was nothing like coming home. The only thing that could have made it better was if he could believe that he and Greta were actually *wanted* here.

"Stop it," Greta called over her shoulder.

They passed by a country pub that was covered in strings of multicoloured Christmas lights. Hans imagined the people inside all wearing festive jumpers, drinking mulled wine, and swapping Secret Santa presents. It was a few weeks until Christmas, but the holiday parties were already in full swing. He wished he could lose himself in that kind of crowd in that moment.

"Stop what?" he asked with a frown she couldn't see.

She shrugged rather than turning around to look at him, which Hans appreciated. They might have been going slower, but she was still taking all the twists and turns at a hell of a lick.

"Stop worrying," his sister said. "You can't control what that woman is going to do any more than when we were kids. You can't stop anyone else in the village from thinking what they will about us, either. So just go with the flow and be grateful she's letting us see Dad at all."

Rage simmered inside Hans. Usually, he considered himself a pretty mellow bloke. But certain things he couldn't forgive or forget. However, if he wanted this visit to go well, he'd at least have to try and pretend to be civil towards Miriam. For the sake of his dad.

"Aren't you anxious about going back?" Hans asked.

Greta shrugged again. "After all this time, we're not going to know anyone besides Dad and that woman. Why care?"

Hans seriously doubted that. Gingerbread was a small village, and a lot of people lived their whole lives there. He and Greta might not recognise anyone after all this time away in London, but everyone else was bound to remember them, especially when they realised the twins were the mayor's children, returned home after a decade away.

After what they'd done.

Hans pushed that thought down. It was in the past. But as they drew closer to the town, it felt like the pain was growing stronger, feeling fresher. Like they were travelling back in time to his darkest days.

But that also meant they were also getting closer back to his brightest light. The one person who had been there for him other than his sister when their whole world had fallen apart.

Dorchester Wild.

Hans bit his lip. Was Chester even still living in Gingerbread? Once upon a time, he and Hans had been inseparable. It was crazy to think that it had now been years since they'd texted. A lump rose in his throat. This weekend wasn't about his former best friend, but it was impossible to come back home and not think of the boy he'd left behind.

He inhaled deeply. He could take the sideways glances from anyone else. He could take his step-mother's fake smiles and sly jabs. He could even take his father's withdrawn indifference. But maybe it would be best if he didn't see Chester. Hans wasn't sure he could look him in the eyes after Hans had pulled away so unfairly, seemingly without cause.

He wished he could take the last ten years back and do it all again.

But that wasn't possible. He needed to focus on the here and now and just get through what was bound to be a difficult and awkward evening. Hans chewed his cold lip as they neared the small bridge that crossed over the babbling River Hesse, signalling that they'd officially entered the village. There was no turning back now, so he'd just have to suck it up and play nice. All that mattered was seeing their dad.

Gingerbread was so small it took no time at all to reach what passed for the high street in the sleepy little village. Like all of the Cotswolds, the houses were notable for their golden-coloured stone and angular grey-slate or thatched roofs.

But on the street where most of the shops and services were located, the line of stone properties was mixed in with a few crooked black-and-white Tudor styles, some places with smooth white walls and brown tiled roofs, and the bank that was three stories high and painted cream with a bold red flat-roof. It was truly a hodgepodge, but the only thing that was missing was any kind of modern chain businesses. Everything was independently owned, and some buildings like The Jewel and The Swan pub had stood for hundreds of years.

As expected, Hans was hit with a wave of sad nostalgia. As the dark afternoon slipped into evening, the gently falling snow was illuminated by the glow of bright, cheerful Christmas lights lining the whole street. Greta pulled her bike to the side, parking it cheekily between a car and a shiny red post box.

Hans grunted and rolled his shoulders as she killed the engine and kicked the bike stand down. Several people with hands full of shopping bags had turned to look at them, probably not used to the guttural roar of the Suzuki Bandit in their sleepy little village. Hans gave a few people sheepish nods and smiles before he remembered he still had his bloody helmet on. By the time he'd wrestled it off and tried to calm his hair back down, the people had moved on with whatever they were doing.

"Nothing's really changed," Greta mused.

Of course when she'd taken her helmet off, her cropped blonde hair looked perfect. No one was going to mistake her for a shaggy beast, unlike Hans. He sighed, giving up on trying to smarten himself up, and handed her his helmet to secure in the bike's lockbox.

"Nope," he admitted as the snow continued to gently fall.

It was all pretty much the same as he remembered from his youth, like the high street had just been waiting for them to come back. A blast of a classic seventies' Christmas song rang out as someone exited the second-hand bookshop, which was as packed to the rafters with haphazardly stacked volumes as it always had been. The pharmacist was advertising cold and flu remedies as well as fragrances and make-up as the 'Perfect gift for Mum!'. Gingerbread didn't have a supermarket. Instead, people were shopping at the butcher's, baker's, and greengrocer's for all their holiday food. Hans wondered if dear old Nancy still remembered everyone's name who came into the haberdashery, and asked how their mother or son or cat was.

Okay. Maybe Gingerbread wasn't the *worst* place in the world. Hans sighed and rubbed the back of his neck as it cracked. He'd spent so long hating the memory of his hometown that he'd honestly forgotten how sweet and kind and charming it was. But he wasn't sure if that brought him comfort or melancholy.

Either way, he was ripped from his thoughts quite dramatically.

No one said anything. No one shouted or screamed as the

little boy ran as fast as his short legs could carry him, sprinting past Hans and straight into the road.

The driver of the approaching car didn't even get time to blast its horn as they slammed on the brakes. Hans was moving before he even thought, dashing into the street and scooping up the boy in his arms as he turned, squeezing his eyes shut and bracing for the impact of the car bumper.

It never came.

But that was when people finally started shouting.

"Jeremy!" a frantic woman's voice screamed as Hans prised his eyelids open. His heart was slamming into his chest as he first saw that the old Volkswagen Polo had stopped mere inches from the backs of his thighs. Then he spied the woman running from the pavement, her hair streaming out from under her bobble hat as she flung her arms out, sobbing as she grabbed the child back from Hans. "Thank you, oh, thank you!" she gasped as she trembled, her face wet with tears.

"Mummy!" the boy, Jeremy, cried happily, clapping his hands. "Big man! White car!" He sounded very pleased with himself.

"You saved him," said the woman, choked with emotion. "I can't thank you enough. You...you *angel.*"

Hans shifted uncomfortably as he realised the young man driving the car had got out to see if everyone was okay. It seemed like anyone who'd been on the street was gawking at them, and people were even leaning out of shop doors to see what was going on.

So much for not getting noticed.

"S'okay," Hans mumbled in embarrassment. "Anyone would have done the same."

The woman took a shuddery breath and shook her head. "No one else even *saw.* Thank you. Merry Christmas. Seriously – you're an angel!" She blinked at him, then frowned. "Oh...my goodness. Are you Hans Jager? The mayor's son?"

Bollocks.

"Uh, yeah," Hans grunted, hoping not too many people could overhear.

The woman in the bobble hat bounced young Jeremy on her hip and nodded. "I was a few years ahead of you at school. I...I'm sorry about everything that happened."

Hans's throat tightened. He'd expected a dirty look, not kindness, and he wasn't quite sure what to do with himself. "T-thanks," he stuttered.

The driver shook his head as he came and joined them. "I was fiddling with my phone," he said to the woman. "I'm so sorry. Are you sure everyone's okay?"

If this had been London, there would have been people blasting their horns and yelling out of their windows by now. As it was, the couple of cars behind the guy's parked one were just sat waiting patiently. But that did mean that more and more people were looking at the driver, the woman, and Hans, and he wasn't keen on anyone else recognising him right then. He took his chance to nod at the woman and back away.

"Merry Christmas," he told her.

She paused in talking to the driver to smile at him again. "Merry Christmas, happy holidays," she said breathlessly.

The little lad waved enthusiastically at Hans as he managed to shuffle back out of the road.

Some people continued walking or went back inside, but others stared openly as Hans went back to Greta. She was leaning against her bike and began to slow clap as he approached.

"You bloody hero, you," she marvelled. "I can't take you anywhere, can I?"

He sighed and ran his hand through his shaggy hair,

brushing away some of the snow that had landed there, and hoping it had calmed down a little from the helmet. A few people were still looking at him from afar, whispering to each other. They were probably wondering who the stranger was, or maybe trying to place where they knew him from. Standing with Greta probably gave them a better chance of recognising the twins, but Hans couldn't really control that. Hans had to say if any of them remembered him, he hadn't recognised a single one of them so far.

He smiled weakly at a few of them, noticing the bobble hat woman taking the runaway boy back across to the safety of the pavement to meet a cross-looking man and an older girl. The man snarled something, making Hans wince, even though he couldn't hear the particular words.

"Come on," said Greta, slapping Hans's shoulder and snapping him back to his senses. "We need to get to the square. It's almost four thirty already, and I'd rather get there early than late. That woman doesn't need any excuses to roll her eyes at us."

Hans exhaled, ready to agree, but then his gaze landed on something that blew all his other nostalgia out of the window. He couldn't believe he'd missed it until now, but in fairness, the whole parade of shops was covered in so many lights and glittering garlands it was perhaps understandable that he'd missed the enticing shop facade until now.

He waggled his eyebrows at Greta, then jutted his chin at where he was looking. "Fancy buying me some hero fudge, sis?"

She frowned and turned to follow his gaze, then gave an exasperated laugh. "You and your sweet tooth. *Okay.* But only because you literally just saved a child's life. Otherwise, you can buy your own tooth-rotting treats.

Hans grinned and bumped shoulders with her as they began to walk to the Candy Cauldron, Gingerbread's old-fashioned-looking sweet shop. The owner was an old crone who had scared the shit out of Hans and Greta as kids, but when they were teenagers it had become his favourite place to loiter. Not Greta's, however. She'd grown out of sweets. That was okay, though. Hans had been lucky to have someone else special to spend their pocket money with on mint humbugs, toffees, and liquorice.

He bit the inside of his cheek and tried to push the thought away. That was a long time ago, but the ache in Hans's heart felt as strong as ever. Chester Wild was in the past, like everything else in this village, and it would only hurt to dwell on it or him any more than he had to.

He shook his head as he practically skipped up to the front door, the golden light glowing warmly from within. The place was packed, unsurprisingly, but behind the customers Hans could see row upon row of glass jars filled with every coloured sweet he could think of. As he opened the door, a bell tinkled above his head, and it was as if he'd never left. Right away, he was accosted with the overpowering rush of sugar in the air. Tangy orange and sharp peppermint mixed with sweet chocolate and creamy vanilla.

"In or out!" a croaky voice snapped from somewhere behind the dozen or so shoppers packed into the small place. "You're letting in all the cold air!"

Greta tutted as she and Hans stepped inside, Hans guiltily shutting the door behind them. "Sorry," he called out as a few people glanced their way.

Sodding hell. He'd only been back in town for ten minutes, and it seemed he couldn't go anywhere without people gawping at him. It was only going to get worse once more people realised who he and his sister were. Most of them probably weren't going to be as understanding as the woman with the bobble hat.

"It's okay," someone whispered conspiratorially as they eased past a few customers. "Don't worry about it. Welcome to the Candy Cauldron! How might I help…"

The man's words died in his throat as he came face-to-face with Hans. He was slim and wearing a chunky-knit taupe cardigan, with dark hair escaping out from the front of a floppy white beanie hat. But it was his startling blue eyes that seized Hans's attention the most.

He'd know those eyes anywhere.

"Hans Jager?" the man asked in disbelief.

So much for Hans not dwelling on the past.

It was standing right in front of him.

2

CHESTER

"Chester Wild?" Hans sputtered as Chester continued to stare at him. "Is that really you?"

Chester finally shook himself and snapped out of his reverie. In a flash, he'd fallen back in time ten years. His heartbeat had sped up, his mouth was dry, and his palms were damp, all after barely two seconds of being back in the presence of the boy he'd been desperately in love with at school.

Well, Hans Jager wasn't a boy anymore. He was a man – one *hell* of a man. That chubby boy had grown into a broad man with a strong, square jaw covered in a short, brown beard. The hair atop his hair was dirty blond and kind of shaggy, but upon clocking the bike leathers, Chester assumed he'd just been wearing a safety helmet.

How did someone so big and rugged also manage to look so adorable? Chester shouldn't really marvel, though. This was Hans. He'd always been Chester's lovable teddy bear.

Until he hadn't been.

They both stood in the middle of the shop, staring at each other as customers moved around them. Nerves and fear warred within Chester against his natural instinct to see Hans again after all this time, which was excitement. But Hans had left Chester behind a long time ago.

Hadn't he?

"Yeah, it's me," said Hans, blinking and shaking his head. "I'm sorry. I should have texted, I just…" He shook his head again and dropped his gaze. "It's been so long. I'm sorry."

Chester couldn't bear to see Hans sad. He never could. Besides, over the years he'd convinced himself that it was for the best that his straight best friend had moved on. Would it really have been better to keep in contact and for Chester to suffer in silence, being tortured every day with loving someone he couldn't have? Hans had never known of Chester's feelings, after all.

So he rallied himself. "Hey, it's okay," he said as he touched Hans's arm, feeling the cold leather of the jacket sleeve. But even that brief contact sent an immediate rush of heat through Chester, not helped by the central heating that Ethel always kept cranked up, despite the risk to the produce melting. Chester smiled and tried not to let his embarrassment show. "You're here now! What a great surprise."

Hans rubbed the back of his neck and met Chester's gaze again with a shy smile. "It's great to see you," he said softly. Chester's heart flipped in his chest.

Before he could get too carried away, he suddenly noticed a blonde woman beside Hans, largely because she shoved her hand in front of his face. "Hi, I'm Greta. I am also here." She arched an eyebrow at him, a smile playing on her lips.

"Oh, of course," Chester spluttered, shaking the proffered hand. "Hans's twin sister, I remember. Wow. You're both here. In the shop where I work. This is…very unexpected." He was babbling, but he couldn't seem to help it. It was like he was afraid that Hans was going to vanish before his eyes again, and chattering nonsense might somehow keep him from leaving.

Hans raised his eyebrows as Chester let Greta's hand go. "You got a job here?" Hans asked, sounding delighted. "Oh, yeah, of course. You asked if you could help us when we walked in."

He shook his head and seemed to be babbling as well. Maybe it was guilt at having not spoken to Chester in years? It couldn't be the same reason Chester was flustered, after all.

"Greta," Hans continued, "do you remember how Chester and I used to practically live in this place? We'd load up on sweets, then go hang out in the woods, or get the bus to Gloucester to go to the cinema."

Greta gave her brother a strange look, then laughed, but not unkindly. "Yes, Hans. I remember your best friend," she said like he was a dummy. "Just because I spent my pocket money on things other than sweets didn't mean I wasn't paying attention to what you got up to." She winked at Chester. "Nice to see you again," she said with genuine affection. Then she nodded at her brother. "You two catch up. I'm going to look at the shiny things and pretend I eat sugar for five minutes."

Hans looked kind of panicked as she left them facing one another. The shop was pretty busy, and they had to move as some customers left, but Chester couldn't help but feel like it was only him and Hans in the whole shop.

It hadn't been a dramatic split that had pulled them apart. That might have been a cleaner break. It was more like as soon as Hans had finished school, he'd left home with Greta for London with no real reason that Chester could understand, and the relationship had begun to crumble.

Which didn't make all that much sense, as Hans had spent the previous three years away at a fancy boarding school that his step-mum had shipped the twins off to, and the two boys hadn't lost touch. They'd texted daily and spent every minute of the holidays together that they could when Hans had returned. Naïvely, Chester had assumed that the closeness they'd had would survive Hans's moving to the city. But it had dwindled to the point where they'd last swapped text messages a few Christmases ago, and that had been it. Nothing.

Until now.

"So, uh," said Chester, trying to keep his spirits up. He was happy to see Hans. He *was.* It was just wholly unexpected, and his heart was having a tough time not falling immediately in love with him again. "How have you been?" Hans wasn't on any social media, either, so Chester really had no idea.

Hans nodded like he was eager for the conversation opening. "Yeah, okay," he said. As soon as he smiled, it was like warm sunshine breaking through wintery clouds. "Not really up to much. I...okay."

He sighed and shook his head at Chester. Chester's stomach dropped. Was Hans going to tell him why he ghosted him? Why he'd left and never come back?

Except the look in Hans's eyes was pleading, and Chester felt his heart melting.

"I feel like a right prat for not messaging you to let you know I was coming," Hans continued. "It was all last minute, and I wasn't sure if you'd even want to see me. I've been a rubbish friend, I know. But...I've missed you. I'm so happy we ran into each other."

Chester bit his lip, feeling all the oxygen rush from his lungs.

He just means as friends.

This was why it had become so difficult as they'd grown older. Hans had absolutely seen Chester as his friend. His best friend, sure, but still just a friend, nonetheless. As they'd drifted apart and their texts had become less frequent, Chester had figured it had probably been for the best at the time, lest his straight best friend realised that Chester had an embarrassingly massive crush on him. Chester had tried to convince himself that all these years apart had dimmed his feelings.

Apparently, he was very, very wrong.

He swallowed and did his best to smile despite his dry mouth. He knew he was supposed to be working, and he was going to get yelled at any second now, but his heart was hammering in his chest, and his tongue felt numb. He was scared of saying the wrong thing. But after years of saying nothing, could anything be really worse than that?

"You're not a rubbish friend," he assured Hans, this time reaching out and giving the briefest of touches to his bare hand. Electricity sparked through him at the skin-to-skin contact, and he tried not to visibly shiver. "But thank you for the apology anyway. I'm glad we still ran into each other regardless. It must be fate."

He hummed a little to show he was joking, but Hans's face lit up. "Fate, yeah," he said, nodding. "Greta and I were supposed to go straight to the market, but I wanted to visit here for old times' sake. Greta doesn't like to eat too much sugar, but I work out so I can eat what I want, and that keeps me happy." He exhaled and shook his head. "Sorry, I'm talking utter nonsense. Being back here is…a lot. But seeing you is good, I promise."

"I bet," said Chester, understanding as best he could.

Gingerbread was his home, it always had been, even after his tragedy. But Hans's tragedy had never seemed to leave him, and Chester suspected it was the driving force behind him moving away.

It felt like a lifetime ago now that Chester had braved approaching a grieving, broken Hans when they'd both been thirteen. Even just recalling that day brought a lump to his throat. Chester had known that kind of pain first-hand, and hated seeing anyone else going through it. He'd only thought he could try and help. He never would have imagined that he'd get a best friend that day.

Nor the love of his life, although it was of course unrequited.

Hans and Chester had had nothing in common up until the moment Hans's mum had been killed in a random horse-riding accident. Hans hadn't been academic, only really interested in playing rugby, whereas Chester had been a dedicated student as well as an avid Pokémon card collector.

He was also an orphan and apparently the only one not afraid to talk to the large crying boy and tell him that one day, it would be okay.

Well, not really okay. But that the pain would change. None of the other children at their small school could relate to the twins' anguish. Chester wished he hadn't been able to either, but he'd lost his mum and dad in a car crash when he was only six. He'd remembered being a small boy, so alone with his nana trying her best to console him, and he couldn't stand for Hans to feel that way too. His sister always seemed strong, but Hans…

…Chester had been drawn to him in that moment, and it appeared after all these years that he still was. Chester loved him through the good days, the bad days, and all the absent days of the past few years.

Even as a lump rose in Chester's throat as he recalled those tough teenage years, he couldn't help but smile. Their relationship had mostly been based on getting into mischief and sharing sweets, but seeing Hans now, it was as if Chester had somehow found his way home, even though Hans was the one who had returned. Chester felt safe and warm, all from just seeing his grown-up best friend.

"I totally get it's a lot to be back," Chester said, "but I hope it's a good feeling. I know this little place can't compare to the bright lights of London, but hopefully, it's not all bad for you here again."

Hans shook his head and looked around the shop. "I thought it was going to be all painful, to be honest. But stepping through that door..." He laughed. "I was always happy in here. With you."

They stared at each other for a lingering moment, and Chester's heart rate began to pick up again. The way Hans was looking at him almost felt charged. Like they could lean closer and...kiss.

Crazy!

He laughed and rubbed the back of his neck, breaking the moment as he looked wildly around the busy store. Luckily, his colleagues were there to deal with other customers, and Ethel was too busy skulking around the till to notice his dilly-dallying. "Yeah. If we were going to meet anywhere, here seems like the perfect place."

Hans laughed too, his cheeks tinged pink. But that was probably just the heat getting to him in those sinfully tight leathers. "And now you work here!" Hans said happily. "That feels apt."

Chester allowed himself to smile. "As assistant manager, no less," he said proudly.

He'd always been a little embarrassed that he'd just stayed in Gingerbread instead of going off and studying or chasing a bigger, better life like Hans had. But Chester loved it here in the village, and he wanted to be close to his nana as she got older, so when a job opening had come up at the Cauldron, he'd jumped at it. This place had a special place in his heart. He remembered coming here as a tiny child with his parents, especially at Christmas. And then it had been his and Hans's special place, of course. To then work here was an honour.

Even if it had meant being employed by Ethel the Hag.

"Wild! Where are you!" she yelled as loud as her raspy voice could let her, as if Chester had summoned her with his thoughts.

If ever there was an anti-smoking campaign that would work on small children, it was seeing what thirty a day had done to Ethel Hex after fifty years. Technically, she was twenty years younger than Chester's sweet nana, but Ethel looked far the worse for wear.

Holiday shoppers practically jumped out of the way of the hunched-over old woman as she and her walking stick clattered their way through the store. She grizzled and hacked a cough into one of her mouldy handkerchiefs that made Chester recoil. Just having that thing on the shop floor was a violation of health and safety, he was certain.

"What you doing, boy?" she shrieked, shuffling to a halt in front of Chester and Hans, then jabbing her walking cane at him.

Chester was used to her nasty ways, though, and didn't miss a beat as he smiled. "Serving a customer, Mrs Hex." Chester doubted the vile beast had ever tricked a poor man into marrying her, but that was what she wanted to be referred to as, and it was easier to call her that than anything else he might be tempted to.

Ethel didn't believe in glasses. She said they were for pansies and communists. Therefore it meant that she had a spectacular squinty stare that she was now turning on poor Hans.

"You!" she squawked. "I know you. The mayor's son. No good troublemaker! I thought you'd died."

Hans's jaw ticked. "No, that would have been my mother," he said, feigning civility. "I'm surprised to see you still here, though. I would have thought you'd joined a coven – *I mean nursing home* – by now." He smiled widely, but it didn't reach his eyes for a second. "You remember my sister, Greta? She is also not dead."

Greta frowned at him as she came back over. For someone who didn't like sweets, she was certainly hugging a lot of shiny plastic bags to her chest. The two women eyed each other with a frown. "Nope, not worth remembering," Ethel announced, already shuffling away. "Too skinny."

Greta raised an eyebrow. "Now I recall why I never came in here with you guys," she said. "Who owns a sweet shop when they hate people – *children* – as much as that?"

Chester shrugged. "I think that's how she gets her kicks, honestly. So, um…" he said, trying to make his segue sound casual and probably failing miserably. "You're back! How come? For how long?"

Please don't vanish from my life again. Even if you are straight, I've missed you so much.

Chester had tried his best to keep their texts going between them. But when Hans had drifted away, Chester had painfully assumed he was moving along with his life. Maybe he had a girlfriend that took up all his time? In any case, Chester had told himself over and over that 'out of sight, out of mind' was a blessing in disguise, and if he let Hans go, then his feelings might fade. He'd been wrong, and now panic was seizing him as he realised there was a very good chance that Hans might disappear on him once again.

The twins looked at one another, and Hans arched an eyebrow. "We probably won't stay long," he said heavily, making Chester's heart sink. "It depends."

"On what?" asked Chester, trying not to sound desperate. But if there was anything he could do to make it easier for Hans to stay longer, he knew he'd do it. Even if he was only torturing himself.

Hans sighed as Greta shrugged. "Family," they said in unison.

"Ah," said Chester. He remembered now. He'd never really forgotten.

When Hans and Greta's mum had passed away, their dad had remarried pretty quickly to a much younger woman. A woman who had wasted no time at all in packing the twins off to boarding school as soon as she had a ring on her finger. Then she'd run them out of town the moment they turned eighteen. Chester wasn't sure of the exact details, but he knew she had something to do with the fact that Hans had packed his bags for London and never looked back. It didn't hurt any less knowing that his best friend's departure hadn't been anything to do with Chester. The result was still the same.

The new Mrs Jager may have driven Hans from Chester's life, but Hans had been the one to decide to leave Chester behind. He wasn't sure what had been different before London and boarding school, and he'd had to conclude that Hans had found a better life in the city.

Without him.

He was about to ask what had changed when the door burst open again, and two small children came running in. A girl held on to a younger boy's hand as they began dashing between people's legs, looking at the jars of sweets on the lower shelves. They bounced in excitement, and Chester recognised them from several visits before. He was pretty sure they were a brother and sister whose parents were going through a slow-motion break-up. That was the trouble with living in such a small town. You knew everyone's business, even if you didn't want to.

Sure enough, as the giddy children bolted past Chester and Hans to smoosh their faces against the jelly baby jars, Chester saw a couple outside who were clearly having a heated row. The man was yelling at a woman in a bobble hat, who kept tearfully checking on the kids through the shop window. Chester had seen her in the shop several times with the kids. Never the dad, who was currently jabbing his finger in her face. This was the first time Chester had seen him, but according to his nana, he was a cold-hearted brute.

"Oh," said Hans with a frown, looking at Greta.

His sister looked between him and the excitable children. "Isn't that the little boy you just saved from running into the road?"

"What?" Chester asked, but before either of them could reply to him, Ethel came barging through the customers, brandishing her walking stick like it was a sword.

"No!" she bellowed with another bout of crackly coughing. "No unaccompanied children in my shop!" The brother and sister snapped their heads towards her, their faces fearful as she banged her stick on the wooden floor. "Out!"

Chester grimaced. "I think their parents are just outside," he tried to protest.

"OUT!" screeched Ethel, spittle flying.

The little boy burst into tears as the girl scowled at Ethel. "My mummy says it's not nice to shout," she said, jutting her little chin out.

Ethel squinted at her. "My mummy always said that bad little girls and boys are tasty in pies." She licked her lips. "Shall I put *you* in a pie?"

The girl gasped as the boy cried harder.

"Okay!" Chester cried loudly and clapped his hands. "Why don't we find your mummy and daddy, okay?"

He ushered the children back out to the cold, where their parents were still having their not-so-quiet argument.

"I'm so sorry," Chester interrupted, embarrassed. "But my boss says they can't be inside unsupervised."

"O-oh, I'm so sorry," stuttered the woman.

The man threw up his hands. "I'm done with this," he barked before turning and walking away.

"Did we make Daddy leave again?" the little girl whispered.

The woman clenched her jaw, then shook her head. "Of course not, Gemma," she said kindly. "Daddy just has a headache. Why don't we go to the market festival by ourselves and bring him back a present?"

The children didn't look convinced, but they each took their mother's hand as they sniffled, and the girl nodded. "Okay, Mummy," she said sadly.

"I'm sorry, again," the bobble hat woman said to Chester.

He waved his hands. "Really, it wasn't a problem," he insisted, despite Ethel's grisly threat. But the three of them were already walking off into the night, heading towards the village square at the bottom of the high street.

He bit his lip, then remembered Hans. Panic rushed through him, like in that minute he might have vanished once more from Chester's life, this time for good. But as Chester spun on his heels, he saw that of course the twins were still inside the shop. Chester sighed in heavy relief.

He wasn't sure how long he could hold on to his best friend this time, but he was going to try.

Even if friendship was all he could ever hope for, it was still hope. Until tonight, Chester wasn't sure he'd ever see Hans Jager again so long as he lived. Fate had given him another chance, and he was going to make the most of it.

No matter what.

3

HANS

HANS WASN'T OBSESSIVELY WATCHING CHESTER THROUGH THE window.

He *wasn't*. What did he think? That Chester was going to disappear on him?

Maybe.

But that made Hans a massive hypocrite. He was the one who'd run off to London ten years ago and allowed their friendship to slide.

It had seemed like an obvious decision back then. His step-mum didn't want him and Greta, his dad had become a shell of his former self, and everyone else…well. It had been made very clear what everyone else in the village had thought of Hans and Greta, and it would only be a matter of time before Chester no doubt started looking at Hans the same way.

London had felt like the perfect opportunity to reinvent themselves. Hans kept telling himself that Chester was better off without him. It had been impossible to let go when he'd come home from school every holiday and Chester had been there, excitedly waiting for Hans's return. When Hans and

Greta reached adulthood and it was clear they couldn't return to Gingerbread, that they weren't wanted, it felt like torture to keep in touch with Chester when they couldn't see each other again.

And then there was the other thing.

At first, Hans had texted on and off because he couldn't bear not to. Because Chester was his best friend, the brightest light in his life. The person he couldn't quite let go of. It had taken Hans years to figure out his feelings might have been something else.

Right around the time that he had finally admitted to himself that he was gay.

That had been the last nail in the coffin. Chester was better off not being his friend if he was going to stay in the village. But more than that, Hans didn't want to ruin what they had when he realised that his feelings might be more than platonic for his best friend. But then he'd been so scared of ruining their friendship, he'd gone and lost it altogether.

But now Chester was here! Or…just outside the door, at least. He was watching the man and woman arguing with a troubled expression on his face and his hands resting protectively on the children's backs. The very same boy Hans had just rescued from running into the road, and now the poor little fellow was crying. But Chester was there, rubbing his back, talking to his mother.

Hans bit his lip, his heart aching.

Chester had always been kind. His and Hans's paths hadn't crossed until they were teenagers. Before then, it didn't seem like they had anything in common, and they had run around with different crowds. But Hans had seen enough of him to know that he wasn't a mean boy. He had been clever and sweet and always there with a smile for people.

And then…

After Mum had died when he and Greta had been thirteen, Hans's friends hadn't been good for much. They got bored of his 'moping' very quickly and stopped inviting him out, then stopped talking to him at all. Even Greta had dealt with her grief in her own way, taking herself off on her pushbike for hours, tiring herself out. It had left Hans with an aching chasm of loss. His entire life had fallen apart overnight, and no one seemed to be there to help him pick up the pieces.

And then Chester had appeared like a miracle sent from heaven.

Everyone had known that Dorchester Wild's parents had died in a car crash when he was six. It was just one of those things. Like how Luke Poole was lactose intolerant or how Ginny Shields also studied ballet and sometimes got to leave school early for auditions. Hans had never really thought about what it meant that Chester was an orphan. *He* had never seemed sad.

Until one day, during lunchtime, Hans had been having a panic attack behind the bike shed. He'd realised it had been a whole month without his mum and that she was never coming back. Nothing he'd tried to do had stopped himself from spiralling, and he'd hidden himself away to cry it out, ashamed at being such a baby in front of all the other boys.

But Chester hadn't treated him like a baby.

He'd found Hans huddled in the dirt, and for a second, Hans had just assumed that Chester would walk away and pretend he'd never seen Hans at all. When he'd taken a deep breath and come to sit beside Hans, slinging an arm around his back, the relief and gratitude had threatened to overwhelm Hans. But instead of feeling crushed from the weight of it all like he had before, he'd suddenly felt like he could breathe for the first time in a month. He'd hugged

Chester like he'd been a life raft, and in some ways, he hadn't let go of him for the next five years.

What might have happened if he'd never moved to London?

No, that was dangerous. He'd promised himself that he wouldn't risk changing what they had. Chester was the best thing in his life. Or at least he had been until Hans had pushed him away. He couldn't have stayed in Gingerbread anyway, not when he and Greta weren't welcome. So it was pointless to imagine if he'd stayed here, even if he and Chester had talked about renting a place together. It was for the best that Hans had left.

Otherwise the last ten years would have been all for nothing.

It had taken Hans a long time to admit he was gay. It had just felt like another element of chaos in his already troubled life, so he'd stubbornly dated women until he was twenty-five. He was so ashamed of all those nice ladies he'd messed around now, but finally coming out had been a massive weight off his shoulders.

But a part of him had always wondered about how he'd really felt towards his childhood best friend. It was easy to say he did love – or he had loved – Chester in a platonic way. Everything was just better with him around, more fun, less complicated. But it had somehow been easier to protect those memories and let the friendship slide away rather than really take a good look at what could have happened if only he'd been brave.

The last thing he'd expected when walking back into the Candy Cauldron had been an answer to that question.

Hans was pretty sure that he'd always loved his best friend. He'd just never realised it.

Now he felt like Dorothy arriving in Oz. Seeing Chester after a decade apart was like suddenly seeing everything in

Technicolor. His heart was thumping, and his cock was throbbing, and they'd only exchanged small talk for a few minutes. He wanted to hold him and touch him and see that wonderful smile all the time.

But now Hans had to go with Greta to meet their estranged father and his horrid wife, and that familiar panic was bubbling up in him. He'd lost Chester ten years ago, but now, suddenly, he'd got him back, and he didn't want to repeat old mistakes.

Just as Chester turned to look back inside the shop, Hans snapped his head away. He didn't want to come across as creepy. But it was like Chester was a magnet, pulling Hans to him. Mercifully, in that moment, Chester put Hans out of his misery. The bell over the door tinkled, and Chester walked back inside, hugging himself and rubbing his arms, watching anxiously as the bobble hat lady walked down the street, hand-in-hand with both her tearful children.

"Earth to Hans," Greta said impatiently.

Hans guiltily dragged his attention back to her. Somehow, they'd moved through the shop and had joined the queue to pay. Greta had a suspiciously large amount of crinkling cellophane bags pressed against her chest, and she was struggling to keep them all in place.

"Oh, shit, sorry. Let me take some of these. Err…are you buying all of this?"

Greta narrowed her eyes. "No. I selected all of this because you either need or deserve it. But you're going to buy it, and then not pay me any petrol money. Deal?"

Hans frowned. That didn't seem fair. The petrol would cost way more. But Greta's job as a courier paid quite a bit better than his at the bakery, and she had That Look in her eyes. The one that said 'I'm the older twin' that Hans never wanted to mess with.

"Okay, thanks," he mumbled with a grin, taking some of

the packets from her before they fell on the floor. But she still had an eyebrow raised at him. "What?" he asked. "Did you say something before as well?" *Whilst I was staring at Chester and realising that I definitely fancy the pants off him.*

She clicked her tongue and smirked affectionately at him. If anyone could smirk with affection, it was her. "I said I'm running off to marry Bella Dalton and co-star in her next movie together. Is that okay?"

He rolled his eyes at her. "Very funny."

"Well, you know I'll always hold a torch for Reyse Hickson, but Bella just has something he doesn't, you know?"

"I can think of a couple of things," Hans said, deadpan. "What did you really ask me?"

He glanced back through the shop, thankful that Chester had been caught by another customer asking about chocolate buttons. Hans was glad Chester hadn't spotted him staring whilst trying to catch his breath and muddle through his feelings, but at the same time, he was anxious for Chester to come back to him. He'd been reminded of what it was like to be around Chester, and now he was like a sugar addict, desperate for his next fix.

Greta snorted. "That."

"What?"

She sighed and shook her head. "That. *Him.* I said I had no idea you were into him before. Did you?"

She knew him too bloody well.

"Uh, no," he said softly. "Not really."

Greta whistled. "Okay, then! That's…something. Something that we will probably have to deal with."

"What? No?" Hans said, tearing his eyes away from Chester and glaring at Greta. "There will be no…*dealing.* I just want to spend some time with him. It's…nice, being around him again."

"Nice, yes." Greta nodded solemnly. "That bulge in your trousers says 'nice'."

"What!" Hans cried, snapping his eyes down. But he should have known Greta couldn't really see anything.

"Made you look," she gloated.

Hans opened his mouth, but the customers in front of them moved, and they were suddenly faced with Ethel the Hag once more.

"Hmm," she groused as the twins dumped all of Greta's hoard onto the counter. "I assume none of this is for you," she said, pointing a crooked finger with a brown nail at Greta. Then she shifted the finger and piercing glare towards Hans. "You were always a fat boy. I remember."

Mortification washed over Hans, reminding him that no matter how big he got, just how small he could feel. But sweets had made him forget the terrible tragedy of his mum's accident for a while, and this had been the special place where he and Chester had escaped the real world every Saturday with their pocket money. Chester never seemed to get bigger, but he also never, *ever* made Hans feel bad for being kind of chubby. In fact, he'd always called him 'Big Guy' and complimented how strong and tough he was. Like Hans was the one protecting Chester and not the other way around.

He wasn't ashamed that he'd done a lot of comfort eating when his mum had died, nor that he was a pretty big guy still. He knew he was fit and that there was a lot of muscle under the cuddly layer. But he hated...*hated* people thinking he was greedy just because he was a little chubby.

Before he could spiral, or before Greta could punch a pensioner, a hand slipped over his shoulder out of nowhere, impossibly warm through his leather jacket.

"Fat isn't a bad word, Ethel," said Chester brightly, stepping around the counter to start scanning Hans and

Greta's purchases. Hans missed his touch immediately. "And you can't be mad at the Jagers for coming back to your *charming* shop the minute they got back into town. Look, they've practically bought one of everything!"

"Humph," grumbled Ethel, watching with beady eyes like she was cataloguing everything Chester beeped. "One of every fudge, at least."

"I'm very sorry for spending so much money in your shop," said Greta through her fakest, brightest smile. "Let's throw in a bag of those Rhubarb and Custards, hey, bro? I might actually eat those."

"They are amazing," Chester confided in her as he grabbed the hard-boiled sweets from the shelf, then dashed back over to continue pricing up the ridiculous shop Greta had done.

Hans had no idea that prices had gone up so much in ten years. He watched with sinking dread as the total kept rising and rising. But then with a flick of her wrist, Greta had her card out, jamming it into the machine. They'd spent so much it had gone over the contactless limit.

"The hag has pissed me off," she murmured into Hans's ear. "And Miriam has pre-emptively pissed me off. I rage bought. You can get me a mulled cider at the market, and we'll call it even."

Hans opened his mouth to protest, but Greta already jabbed in her PIN. Then she sighed and relaxed. "All done," she said cheerfully.

Except they weren't.

"Huh-hem!" Ethel uttered like she was clearing her throat. Then she smiled so much it looked painful, showing off her tombstone-like teeth. She gestured demurely to the charity box shackled to the till. "Spare a penny for the starving children?" she simpered.

Hans had never understood why the old crone cared a

hundred times more about poor children halfway across the world when she practically chased the ones in her shop out with a broom. But regardless, he delved into his pocket before Greta even understood what Ethel had not-so-subtly hinted at, dropping all the coins he had into the box. He might not have any love for her, but he'd always given generously to her grubby charity box, knowing that he was assisting children in even more desperate situations than he'd been in.

Greta frowned, watching Hans as he dropped the coins one by one through the slot. "What?" he mouthed.

She shook her head, then flicked her gaze from the charity box to Chester with the focus of a nuclear missile. "Chester," she said as he finished bagging up their purchases. "If I may be so bold, can I ask when do you finish your shift?"

Chester looked like a deer in headlights. "Greta, I think you're awesome, but, um…I'm so sorry, but I'm, uh, very gay…"

Greta blinked slowly. "And my evening plans involve streaming the new *Fallen Angels Club* movie and this candy cane."

She waggled her eyebrows suggestively as she dangled the curved rod of hard candy in front of him before dropping it into the paper bag he'd been packing for them. Chester's eyes widened, Ethel looked like her heart might have finally given out, and the middle-aged woman behind them in the queue snorted in delight.

Hans wasn't sure which was worse: that his sister had announced she was going to use a candy cane as a dildo later or that she was almost certainly serious.

"Right," said Chester with a nod. "Sorry, my mistake. I do love Bella Dalton."

"Who doesn't?" Greta winked. "No harm done. But we have to go to a horrible thing right now, and I think my brother might like his former best friend by his side, but he's too shy to ask."

"No! What?" Hans spluttered. "That's not…*I should have eaten you in the womb,*" he hissed.

She just batted her eyelashes at him. "Oh, *please,*" was all she said. That could have meant 'we both know you'd have been screwed in this life without me' or 'as *if* you'd be the cannibal in this family'.

She had a point on both counts.

"You're holding customers up!" Ethel barked.

Chester flashed his most polite, beaming smile at her. Hans recognised that look from years in customer service himself. "I'm *so* sorry, of course! Let's just move this over here, and Ethel, you can serve this lovely lady next, hm?"

Hans noticed when they stepped aside and the woman behind them placed her items down, she'd also added a candy cane to her purchases.

"Look," said Greta to Chester in That Voice as they wandered towards the front door. "I'm very sorry. That was shitty of me. I'm on edge, but that's no excuse. I shouldn't have put you on the spot like that." She ran her hand through her short hair. "However, the fact remains that I think it'd be cool if you came to the grand opening of the market with us. Hans knows he's an idiot for letting your friendship limp into obscurity, but we don't have time for you to go down the pub, and I'm not sitting by whilst he's too shy to say anything himself. We have to go see the hell-beast Miriam and our dad. So why not kill two birds with one stone? You guys can catch up, and Chester, if you don't mind, your presence might make Miriam behave. She's always better in front of strangers."

"Oh, no, you don't have to…" Hans spluttered, shaking his head in horror. As much as he wanted to spend time with Chester, he didn't want him to have to deal with his wicked step-mum. He'd never even brought Chester home, because by the time they'd become friends, Miriam had already moved in. And Greta had a point. He *was* shy. But surely inflicting their family drama on Chester wasn't the answer.

But Chester's expression looked hurt. "It's fine," he said in a small voice. "I don't want to impose."

Shit. "No, that's not what I meant," Hans tried to explain hastily. "I'd love to catch up. I just didn't want you to feel like a human shield." He threw Greta a dirty look, but she just smirked proudly.

Chester, on the other hand, looked relieved. "Don't be silly, big guy," he chastised. The use of his old nickname made pleasurable heat rush through Hans. Chester lightly slapped Hans's arm. "It won't feel like that. If she'll behave better with me there, that's just a bonus. I'd…it would be nice to catch up. Really nice."

Fuck. Hans tried not to tremble too obviously. Spending time with Chester would be more than 'really nice'. *So* much more.

"Well, okay then," said Hans, ignoring Greta's smug look from behind Chester. "What time do you finish up? You could call me, and we could meet in the market, maybe? My, um, number hasn't changed." *I just stopped contacting you on it, like a twat.*

But Chester smiled. Was he blushing? No. His cheeks were probably just rosy from stepping outside, then coming back into the heated room.

"I'm actually just finishing my shift for the day," he said, his eyes bright as he bit his lip.

Whoa. Something flipped inside Hans's chest and squirmed in his belly. Just from one look. But that was crazy. Chester was just being friendly. He'd never given any indication that he had feelings for Hans back at school, even though he'd come out the summer they'd turned sixteen. He was just glad to see Hans after all these years.

Right?

"You've got three minutes left, Wild!" Ethel screeched, scaring a young boy into ripping a bag of chocolate coins open and scattering them across the wooden floor.

Chester inhaled as he plastered a smile on his face. "Of course, Ethel," he said through a clamped jaw. But then he relaxed a little. "I'll meet you both out front?" he said hopefully as he began edging towards the chocolate coin disaster zone.

"Of course," Hans assured him. Chester's question had suggested there was a chance that Hans wouldn't wait for him.

After ten years apart, there was absolutely no chance of that.

4

CHESTER

The Christmas market was one of the highlights of Gingerbread's calendar. Tourists came from far and wide to their humble little village to delight in the German-inspired event, and the stall owners themselves came from even further afield to tout their wares. Every year, the village square became packed to the brim with people selling beautiful handmade crafts and delicious food and drinks.

But this year was easily the best yet, and it hadn't even really begun.

Chester took a peek over at Hans as they walked with Greta up to the square. They'd visited the market a couple of times as teenagers, but this was completely different. It was like there was electricity in the air as well as the scent of cinnamon and the cold, drifting snowflakes, although it was snowing much less now. In fact, it had almost stopped entirely. Chester kept telling himself to stop getting his hopes up, but it was difficult. Christmas was the time to hope.

They may have fallen out of contact, but now Chester had to wonder if he'd still been on Hans's mind, even if he'd been out of sight. Chester had certainly never forgotten about his former best friend. Only now, something unthinkable was happening.

He was allowing himself to give in to his ridiculous fantasies for the first time in his life.

Hans was almost certainly straight. Chester had no reason to believe otherwise. But the way he kept smiling at Chester gave him a moment's pause. Sure, he was probably just happy to see his old friend. Chester knew they never would have become close if it hadn't been for Hans's tragic circumstances. It made it easier to understand why the friendship had failed after Hans's move to London. Chester was probably a reminder of the most painful time in Hans's life.

Except that was years ago now, and Hans was happily chatting to Chester about some event in London called Winter Wonderland that was like Gingerbread's Christmas market but a hundred times bigger.

"…queues for miles and everything costs a fortune," Hans was saying as they made their way into the busy throng of people already sampling all that the village square had to offer. Various Christmas songs drifted through the air, competing to be heard over the shrill merry-go-round organ that was pumping out slightly off-key chords as the children whirled round and round. "Don't get me wrong. It's brilliant," Hans carried on. "I'd bet you'd love it. But a fiver for a thimble of mulled wine is a bit much. Oh! Speaking of which, anyone want mulled cider?"

He pointed excitedly to a nearby stand, and Chester's heart ached. That was the earnest puppy of a boy he remembered. Not to mention how nice it was to hear that Hans thought Chester would love something from his new life. It didn't seem like Hans had changed much on the inside, even if the outside…

Well, Chester could only tell so much through the bike leathers, but he could see the basic outline of those shoulders and that *arse*.

He bit his lip and realised Greta had answered her brother, saying she could have one so long as she also had food, as she still had to drive them to their childhood home. So Chester said the same as he also had to drive, not dwelling on the idea of parting ways later that evening and going home to his dark, empty flat.

Mentioning the Jager's home made Chester recall how normal it had felt at the time that he'd never been there. Hans always said it was stuffy and boring, and how much nicer it was at Chester's nana's house. That was where Chester had grown up after the accident, and he thought his nana was the best. She always had scones baked for when she knew Hans was going to visit, and the two of them always had fun, no matter where they went.

But now, as an adult, Chester had to wonder if Hans had been protecting Chester from Miriam. If she had enough power over the twins' father to uproot their lives like she had, maybe it was best that he'd never met their step-mum face-to-face.

He shook himself as Hans went to join the line for the hot cider stall. It was only then that he realised that he'd been left with Greta. Alone.

He tried not to jump. "Oh, so, uh, hi," he rambled weakly. "It's nice to have you both back here. I hope everything's all right with your family?"

Greta sighed and folded her arms. "Not really. Our step-mother has deigned to allow us to visit our father, so that can only mean one thing."

"He misses you?" Chester suggested feebly.

Greta arched an eyebrow. "That he's dying."

Chester laughed until he realised she wasn't. "Oh – shit,

fuck," he blurted out, suddenly feeling hot with shame despite the cold night air. "You're not kidding. Holy crap, I'm so sorry."

She gave him a one-armed shrug and looked over at Hans, who appeared to be making the middle-aged lady serving the mulled cider laugh.

"We don't have many details," Greta continued. "Apparently, the hospital is running tests. But Dad said in his text that the doctor told him it might not be a bad idea to get his affairs in order, so…here we are to have dinner with them after this ceremony. As ordered."

She finished speaking just as Hans approached. She offered him a big smile as she reached out to take one of the three plastic pint glasses Hans was holding between his fingers. Chester did likewise so none of the cups fell to the cobblestone ground.

"Thanks," he said breathlessly.

Hans grinned, taking a sip of his own hot beverage. "No problem. What were you two talking about?"

Chester wasn't sure if he imagined the slight hint of tension to his question, and immediately wondered what Hans might be worried about his sister discussing with him. What did Greta think of their friendship? Did she have an opinion on their estrangement?

"The creative uses of candy canes," Greta said, licking a drop of cider from the lip of her plastic pint glass.

Chester snorted, his fears allayed for a moment.

Hans shuddered. "I wish you'd been adopted," he grumbled.

"Love you, too," she said with a grin, then began weaving her way through the crowd.

There was a small stage set up in front of the mayor's office that she was apparently heading towards, and Chester found himself following her by Hans's side.

"So, um," he began, not really sure what he wanted to say. Was it okay to repeat what Greta had told him? He cradled his hot cider between gloved hands and tried to think of a way to finish his sentence. What did he even want to ask? All he knew was that he was so happy to have Hans back, but… for how long?

Hans saved him by sighing and shaking his head. "I know I said it before, but I really am sorry for being so shit," he said as they made their way through the throng.

Greta was several feet ahead now, carving a path, leaving Chester to feel like he had a little privacy with his best friend for the first time in ten years.

"It's okay," said Chester reflexively. It wasn't, but he didn't want to waste his time with Hans mulling over the way their relationship had broken down.

Hans rubbed his hand over the scruff on his chin, then took another sip of cider. "It's not okay, though. I'm sorry for leaving so abruptly. For not making more of an effort. For never even trying to come back. I realise now how stupid that was. I love hanging out with you, and it's always so easy." He grinned and bumped Chester's shoulder with his own. "I feel like I've gone back in time. Like I never left. We've just picked up where we left off, don't you think?"

But you did leave, Chester almost blurted out. *You were my everything, and then you were gone.*

He bit his lip and tried to compose his response. "It's like old times," he agreed. "I did miss you a lot. But I know you were getting on with your life."

Hans scoffed and scowled into his cider. "Dunno why I thought my life would be better without you in it," he mumbled. Then he seemed to realise what he'd said, and glanced over at Chester. "I just mean, I got lazy. I should have never stopped texting. I'm sure that hurt your feelings, so, please. Let me apologise."

Chester felt like his heart was in his mouth. It was too easy to read more into those words than could possibly be there, so he tried to stay casual and not announce just how in love with Hans he had been then and still was now.

He bumped their shoulders back, and they shared a smile. "Yeah, it hurt when we stopped texting and calling. But it takes two to tango, and I let the friendship fade just as much. So…thank you for apologising, but I'm sorry, too." He gave a nervous chuckle. "I could have always tried to brave London," he added weakly, but before he'd even finished speaking, Hans barked out a much louder laugh.

"You? In London? You'd *hate* it. Except for Winter Wonderland. Maybe we could do that one day."

Chester was torn between embarrassment at how true that was, pride at how well Hans apparently still knew him, and joy at the idea that they might do something together in the future. It was a throwaway comment and a small hope, but he was clinging to it.

He was sad they'd lost all those years, especially when there had been a time when they'd spoken every single day without fail. But people grew up and grew apart. Chester didn't want to dwell on the past, particularly when he didn't know how much present they were going to get.

He rallied himself to say something positive. But in that moment, something bumped into his legs. "Oops! Sorry!" a little voice squeaked. He looked down and was surprised to see the little girl and boy from the shop earlier. They were red-faced and out of breath, bouncing and twirling around giddily. Unsurprisingly, their stressed and tired-looking mother in the bobble hat wasn't far behind them.

"Gemma! Jeremy! Apologise to the man!" she said, sounding like she was about to burst into tears as she ushered the children away from Chester's legs. "I'm so – oh… *gosh.*" She grimaced like she'd almost said something much worse in front of the children. "I'm sorry. We're bothering you again." Her eyes slid towards Hans. *"And* you, too! I'm so embarrassed."

Chester remembered Greta saying something about Hans saving the boy from being in the road. But he could ask about that later. The woman did indeed look like she was going to crumble on the spot, and Chester was already waving his hands. They couldn't have that. Her husband was clearly a dickhead, and she could probably do with a little kindness just then.

"No, no! It's fine!" he assured her and her kids, who were gawping up at him with open mouths and wide eyes. "I'm actually really happy I ran into you. You forgot these earlier."

He'd heard the mum saying they were going to be coming to the market, so on the very slim chance Chester saw the little family, he'd grabbed a couple of things from the shop as he'd run away from Ethel's never-ending grousing. With a flourish, he produced three chocolate Father Christmas lollies from his bag and held them out to the bobble hat mum. They'd definitely bought chocolate from the shop before, so he was almost certain that they didn't have any allergies. But he also had backup candy canes, just in case.

"I-I don't think I did?" said the mum uncertainly. "We didn't have time to buy anything."

"But, Mummy," said the girl in a pleading voice. "Those are the *best* chocolates. We love them."

"I know, sweetie," said the bobble hat woman as she began rummaging in her bag. "I can pay for them now…"

Chester gave her a sympathetic smile and held the lollies closer to her, catching her attention again. "Trust me, they're already yours," he said with a wink. "I promise."

"Oh…" said the mum, reaching out a trembling hand. "A-are you sure? That's very kind of you."

Chester blew a raspberry that seemed very loud when he

realised Hans was watching him. He didn't want to make a big deal out of it, but with Hans there, everything felt larger than life. "O-of course," he stuttered. "I'm very sorry about the, uh, misunderstanding with my boss. She means well, but she's a bit of a stickler for the rules."

"Lock-lock!" the little boy cried, extending his small arms upwards and making grabby hands towards the chocolate. Chester smiled at the mum, who shook herself, laughed, then nodded.

"Yes, thank you," she blurted out. "That's so thoughtful of you. I've had a…well, it's been a tough evening. We really appreciate your thoughtfulness."

Chester happily watched her hand out the 'lock-lock', and the children excitedly unwrapping their gifts. "Thank you!" the girl chirped without being prompted.

"You're very welcome," Chester said, glad he'd been impulsive.

After Chester watched the threesome wander off, all happily enjoying their lollies, he turned back to Hans. He was staring at him like he'd just sprouted horns.

"What?" Chester asked, suddenly self-conscious. Was Hans judging him for 'liberating' the chocolate from the shop? Because Chester had already promised himself that he would deduct the amount from his own paycheque when he was next back in for work.

Hans shook his head. "Nothing," he said faintly. "That was just…very sweet of you."

Heat threatened to creep onto Chester's face despite the cold night air. What did that mean? Was 'sweet' a good thing, or was that something you'd say to a friend you saw more like a brother?

Or was that the same twinkle that Chester swore he kept seeing in Hans's eyes? The one that looked like it could be more than just friendly appreciation? No, surely not.

"Oh…it was nothing," said Chester before the pause got awkward. He rubbed the back of his neck.

Hans was still smiling and went to say something, when all of a sudden, his attention was snapped towards the direction of the stage. His expression suddenly dropped as his eyes widened. "Oh, fuck," he rasped.

They were still several feet away, but from the side of the makeshift structure emerged an immaculately dressed woman that Chester guessed was in her mid-to-late thirties. Blonde curls escaped from a dove-grey Russian Cossack hat, its fur fluttering as she sashayed forwards in a billowing floor-length black fur-trim coat, cut to perfectly accentuate her slim figure as she effortlessly coasted along the cobblestoned ground in four-inch stilettos.

"Greta, darling," her voice rang out like a bell, clearly cutting through the din of the market. Greta was a few feet ahead of Chester and Hans and turned from where she was looking at a stall that sold blown-glass ornaments. The woman opened her arms wide and pulled Greta to embrace her like a long-lost friend, apparently whether Greta wanted to hug or not. "It's been too long. Your father is simply beside himself to see you, finally."

Miriam Jager. The mayor's second wife. It had taken a moment to recognise her under all those dead animals.

Chester felt Hans tense up beside him, even though they were a few feet away. Miriam was still determinedly embracing Greta, who had frozen in place. The woman smiled crimson lips over perfectly white, straight teeth, her gaze shifting to look over Greta's shoulder.

Chester could have sworn her eyes dilated as she spied Hans.

"And your brother is here, too!" Miriam cried, finally releasing Greta from her clutches. "One big happy family!"

Chester wasn't sure what to do with himself. He wanted

to be there for Hans, but illogical panic was rising in him like a flooding well. This was the woman who'd done everything to take Hans away from him, and she probably didn't even know Chester existed. She'd just been so desperate to have the mayor all to herself that she'd kicked the twins out on their own. Or so Chester had assumed. He'd never really known the full story. Hans never wanted to talk about his mum or his step-mum. The whole situation had been too painful, and Chester had respected that.

He wished he was a bit more prepared now, though.

Whatever the true reason, the effect had been the same. Hans had left, and there was clearly no love lost between him and this shameless fake woman. Chester was irrationally fearful that she'd do the same thing now. Chester would do anything not to lose Hans again so soon, but just seeing Miriam up close made Chester feel powerless.

Of course, he'd seen her countless times over the years at these sorts of ceremonial events and about town. But he'd never once spoken to her directly. She'd certainly never visited the sweet shop whilst Chester had been working. If Chester had to guess, he'd say Miriam was the kind of miserable person always on a never-ending diet, so their paths hadn't ever crossed.

It looked like they were about to now, though.

"Miriam," Hans said tersely.

It was all Chester could do not to move closer and wrap his arm around Hans's waist, like when they were boys and such a gesture would have felt innocent. But he wasn't sure if that would help the situation or not. Probably not, so he stayed as he was.

Miriam grasped her gloved hand around Greta's bicep and practically dragged her over to where Hans and Chester were standing. "You finally made it!" she said, shaking her head. "We were expecting you earlier," she added in a chiding tone.

Chester didn't miss that she'd said 'finally' twice now, like it wasn't her who had banished the twins off to boarding school and no doubt encouraged them to leave for good at eighteen. Nana had always called Miriam Jager a gold digger who had only married Hans's dad for money and power, and Chester couldn't say he disagreed with that assessment.

"Dad said to meet you both for the market opening ceremony," said Hans, offering her a thin smile. "That's here and now. Where is he?"

Miriam's laugh was like a tinkling bell as she waved her hand absently, indicating the currently empty stage behind her. "Oh, you know. Busy, busy."

"I thought he wasn't feeling well," said Greta, pulling her arm free with a scowl.

Miriam's smile didn't meet her eyes. "Let's not be crude, dear. There's no need to talk of private family matters in front of this young gentleman, whoever he is."

Chester realised she meant him. She was looking him up and down with curiosity that bordered on disdain, despite the fixed smile still being in place.

He jumped to life, determined not to let Hans or Greta down with poor manners. "Dorchester Wild," he said, offering her his gloved hand to shake. Belatedly, he realised there was a thread coming loose from the thumb, but there was no turning back now. "It's a pleasure to meet you, Mrs Jager."

Miriam raised her perfect eyebrows and gave him just her fingertips to shake. "Charmed," she said with another fixed smile on her shiny red lips. "And you're a friend of Greta's, I assume?"

"Oh, um, more Hans, actually," said Chester, desperate not to put his foot in his mouth. "We went to school together before…uh…" *Before you shipped them off to the greyest, strictest boarding school you could find in the country.*

"Chester was my *best* friend," said Hans firmly to Miriam. And then he did something totally shocking. He pulled Chester to him in a sideways hug. It only lasted a few seconds, but Chester's body tingled all over from it. "It's wonderful to see him again after all this time."

Apparently, Miriam didn't need any of them to carry on her conversation, as she ignored both Chester and Hans to focus back on Greta.

"Pity," she said with a pout. "I *did* tell your father you were both welcome to bring a boyfriend," she said pointedly at Greta, then looked at Hans, "or a girlfriend. But Johan tells me you never seem to have anyone special in your lives." She tutted and sighed, still pouting and blinking her long eyelashes like this was the worst tragedy that could befall them.

"Actually, I've had a lot of special girlfriends," said Greta brightly. "Sometimes several at the same time."

Hans spluttered into what was left of his cider. He'd drunk almost all of it since Miriam had appeared. "Yeah, I'm not sure what Dad would know," he mumbled. "It's not like we've exchanged more than Christmas and birthday cards in the last ten years. But I've dated a lot."

Chester tried to remind himself that was a good thing Hans hadn't been lonely, and he was proud of his friend for standing up to Miriam. It was important not to get irrationally jealous over all those women Hans had dated that weren't him.

He rallied himself and smiled. "It's cheaper to be single over the holidays, anyway," said Chester in an attempt to break the mounting tension. "Less presents to buy."

Not that he'd really know. It had been years since his last boyfriend. He'd exhausted what few men Gingerbread had to offer, and the few times he'd tried to date guys from other towns had always fizzled out.

Greta snorted. "Oh, I'm liking you better and better, Wild. We should have hung out more back in the day."

Was it Chester's imagination, or did Hans take a tiny, possessive step closer to him again?

"Well, now's your chance," said Miriam to Greta, happily clapping her hands. "You know it's important for your father to have a strong family image for the village. If you're going to be back in his life, I think it would be lovely for you to have a nice little boyfriend by your side."

Chester, Hans, and Greta all stared at her, the tension in the air growing.

"Or girlfriend," Greta said dryly.

Miriam laughed like she'd said something extremely funny. "Well, uh, yes. You know your father is a *modern* man." She winked using her whole face. "We have to say that sort of thing these days and wave those rainbow flags, don't we?" Another tinkling laugh as she wiped a tear from her eye. "That's fine for other people, yes, yes. But you know it would make your father happy to be settled down in a *traditional* manner."

"I honestly wouldn't know," said Greta with a smile like a snake about to pounce. "I haven't had a conversation with him in years. *Is* he a modern man?"

It was like watching a tennis match, except then Hans jumped in too. "We hope so. Because that's important to *both* of us," he said pointedly.

Something rinsed through Chester, leaving a tingling sensation behind. Was Hans just saying that to support his sister…or did he mean himself as well?

Miriam waved her fingers, a flash of annoyance crossing her face for just a second before the big, fixed smile came back. "This is all hypothetical, though. As you don't have anyone here with you, we'll just, um, gloss over that if anyone asks."

"Gloss over our sexuality?" Hans spluttered. He crumpled the empty plastic cup in his hand, then apparently didn't know what to do with it, so he stuffed it into his jacket pocket. "No, I'm sorry, Miriam, but this is who we are. If Dad – and *you* – want us back here to show the whole village we support him now he's sick, you're going to have to accept us as who we are. If I had a boyfriend here, I'd expect you to be courteous to him."

His eyes were blazing, and Chester was proud of him, definitely. Just in a detached sort of way. Because all the blood had rushed from his head, and he was feeling extremely dizzy.

Hans *was* into men? Was that what he was saying? It really sounded like it. Or was he just trying to make a hypothetical point and get back at the step-mother who had pushed him out and the father who had let him go?

For the first time, Miriam seemed to flounder. A few people around them were turning their heads to look at Hans's raised voice. Miriam was flapping her hands slightly as her smile looked like it was going to crack off her face from the strain.

"Hello, Elizabeth. Hello, Terry." She inclined her head to a couple walking past. "Yes, yes, Hans. Of *course* we would support your, um, boyfriend. If you had one. Gingerbread is *progressive.* The Best Small Town Survey said so last year. We even have some Black families now! Isn't that adorable?"

Hans clenched his jaw, Greta's eyebrows shot up in disbelief, and anger washed through Chester. He'd wanted Gingerbread to be more inclusive his whole life. And now this woman was only considering being more welcoming to outsiders just so the village could get an award or something? A higher rating on some points system that treated people like Pokémon cards to be collected?

"Yes, I told Hans it would be fine for him to come back home," Chester said firmly. "Gingerbread *is* more accepting now than when he and Greta were last here, a long, *long* time ago."

He felt himself trembling a little as he met Miriam's icy stare. "Oh, really," she said coolly. "And what is it to you, Darren?"

"Dorchester," he corrected sharply.

She smirked. "Right. Are you my step-son's boyfriend? Is that why we're all having this irrelevant and slightly baffling discussion?"

Chester wasn't sure what came over him. He was furious and determined to protect Hans just like he had when they were boys. Except Chester hadn't had any power to stop Miriam fucking with Hans's life back then.

Now, apparently, he did. Even though it was an insane idea. Even though if he'd thought about it for more than a second, he would never have plunged Hans into a situation like this without asking. But Hans was his best friend, and Chester was sure he could tell a little lie if it meant protecting Hans the only way he could think of in that moment.

"Yes," he said loudly, breaking into a smile as he linked his arm through Hans's arm. "I'm his boyfriend, and we're very, *very* happy together."

5

———

HANS

THE EXPRESSION ON GRETA'S FACE WOULD HAVE BEEN hilarious if Hans hadn't been so busy trying not to have a heart attack. He'd been so riled up after recklessly pulling Chester to his side to prove a point and already wondering how best to apologise about that, when Chester had gone and one-upped him. Or maybe ten-upped him.

Had he really just said they were *boyfriends?* Hans's heart fluttered, liking the sound of that a little more than it should have. Once again they stood side-by-side, but this time with their arms around one another.

His heart wasn't the only body part excited by the close contact.

"Uh, yeah. Yes," Hans spluttered, looking at Chester, feeling his eyes grow wide. The cider was thrumming in his veins and making him a little lightheaded. Also slightly reckless. "Boyfriend. I mean…we hadn't talked about…that word…yet. But is that all right with you, Chester?"

Hans nodded, actually trying to ask if Chester was seriously okay with pretending to be Hans's boyfriend simply to spite his awful step-mother. Chester's eyes searched Hans's for a second before his smile got bigger, and he nodded as well.

"Yes, of course. If-if that's what *you* want?"

Something strange happened in Hans's chest. Obviously, Chester was double-checking it was okay to proceed with the charade. But for just a moment, Hans imaged he was asking if he wanted to be boyfriends.

This was why Hans had let their relationship slide, especially over the last three years. Because he was too afraid of what his own feelings could be and didn't want to risk changing their dear friendship into something more that could potentially ruin it all. Obviously, that had backfired into making the friendship disappear almost entirely. But now it was crystal clear how he felt, and it was undoubtedly more than just friendship. Was this a huge mistake? He was so uncertain of how to handle his emotions already, without throwing this charade into the mix.

Hans didn't exactly have a lot of confidence with relationships as it was. Deep down, he'd always been sort of faking it with the women he'd dated, and the guys after that had only lasted a few hook-ups or dates before they'd fizzled out. It was as if Hans had always been holding something back, too afraid to really commit. So how was he supposed to pretend now with Chester? Was this even a good idea?

Yes. The aghast look on Miriam's face was worth it. And anyway, Hans wasn't going to embarrass Chester now by contradicting him. Besides...maybe pretending would be a safe way to explore his feelings for Chester without blowing everything?

And there was a tiny chance that maybe Chester wanted to pretend, too.

No, that was ridiculous. In any case, the point here was to

get one over on Miriam, and Hans couldn't pass that up. After all, who was it really going to hurt? They'd make her and his father eat humble pie, then leave town once more, probably for good this time.

The idea of leaving Chester again drove a knife through his heart, but he could deal with that later. Right now, he snapped himself out of his thoughts, hoping he hadn't paused for too long. "Yes," he breathed, beaming at Chester. "That is what I want."

Greta tutted, pulling Hans's gaze away from Chester's dazzling blue eyes. "Well, if I'd known this was going to happen, I would have brought Bella with me, too." She fluttered her eyelashes at a very stunned-looking Miriam. "Bella is my definitely real girlfriend, and she is very sorry to have missed all of this."

Hans scowled at her. He knew she was just playing around, but he didn't want Miriam to doubt their little charade even a bit. It would embarrass Chester and make Miriam even more insufferable than she already was.

Luckily, Miriam seemed to have been in some kind of trance that she only just blinked her way out of. She'd probably been frantically computing how to spin this so it wouldn't be a PR disaster in her eyes.

"Y-your boyfriend," she stuttered, her fake smile stretching over her teeth. "Well, that's, um, yes. That's wonderful, isn't it? Uh, well…"

"Miriam?" An older woman in a flowery coat bustled over to them. "Is that Hans and Greta? It's so wonderful to see you both! Gosh, it's been so long. Don't you both look well."

After getting over the surprise of yet another person being nice to them instead of hostile, Hans realised he recognised the woman. She was the kind lady who ran the haberdashery. The last time Hans remembered seeing her, though, he was sure she'd shaken her head and turned away. Was her delight now genuine?

"Hi, Miss Nancy," he said, trying not to let his confusion show. If she was going to be pleasant, so could he. "How's the shop doing?"

Nancy wagged a crooked finger at him. "Marvellous. You must promise to come see me. And with Mr Wild here. Oh, I always thought you both made a charming pair as youngsters. Is this something official, now?"

She'd thought *what* about them as kids? Hans knew it was ridiculous, but the idea that anyone might have regarded them as a potential couple back in the day made him feel all kinds of silly things. Pride. Hope. Longing for what might have been.

"It's very new," Hans said, trying not to mumble as he smiled. He also attempted to remind his stupid heart that this was just pretending.

Nancy looked at their linked arms and beamed, then grinned and elbowed Miriam's side in a conspiratorial manner. Miriam made a face like she'd swallowed a lemon before schooling her features.

"Uh, yes, official," she managed to stammer. "Apparently so. Johan and I are *very* proud to support our gay son." Hans tried not to flinch at the idea that this woman could ever be his mum. He didn't want to cause a scene in front of sweet Miss Nancy.

Greta waved in her face. "And your bisexual daughter as well. Right, *Mum?*"

Miriam looked like she was going to explode or pass out. "Of course," she said through clenched teeth.

Nancy didn't seem to notice. In fact, she was all of a titter. "Oh, that's simply wonderful. Good on you both!" She looked between the twins and Chester. "Did you know I have another grandson now, not a granddaughter? Isn't that lovely? My Holly's eldest. You know Jack, don't you, Chester? He runs the town choir. He's very handsome." She elbowed Miriam again. "I say, Miriam. Wouldn't it be just spiffy to have one of those parade things that the big towns and cities have?"

"A Pride? In Gingerbread?" Greta spluttered, glee lighting up her features. "Yes, Miriam. Wouldn't that be something great to bring up at the next council meeting?"

"That's an...idea," said Miriam. She swallowed and blinked, never losing her strained smile. "I do apologise, Nancy, but we simply must go find Johan now. He's eager to see the children. It was lovely to see you, as always," she simpered.

Nancy didn't seem to realise she was being patronised, however, and just gave the group a cheery wave and a smile. "You, too, Miriam. See you at Pilates class! Hans, Greta, please promise you'll pop by my shop before you leave. I've got some lovely sparkly rainbow material. It's like a mermaid's tail! Maybe you'd like some? Golly, we have missed you here in town."

She reached over and squeezed Hans's arm, most likely because he was closer to her than Greta. But the motherly affection of the action made his throat tighten, reminding him of why they had been away so long in the first place. But he was so confused. Why was she being so nice and inviting them to her shop? Didn't she think the same dreadful thing as everyone else in town?

Didn't she know that their mum's death had been Hans and Greta's fault?

Before that familiar grief could overwhelm him, there was Chester by Hans's side, like he always had been before. He really was Hans's rock, and it was crazy to think Hans had pushed him away over the last decade simply out of fear for what *could* happen.

"I'll bring him by, Miss Nancy," said Chester cheerfully, hugging Hans closer to his side. "Don't worry."

Nancy sighed and placed a hand over her heart. "Adorable," she said again before vanishing into the market crowd. Hans felt a twinge of guilt at lying to her about him and Chester being boyfriends amidst all his other swirling feelings, but there wasn't much that could be done about it in that moment.

When it was just the twins, Chester, and Miriam again, an uneasy air settled between them. It was like chess. It was anyone's guess who was going to move where next. Hans could practically see the cogs turning in Miriam's head as she planned how to handle this spanner in the works. Hans and Chester might have earned a point for their boyfriend charade in front of Nancy, but he had no doubt that he'd pay for it later in some way.

All Miriam did was play games. Could she sense that Hans and Chester were pulling her leg with this boyfriend business? Hans knew he wasn't that good an actor. But on the other hand, he was pretty sure she'd rather die than admit weakness, so when her face suddenly brightened with fake joy once again, he wasn't surprised.

"Well, then. This is marvellous, isn't it?" She wrinkled her nose like a bunny rabbit. "Why don't we go find your father before it's time to go onstage for the opening ceremony? The village is going to be so *happy* to see you two join him this year."

The accusation in her tone was clearly there that the twins hadn't been around to support their father for years, which was so typical of Miriam to try and make them feel guilty for something *she'd* been responsible for. Hans was convinced that this woman lived in her own fantasy that rewrote the facts on a regular basis to suit whatever narcissistic lie she was telling herself that day.

But the truth was it wasn't just her. Their father hadn't been the same man after their mum's death. He'd withdrawn from the twins and seemed happiest to be bossed around by Miriam. He'd allowed her to send them off to that dreary boarding school, then left them to fend for themselves in the world without any financial support, let alone paying for university like they'd thought he would. Hans had spent as many years as angry at his dad as he had at Miriam, the universe for taking his mum away, and for his own part in her death.

But then there had always been a Christmas or birthday card from his dad. They never said much, but the fact that he never skipped a single year meant *something*, Hans was sure. Enough to get him back to Gingerbread to see him now and put up with Miriam's bullshit.

So Hans just beamed at her. "Sounds wonderful," he enthused, just as fake as she was being.

"Positively spiffy," Greta agreed, trying to outdo his cheeriness. She held out her hand and indicated that Miriam should lead the way. "After you!"

Miriam looked like she might be about to say something. Her lip almost curled, her facade dropping for a fraction of a second. But then she snapped her jaw shut and smiled like a viper before spinning aggressively around and stomping off on her pencil-thin heels, somehow still gliding along the centuries' old, uneven cobblestones. Greta threw Hans a quick look, then followed swiftly after her.

That look clearly said 'sort your shit out, *now*'. Hans reluctantly had to agree, but before he could open his mouth, Chester whirled on him.

"Oh my goodness, I'm *so* sorry!" he hissed. His eyes went as wide as saucers, and he clutched at his chest. "I panicked. Please don't hate me for springing such a ridiculous idea on you!"

All the other feelings flying around Hans's head melted away like marshmallows in hot chocolate. "I could *never* hate you, Chester," he said, squeezing his hand. "I actually think it's a pretty hilarious idea. Just the kind of lark we used to get up to back in the day. And, well, it's also kind of sweet," he added in a mumble. He begged himself not to blush. He couldn't give too much away about his true feelings. That would complicate their relationship when it was already so fragile. "It certainly put a look on her face," he said instead.

Chester laughed, looking relieved. "I thought her whole head was going to spin around her neck," he said giddily. Then he bit his lip and glanced out over the mass of people in the square, then back to Hans. "So, you're, uh, gay? Or bi?" His question was tentative, like he thought he might spook Hans by asking. Which was fair enough, but it still made Hans's chest hurt a little. He didn't want Chester thinking he couldn't talk to him.

"Yeah," he said gently. "Gay. I took a little longer than you to figure it out. Sorry."

Chester caught his gaze again, but he wasn't angry. If anything, he looked happy and maybe a little excited. "Why would you be sorry?" he asked enthusiastically. "That's great! I'm happy for you. So, um, *this* is really okay with you?" He held up their still entwined hands and raised his eyebrows.

Hans's breath caught in his throat. He was still reeling from how his attraction for his best friend had hit him like a train. He'd suspected it for a while, but now he knew for sure it was definitely more than just platonic. Was that attraction okay? Was it okay to pretend? And how did Chester feel? Surely if he'd had nurtured feelings for Hans when they were teenagers, Hans would have realised – right? But could he feel differently now?

Hans shook himself mentally. He could try and untangle all that later. For now, he'd meant what he'd said. "Yeah, totally fine. We only have to pretend for an hour or whatever, after all. It'll be fun! You always know how to rescue me, don't you? Even after all these years."

Was it his imagination, or did Chester blush at the compliment?

He was pulled from his musing as his name was barked from several feet away. "Hans, darling," Miriam hollered, making several people turn and look at him. Hans tried to shrink away from their curiosity. Miriam clicked her fingers from beside the stage, still wearing that bright fake smile. Greta rolled her eyes. "Here, please!" Miriam said.

Hans ground his teeth. "You'd think I was still thirteen," he muttered.

Chester gave his hand a comforting squeeze. "But you're not," he said firmly. "So let's go over there and face her together. This isn't about her. It's about your dad."

Hans gave him a lopsided smile. "Greta told you about that, huh?"

Chester rubbed his arm. "Pretty much. I'm really sorry to hear he's not well."

Hans had so many mixed feelings about his father. Honestly, he was a sweet man who had been grief-stricken in the wake of Hans's mum's death, then swindled by a shiny, overbearing gold-digger. He wasn't the first and he wouldn't be the last to be taken advantage of like that.

But Hans didn't want his dad to pass away with this bitterness hanging between them. He still remembered the kind man who had taught him and Greta to ride their bikes, who had read to them as small children, who had tried to stay strong when he'd told them their mother was really gone. For his father's sake, Hans rolled his shoulders back and nodded at Chester.

"Let's go," he said.

Johan Jager was a homely-looking man with thinning

white hair, ruddy cheeks, turkey jowls, and bright blue eyes that twinkled behind slim-framed glasses. He'd aged quite a bit over the past decade, but as soon as Hans saw him emerge from behind the stage area, he immediately felt like he was really home.

At his feet was a bouncing ball of fluff. Hans paused in his stride as his eyebrows shot into his hair. His father had a *puppy?* Miriam had actually allowed that? She'd loathed all animals when Hans had lived with her. They weren't diamonds or fast cars, so what did she care?

The only thing Hans remembered his dad putting his foot down about was not getting rid of his mum's young horse, the one that had thrown her. It hadn't been Peanut Butter's fault after all, and Hans was glad that his dad hadn't sold him after the accident. He hoped the horse was still in the stables at the family estate.

Either way, his dad really must be dying if Miriam had allowed him to get a dog. But the fact that the chocolate-coloured puppy was on a lead in Johan's hand certainly suggested that they belonged to Johan. The little tyke was jumping around his legs and wagging their tail frantically as they tried to say hello to everyone they met.

Including Greta.

Hans stopped walking altogether as he watched his dad break into a tearfully happy smile and throw his arms around his sister.

What the hell?

This man had shown them the barest affection after the accident. Hans could sort of understand why, after what the twins had done. If not for them, their mum might still be alive. Hans understood that his dad couldn't get rid of them quickly enough when they were teenagers, but then he'd never missed cards for either of them at Christmas or on their birthday. It had confused Hans for a while now, and honestly, in that moment, he was baffled.

So was Greta, it seemed, as she didn't seem to know what to do. She awkwardly patted their dad on his back as the bag from Candy Cauldron swung between them, dangling from her hand. The puppy sniffed at it with extreme interest.

"Okay, yes, that's lovely," said Miriam loudly, shooing them part. The curly-haired puppy barked, and she shot them a narrowed look with a snarl.

Yep, she still hated animals apparently.

Hans's dad laughed and let Greta go, looking down at the puppy with affection. "Sorry, he's a bit excited. Aren't you, Dodger?"

"Dodger?" Greta repeated.

Their dad nodded proudly. "Short for Jammie Dodger," he told her with a wink. "He's a cockapoo and he's six months old. Isn't he marvellous?"

Hans's mind faltered. *Jammie Dodger?* That was his dad's favourite biscuit, so maybe it wasn't so surprising he'd chosen that name. But that wasn't what made his brain hiccup. It was the fact that his mum's favourite flavour was always peanut butter, and they used to say 'peanut butter and Jammie Dodgers' instead of peanut butter and jam. It was their way of saying that they were 'two peas in a pod'.

It was their way of saying 'I love you'.

Was that intentional? Miriam couldn't possibly know that. She'd have pitched a fit. No, it had to be a coincidence. Dad had probably forgotten all about that and just named the puppy after his favourite treat. They probably didn't even have the horse still.

He was pulled from his musings as his dad looked up and caught sight of him. For a second, time seemed to stop as they stared at each other. Then Johan broke into another watery smile and crossed the couple of feet between them to throw his arms around Hans and clap him solidly on the back.

"Dad," mumbled Hans into his father's waxy Barbour jacket. Hans was so much bigger than him now compared to how he remembered being hugged as a child. He'd grown and his dad had shrunk, so the effect was quite drastic. Still, being embraced by a parent for the first time in over a decade suddenly made Hans feel small and delicate, like he might break.

"It's so good to see you, my boy," Johan said thickly. He squeezed Hans tightly, then cleared his throat before releasing him. "And this can't be Dorchester Wild, can it? Look at you!"

Obviously, Hans's dad didn't frequent the Candy Cauldron that much if he hadn't seen Chester recently. They'd both been living in the village this whole time, after all. But he looked genuinely happy to see Chester, and clearly remembered him being Hans's best friend, even though Miriam didn't.

As they shook hands, the woman in question loomed. Long fingers wrapped over Hans's dad's shoulder as she peered from behind him, her crimson lips smiling wide. "Yes, dear," she said in a far too cheerful voice. "This is Hans's little boyfriend, apparently. Isn't that a surprise?"

Hans bristled. How fucking *dare* she out him as gay. That was his decision, his right, not to mention a moment he could never get back between him and his only surviving parent.

Before Hans could get up in arms about both those things, he realised his dad's face had dropped in shock as he looked between Hans and Chester. "Is this true?" he rasped, and Hans prepared himself for an onslaught. But his dad's smile came back even broader, and his eyes glistened as he clasped both Hans and Chester on their shoulders. "My goodness. I'm so happy to know you've found someone special, my boy. And such a kind friend from the good old days! How did this come about?"

Hans was so astonished that his jaw had gone slack. His dad didn't seem to have a problem with Hans supposedly having a boyfriend at all, despite everything Miriam had been saying. He just seemed delighted that Hans had a partner, regardless of their gender. Miriam looked just as stunned at his reaction. Then her jaw clenched like she was barely holding back her anger.

Then Hans realised he'd asked how Chester and he had got together, and Hans really didn't have a good answer. Not when they hadn't seen each other in ten years. They really should have come up with a lie to tell, but they'd barely had time to wrap their heads around this idea themselves.

Just as his mouth started to flap, Chester squeezed his hand again and jumped in. "It's all very new, sir," he said. Hans looked at how he beamed when he talked, and shivered as Chester easily slipped his hand back into Hans's. "We started talking again a few months ago," Chester lied, "and when Hans said he was coming back for the market opening ceremony, I think we knew our feelings had changed since boyhood." He blushed, and Hans wondered how good an actor his friend really was. "When we saw each other, we decided to stop wasting time and make it official."

Hans swallowed, realising with a jolt that he liked that tall tale a *lot*. In fact, he kind of wanted it to be true quite badly.

In that moment it struck him that he might have to say something to Chester about how he was feeling. But their relationship was still so fragile after so many years apart, and he was afraid. He'd rather have Chester back as a friend than not in his life at all. And if they only had a bit of time this evening, that could make things awkward and complicated.

But maybe...if they started texting again when Hans went

back to London, he could be patient. Maybe see what happened? The thought warmed him despite the cold night air.

"Well, that's marvellous," said his dad, sounding incredulous but also genuinely happy. Dodger was looking up at them, wagging his tail furiously, as if he was giving his approval too. Johan turned to face Miriam, who quickly smiled when she realised he was looking her way. "Isn't that just lovely, dear?"

Miriam hummed.

"It's excellent," agreed Greta, looking thoroughly amused.

"And what about you, darling?" their dad asked her. "Do you have a boyfriend, or, um, a girlfriend?" He seemed so earnest that Hans didn't blame Greta's expression for softening.

"No one here with me, Dad," she said, touching his arm. "But maybe I'll bring a nice girl next Christmas, yeah?"

He nodded and smiled as he looked between his kids. Did he even have until next Christmas?

Before Hans could worry about that too much, his dad piped up again, nodding at Chester. "This is just fantastic, really. And I'm sure Hans has invited you to dinner already?"

Hans froze. He really hadn't been thinking beyond this stupid opening ceremony, which seemed pointless to him, as the market was already *open,* and why would people care if they mayor's grown children were standing beside him for once? But then they were supposed to go back to the house for a dinner that was bound to be beyond painful, with Miriam monitoring every word they said, then stay the night and head back to London in the morning.

He'd just imagined that he and Chester would hold hands and keep up this charade for however long they were at the market, then go their separate ways. It somehow felt safer to pretend here with so many people around, as well as sights and sounds to distract everyone. But an intimate family dinner? How were they supposed to keep this charade up there when Hans was wrestling with whether or not he wanted this pretend relationship to be real?

"Oh, uh…" he began to say.

"Oh, I don't think there's any need for that, Johan," Miriam said with a mildly hysterical titter. "We've only prepared dinner for four people."

Hans's dad scoffed. "We've got enough food and drink to feed an army. You always outdo yourself, darling. No, I must insist you join us, Dorchester. I'd be delighted to get to know you better. I always thought you made Hans happy as a boy, but this development is such a delightful surprise."

Hans felt a pang of guilt for lying to his father and giving him false hope. Just because he didn't *look* particularly ill didn't mean he wasn't. And here Hans was, duping him. But also…his dad really thought that? Hans didn't think his dad had particularly noticed he had a best friend, and Hans had been careful to keep Chester away from the family house and all its tragic drama. Maybe he hadn't been quite as withdrawn as Hans had remembered.

Besides, what Johan didn't know wouldn't hurt him. Hans was so happy that his dad hadn't had even a hint of the homophobic reaction they'd seen from Miriam. In fact, the growing horror on her face as it became clear that the dinner invitation was a very real one made Hans think maybe this wasn't such a terrible idea after all.

He turned to Chester, who was watching Hans, apparently waiting for his cue. "Well," said Hans. This time it was his turn to squeeze Chester's hand. "Of course I'd love to have you there. But only if you haven't got plans?"

Chester blinked a couple of times. The snow had eased considerably, but he still had a couple of delicate snowflakes caught in his eyelashes. He looked angelic as he searched

Hans's face with earnest eyes. Then a sweet smile crept onto his mouth. "I'd love that," he said quietly.

A shiver ran down Hans's spine. It had only been fifteen minutes at most since they'd started this charade, but it was becoming increasingly difficult to remember that they were just pretending.

Or were they? He guessed he was going to get a little longer that night to find out.

6

CHESTER

THIS HAD TO BE SOME KIND OF DREAM. THE MOST CHESTER had previously had to look forward to when he'd woken up that morning had been a long, unpleasant shift with Ethel breathing her rancid breath down his neck, then a hot chocolate back in his sad, empty flat before a microwave dinner and an early night.

Now he was watching Hans stand awkwardly onstage with the rest of his family, waiting for them to finish the ceremony so they could all have dinner together. He'd even been trusted to look after Dodger whilst Mr Jager was giving his speech, and the puppy was alternating between straining against his lead as he tried to get back to his daddy, and jumping up Chester's legs for attention.

Chester's heart warmed as he fussed the puppy's head. This family dynamic was such a minefield to navigate, but one thing was for certain, and that was Chester was going to make the most of this crazy charade whilst it lasted.

He bit his lip and tried to make his heart listen to his brain. *This isn't real*, he told himself. He needed to be satisfied with having Hans back for just one evening. They might possibly rekindle their friendship online or over the phone, but that was it. Just because Hans was apparently very much gay didn't mean they were going to automatically become boyfriends. That was crazy. Chester needed to get a grip.

But his stupid heart didn't seem to want to listen. It was thumping away in his chest, and his hands were tingling, despite the gloves he was wearing. He was hot and cold all at once, slightly trembly on wobbly legs and yet floating on air.

He hadn't ruined things by suggesting this farfetched ruse. In fact, now he knew what it was like to hold hands with Hans, to be hugged by his side. But more than that, he'd seen the way Hans had looked at him with those searching eyes. Logically, Chester knew it was all part of the charade, but again it appeared his stupid heart wasn't getting the memo. It positively fluttered every time he felt Hans's gaze roaming over him.

Mr Jager had been on the microphone for a few minutes now, officially welcoming everyone to Gingerbread's annual Christmas market. It was the same every year. They waited for the first Friday of December to have the little ceremony, but it didn't make much difference to the stall sellers who had all already been trading for most of the week.

This afternoon was just the deadline for them all to set up, and the evening would be filled with live entertainment of staggeringly varying quality. Chester usually enjoyed the kids' choirs and the bands made up of young adults and teenagers who did reasonable covers of Christmas rock songs. But he could see 'Magic Michael', the local accordion player, limbering up to follow the Jagers onstage, and Chester wondered how fast he could get Hans to run.

Speaking of which, Chester watched with sympathy but also amusement as Hans didn't seem to know what to do with his big hands as his dad carried on with his usual patter. By the way he was fidgeting, he was clearly uncomfortable being on a raised stage in front of a crowd. He kept biting his lip and glancing at his dad, like he was trying to telepathically ask him to hurry up.

And when he wasn't looking at his dad or his shoes, his gaze kept flicking back to meet Chester's.

Every time their eyes met, it was like the New Year's fireworks started going off early in Chester's heart. Hans's mouth would twitch just a fraction before his eyes roamed again, but every little smile was like Chester had been plunged into a warm bath. After a decade apart, he'd really tried to convince himself that the connection he remembered between them couldn't be that strong. Otherwise, why would it have faded away?

It was definitely still as strong. And not just emotionally. It had been difficult at times when they'd been teenagers for Chester not to get too excited in the trouser department just from looking at Hans. He'd always put that down to raging teenage hormones, but right now he was certainly still feeling some kind of thickening down below, and he shifted his weight to try and give his eager cock some more room in his jeans.

"Down, boy," he muttered to himself.

Dodger looked up and crooked his head as if to say 'Oi! I was behaving for once!'

The audience laughed warmly but not exactly enthusiastically as Johan told the same old dad jokes he inflicted on them every year. Hans looked as if he groaned, even though Chester couldn't hear him from where he was standing. But he liked watching Hans catch his sister's eye and how they both snickered.

Every Christmas, Chester found himself torn but ultimately watching on as Hans's estranged dad and step-mum stood up on this stage. It was the same at the summer fair, the Easter festival, bonfire night. In fact, any time they were required to speak publicly, Chester would watch. He'd be dishonest if he said he didn't harbour some resentment towards them for chasing Hans away.

But at the same time, seeing his parents had somehow felt like as close as Chester could get to Hans, and he hadn't been ready to quite let go of that connection. It had felt a little like betrayal to get his Hans fix from the very people who had driven him away from Chester, but he was only human, and it had been the best he could do.

Until now, of course. Now Hans was right in front of Chester, shuffling his hands between his jacket pockets, his trouser pockets, cupped behind or in front of him, or just hanging by his sides. His cheeks were red, probably from a combination of the cold and embarrassment, and his dirty blond hair was kind of wild around his ears.

Fuck. What Chester wouldn't do to grab that hair and nuzzle his face against Hans's soft-looking beard. He hadn't had that when he'd left at eighteen, that was for sure.

My teddy bear, Chester thought privately, daring to recall his special, secret nickname for his crush that he'd never told another living soul. But Hans was more of a teddy bear than ever, and Chester had to try very hard to listen to what was being said rather than picturing cuddling Hans.

Naked.

Mr Jager got Chester's attention back as he actually turned and looked at Hans, drawing the eyes of the crowd to him as well. "I am very honoured to share the stage tonight with all my family," said Johan, gesturing to his left and right, and to all intents and purposes, sounding sincere. "My *whole* family."

Greta hadn't moved an inch since she'd walked up onstage, and was staring out into the audience as if to challenge anyone as to *why* she and her brother hadn't been present for the past ten years.

Miriam, on the other hand, was preening like a doll – polished, glossy, and hard. She swished her floor-length coat back and forth like a little girl, then flicked her hair as she expertly snatched the mic from Johan's hand before the poor man apparently knew what hit him.

"So true, darling. So true. Christmas *is* about family, after all. And nothing is more important to us than our children. We're so glad they could find time in their *very* busy schedules to join us this year. They work in London, don't you know?" She giggled and winked, handing the mic back to Johan.

There was an awkward lack of response from the crowd as Chester balled his fists. *She* was the reason they'd never come back, and she was definitely not their mum. It made his blood boil. Some people in town had certainly thought it had been odd and unkind that the twins had moved away as soon as they could. Like they'd abandoned Gingerbread as well as their father, its mayor. But over time, Chester felt like they'd come to forgive Hans and Greta, and personally, Chester couldn't blame them from wanting to get away from Miriam.

Even if it had broken his heart.

It was never exactly abuse. Chester remembered how Hans had been incredibly distressed when she'd appeared out of nowhere mere months after his mother's death. He'd told Chester how she'd been all sweetness and smiles in front of Johan but shown a disturbing coldness whenever she was left alone with the twins.

Nothing they could have reported to their father, other than a lack of warmth. But somehow, she had sweet-talked her way into Johan's heart and convinced him that the best thing for the children would be a 'superior education' and to 'fend for themselves out in the world'. It made Chester heartsick to think of her lack of empathy as she'd pushed them out of Gingerbread for good the second they'd finished school. What power did she have over Johan and his children?

Chester shook his head. He didn't care about Miriam beyond how she made Hans feel. In fact, he didn't really care about anything beyond Hans in that moment. Chester couldn't help but feel like he'd been given a second chance with his first love, the one that had got away.

He'd always thought of Hans as his first love, even though it had been unrequited. But the truth was, none of the guys he'd dated during his twenties had ever lived up to the easy, loving relationship he and Hans had shared as just friends.

It made Chester wonder now if he'd ever really loved any of those other men. He'd thought he had at the time, but now he wasn't sure if any of them really measured up to Hans.

Did that make Hans his *only* love?

That was a tricky line of thought. Hans could still be just as unavailable to him as he had been when they were teenagers. Just because he was gay didn't mean he'd suddenly be attracted to Chester. But it certainly gave Chester more of a chance than he'd ever had before. He'd never dared to believe it could be possible, even when he'd given in to his late-night fantasies. But now it was real.

Did that mean Chester might have a chance with him after all? Even just daring to think that made him feel faint. It had been completely forbidden to entertain that notion for so long. But Chester's heart raced nonetheless, and his throat became tight. He'd gone from a snowball's chance in hell of getting with his best friend to a very slim 'maybe'. But apparently, that was enough to make him as giddy as the kids that came into the sweet shop.

Or would admitting his crush out loud just ruin everything they'd managed to get back this evening? There was no reason for Hans to reciprocate Chester's feelings just because he was gay, too. It was too soon to tell. Chester just needed to be patient and see where this tentatively rekindled friendship led them.

He watched the family wave goodbye as the audience clapped politely, and at the side of the stage, 'Magic Michael' pushed through several older women in tap shoes to get up on the stage. Chester winced as he began blasting out the first few off-key notes from the instrument hung around his neck, and Chester gathered up the few bags he'd been left to watch and moved himself and an already whimpering Dodger a little further from the stage.

"Well," said Johan. He clapped his hands as he and the rest of the family approached Chester. Dodger whined and tugged against his collar, eager to get back to his dad, so Chester handed the lead over as soon as Johan was close enough. "Now that's over and done with, shall we head back to the house?"

Although he was looking older and frailer these days, Chester couldn't say he looked particularly sick. But not all illnesses were visible, so he shouldn't pry. He just hoped that Hans might get more time to reconnect with his dad if that was what he wanted.

"Darling, are you *sure* this is a good idea?" said Miriam through a smile that barely concealed her gritted teeth. She patted Johan's shoulder and flicked a disdainful look at Chester that he almost didn't catch, it was so quick. "I thought you wanted to discuss certain *matters* with the children?"

"We haven't been children the entire time you've known us," said Greta, raising an eyebrow.

Hans moved to stand next to Chester, and he couldn't help the thrill that ran through him at the protective motion.

"I'd rather not put Chester in an awkward position," he said, glancing at Chester and then his dad.

But Johan shook his head. "Oh, that can wait," he said dismissively to Miriam. He looked sadly at Hans as he squeezed his shoulder. "It's been far too long already that we've been apart. I know I let you kids down, and I'd like to make up for that."

"Johan," said Miriam sharply, her eyes darting around the crowd before she fixed a smile on her husband again. "Let's not...there's no need to go over that here, like you said. Let bygones be bygones and all that. Tonight is about happiness and celebration."

Hans frowned. "Well, which is it?" he said, looking genuinely confused. "Are we going to talk about Dad's illness and the past ten years or not? I thought that's why we'd come here."

Chester knew that was why Hans was back, not for him. But as soon as he'd spoken, Hans turned to glance at him and squeeze his hand. Chester might have just been imagining things and giving in to wishful thinking, but he couldn't help but feel like Hans was trying to tell him that his parents weren't the *only* reason he was back in town. Not now, anyway.

"Well," said Johan in a placating tone, smiling at his children. "I'm also keen to hear what everyone's been up to and have a good old chin wag. And *of* course Hans's boyfriend is invited. I would rather try and make up for some lost time today, and then we can perhaps discuss some more practical details in the morning. What do you say, kids?"

Greta blinked at him, looking surprised. "Uh, sure. I'm still up for dinner. It's the reason we came here, after all."

Miriam still looked like she wanted to stop the whole thing, which Chester really couldn't understand. She and

Johan were the ones who had invited the kids back here. Why was she suddenly getting cold feet?

Unless *she* hadn't wanted them to come, and it was all Johan's idea? Maybe he was having a change of heart after all these years?

"I think you should go to dinner," said Chester to Hans earnestly, not wanting to stand in the way of any reunion. "And if it's just a family affair, I understand."

Hans frowned, then appeared to make a decision. "Okay, yeah. I'm still on for dinner. But I'd really like Chester there. We've also had too long apart, and I'd appreciate as much time as we can get together."

"Maybe Chester would like to sleep over as well?" Greta said, waggling her eyebrows.

Chester almost died on the spot. They were *not* ready for that conversation yet. Hans looked like he was going to combust from embarrassment.

Chester tried not to take that as him being horrified at the idea of sleeping with Chester, but maybe it was. Chester did his best to keep smiling and support his *friend* like he'd promised, and not take it too personally.

Hans's dad didn't seem to have noticed anything was amiss, probably because Dodger had wrapped his lead around Miriam's legs and was currently trying to topple her off her four-inch heels. Chester knew he liked this dog.

"Of course, of course," said Johan when Miriam was in less danger of hitting the cobbles. "Have you got transportation, Chester?"

"I've got my car," Chester said quickly. If he could drive Hans, that would be more time they could spend alone, which Chester was desperate for.

Hans beamed. "Oh, yeah, brilliant." He nodded at his sister and dad. "Maybe we could meet you all at the house. If we've got some time until dinner's ready, I'd like to take Chester around the market for a bit."

Chester tried very hard to tell his heart that this was just part of the charade, and Hans wasn't really planning on taking him on a little date. But god damn it, that *really* sounded like a date.

Oh – wait. Hans probably just wanted to go over their cover story more. They'd bluffed it with an earlier question, but they'd need to learn a bit more about each other's lives if they were going to fake this properly. Their ruse wouldn't go very far if Chester had no idea about the last ten years of Hans's life in London.

Except Greta seemed to think it was a date, too. "Aww, look at you two, all loved up." She smirked as she smacked Hans's arm. "It's gross. Yes, please get it out of your system before we have to sit down to dinner. You can make all the kissy faces you want here and other people can suffer instead."

"Love you too, sis," said Hans in exasperation.

But Johan clapped his hands together, and Dodger barked happily. "Excellent plan. Yes. Greta, do you want to meet us at the house when you're ready, too? Miriam and I will go see that everything's been set up just right. I want you two to feel right at home again," he added warmly.

"Oh, so long as you have some means of reaching the house, Greta," said Miriam with false concern. "I'm taking Johan home in the Porsche, and it only has two seats, don't you know? There's barely room for the dog!"

The way she shrieked with laughter told Chester that she'd rather leave poor Dodger out on the road than have him in her car. She always seemed to have some flashy sports car that she was driving too fast in, even before she got with Hans's dad. In fact, she seemed to delight in revving the engine when she was driving down the highway and scaring the shit out of pedestrians. Horrid woman.

There was no denying that there was a strange vibe in the air, and Chester felt like a lot wasn't being spoken aloud. But he wasn't sure what, and everyone seemed keen to go their separate ways and regroup for now. And he was definitely eager to get Hans to himself for the first time in a decade, so he happily bid them all goodbye. Chester spotted Greta throwing Hans an amused grin as she melted into the crowd, and tried to ignore the daggers that Miriam cast behind Johan's back at all three of them.

And then Chester had Hans all to himself.

Now what the hell did he do with him?

"Do you want to actually look around the market?" Chester asked tentatively.

To his relief, Hans blew out a breath and half-smiled. "Yeah, that sounds nice," he said, sounding genuine. Then looked down at Chester's arm and bit his lip. "Do you, uh, think we should hold hands? Just to keep up the act in case anyone, y'know, uh, sees."

Hans wanted to hold hands, even when there wasn't his family around to see? Chester admitted that they could come back at any second, but…well, it was difficult for his heart not to soar and for his hopes not to leap up. There was nothing more he'd like to do than hold hands again with the love of his life, even just for a little while, even if it was just – supposedly – for pretend.

And he couldn't help but wonder if Hans was really asking to keep up their ruse or just because he *wanted* to.

Either way, Chester licked his lips and couldn't stop the small smile that crept onto his face. "I'd like that, Hans," he said sincerely.

Hans huffed and gave him a dorky smile, looking at him through his lashes as he threaded their fingers together.

"Cool," he mumbled, but was it Chester's imagination, or did he seem utterly delighted?

Still my adorable teddy bear, Chester thought with deep fondness, unable to ignore how deeply *right* holding hands with Hans felt.

He might not be able to enjoy that feeling for more than a night, but he was going to make the most of it whilst he could.

7

CHESTER

No matter how many times Chester tried to tell himself otherwise, his heart kept insisting that this felt like a real date. The snow had stopped falling, but the night was still magical with all the twinkling lights and scents of nutmeg and spiced apple in the air.

For a while they just browsed the stalls, admiring the wares. Chester insisted on getting Hans another mulled cider, as he didn't have to drive like Chester did. But then Hans surprised Chester with a bag of delicious roasted chestnuts. They'd once shared a bag at the market as teenagers, and Chester wondered if Hans had remembered and bought them on purpose. But he was too cowardly to ask aloud, in case it broke the magical spell they were under.

It was crazy, but Chester couldn't actually remember the last time he'd seen Hans before he left. There hadn't been any big, tearful goodbye that he could recall. It was just as if Hans had been there one day, and then the next, he was gone. At first, that assured Chester that he'd be back, that nothing much would change in their lives. But after a few years, he wished he'd had something to explain why everything had indeed changed, a concrete event he could look back on and pinpoint as the moment where it had all gone wrong.

Now, though, that didn't seem so important. All those sleepless nights missing the one person that meant the most to him had all been washed away the moment that Hans Jager had walked back into Chester's life and told him that he was sorry. That he'd missed him.

Yes, everything was up in the air. Chester wasn't sure how much they were really pretending right now and how much he was simply relishing spending time with his favourite person in a way that felt like he'd never left. He had no idea what the future held or how much he should or shouldn't get his hopes up. He had no idea what the hell was going on with Hans's strange and complicated family. All he knew was that he could have spent all night playing hoopla and sampling mince pies with his best friend. But the reality was they had a job to do and not long to do it in.

"So," he said in what he hoped was a jovial tone as they walked away from a stall with incredible handmade marionette puppets. "If I'm your fake boyfriend, what do I need to know?"

Hans chuckled and sipped his mulled cider from the flimsy plastic cup it had come in. Chester had reminded him to throw the other crumpled one away and wipe the inside of his pocket out with a tissue to clean off any stray droplets of drink. It wasn't that Hans couldn't look after or think for himself, but Chester loved looking after him in a way that ran deep into his bones. He always had. And by the way Hans blushed at him and happily did as he was told, Chester couldn't help but think he felt the same.

Their dynamic was perfect. Was it really reckless of Chester to think it could only be improved by taking their relationship up a notch?

He was distracted by Hans's reply. He needed to pay

attention if he was going to convince the Jagers that they were really dating.

"I mean, what's there to know?" said Hans with a sigh. "I just work at a bakery, live in a house share with some other gay guys. Pretty much all the same as I told you when we last…since I stopped talking to you. Um, except the gay part. You didn't know that. Fucking hell." He flicked a sheepish look Chester's way. "I, um, only came out a few years ago. When I was twenty-five. I guess I was in denial or something for a while. I just wanted something in my life to be *easy*. You know?"

"Yeah," said Chester softly. "I do."

For him, staying in the closet had never been an option. He'd been fascinated by boys since he was a small child, and once he understood what gay was, he knew that was him. It did give him a little comfort, thinking about how his parents must have known that about him before they passed, and they had still loved him unconditionally. He had no doubt they would have supported his coming out as a teenager, just like his nana had.

But that wasn't to say things were *easy*. Sometimes, Chester would have given anything not to be the nerdy, gay orphan, the boy who everyone knew and pitied in the village. But this was who he was, and there was a strength that came from that. Chester hoped that was what Hans had come to realise at twenty-five. Accepting your authentic self was powerful.

"I'm glad you got there eventually," Chester carried on, rubbing his thumb over the back of Hans's hand. He was pleased when Hans smiled at him again.

"Me too," Hans agreed. "But it was selfish to cut you out. I should have shared that time in my life with you, not run away."

He shook his head and looked sad again, and Chester decided enough was enough. "No, stop," he said.

He pulled Hans over to a dark corner by a stall selling toffee liqueur in glass bottles shaped like angels. The glow of multicoloured Christmas lights reflected off Hans's face, picking out individual strands of his beard which almost threatened to distract Chester too much. He wanted to nuzzle it *so* badly. But he snapped himself back into the moment.

"We can't keep beating ourselves up over the last ten years," Chester insisted. "Life happens. We both pulled away from each other for a while. However, we're here now, and we can control what happens next. But you don't ever have to explain to me that coming out was a big deal that you had to sort through in your own way. I'm happy for you, and I'm glad it's another experience we can share together, as friends."

He probably shouldn't have said the last part. It was pointing to the elephant in the room. They were both gay and therefore could theoretically be attracted to each other. But they had to get through the dinner and whatever revelations Hans's family had in store first. Then they could riffle through their feelings and maybe see where the future took them.

"We can really do that?" Hans said faintly, shaking his head as he stared at Chester. "Start again? Or…rather just keep going. Like nothing happened?"

Chester shrugged. "Not exactly," he said. "A lot's happened. But I think we need to stop lingering and start moving forwards again. We've both said we're sorry. Now I think we should make the most of the night, don't you?"

Hans licked his lips. "Okay," he murmured.

His mouth glistened in the fairy lights. Chester suddenly

realised how close they were in this dark corner, and he still had his hand on Hans's arm where he'd pulled them over. Hans smelled so good, all woodsy and musky and, of course, sweet. His teddy bear was always sweet. From the cider and chocolate and whatever else he'd been sampling in the market, he was like Chester's own pick 'n' mix. A buffet of delight…

…and they were too close!

Chester jumped away and walked back out into the main path of the market, shoving his gloved hands into his pockets and laughing awkwardly. "Okay, great. No more self-flagellating, then. Let's work out this dastardly ruse of ours. I said we started texting again a few months ago. I guess the rest is history now?"

Hans came out of their little hidey-hole with a strange look on his face that Chester couldn't quite place. But then he smiled and nodded. "Sounds good," he said. They fell into step, walking together. When Chester slipped his hand back into Hans's, he didn't act like it was anything unusual. In fact, it felt perfectly natural.

For a while, they just ambled by the stalls, side-by-side, until Chester felt like the intense moment had been forgotten. "So, a bakery?" he asked. "That sounds fun."

Hans shrugged, but a small smile crept onto his face. "I mostly just make bread rolls. But sometimes, I get to help out with the cakes and pastries." A blush *definitely* blossomed on his cheeks at that. "That's what I really love. Sweet things. I don't have to tell you that, though, do I?" He laughed, rich and hearty, and Chester's heart ached in a good way. Where their hands were connected felt electric, simmering with heat, even through Chester's glove. "One day, I'd like to have my own place. It such a silly, simple thing. But cookies and sticky buns make people so happy, you know?"

"Everyone needs a little sweet treat in their life, I think," Chester told Hans. He still knew Hans so well after all this time, and it reminded him that the future didn't have to be this scary, complicated thing. Maybe a part of it could just be baking, like Hans said.

In Chester's dreams, *Hans* was his sweet treat.

Hans cleared his throat, and Chester realised he'd been staring at him, probably with a dopey look on his face. He looked away but couldn't stop the grin from spreading on his face or the tingles that flew over his skin.

"How about you, then?" Hans asked. "I can't believe you ended up working at the Candy Cauldron. How is it dealing with Ethel day in, day out?"

He winced, and Chester couldn't blame him. "Honestly," Chester said as they wove their way through the crowd, *still* holding hands, "I love everything about my job aside from her."

"I mean, that's not hard to believe," said Hans with warm affection, making it clear he was sympathetic of Chester's plight.

Chester sighed, not just because he was thinking of Ethel. They'd kind of run out of stalls to look at, and Hans's cider was almost done. As much as Chester didn't want the moment to end, he knew they had a dinner to get to.

"Should we start making our way to my car?" he asked reluctantly.

"Hm? Oh, yeah," said Hans, his face dropping a little. Chester couldn't help but hope that was because he'd been enjoying their not-date as well and didn't want it to end either. "Sure, lead the way."

There was every chance, however, that this was just the start of something special between them again...just friendship, or something more...

Chester winced internally. What was he thinking? Hans's life was in London, and Chester had no plans to leave Gingerbread. What did he think was going on here?

No, he needed to remember that whatever was happening was just for an evening. Hans wasn't moving back to Gingerbread, not with his step-mother making his life unbearable here, and Chester had no intention of abandoning his village or his nana. He had no plans for uprooting his whole life. Besides, the store would fall apart without him. Sure, they could maybe get another assistant manager, but this was his *home*.

Things weren't going back to the good old days. Hans was still going to be almost a hundred miles away in London, which would be fine for a casual friendship, but nothing like what they had before. Certainly not a romantic relationship. Chester needed to stop getting his hopes up.

If only his heart would get that memo.

"Yeah, uh, Ethel," he said, wrangling his head back into the previous conversation. "She's the same as she always was. I thought I could improve things from the inside, but it's like she hates everything about the business and isn't interested in any kind of change or improvement. If it weren't for me, everyone would be out of a job, and a shop that's stood for hundreds of years would go under – I'm not joking."

He blew a raspberry to show his frustration. But then Hans squeezed his hand, making Chester's heart flutter, and he looked over into his friend's big brown eyes, warm with fondness.

"I bet you've got loads of ideas," Hans said warmly. "You always did like to think outside of the box."

It was Chester's turn to blush. "Uh, I – well," he stammered, biting his lip in pleasure at the praise. "I'd really *love* to make the entire shop vegan friendly. I think using gelatine in sweets in this day and age is barbaric, and vegan chocolate has been around for years. We could totally offer both dairy and non-dairy options. And a better nut-free range. When I picked up those lollies for those kids, I also grabbed a bunch of candy canes as well in case they had any allergies. But I'd like to make *every* kid feel welcome in the shop. Make it a haven, like it was for us."

For a second, Hans didn't say anything, so Chester glanced over to see his friend beaming at him. "That's so kind," said Hans, shaking his head. "You and your big old heart, always taking care of other people. I'm not even surprised."

"Yeah, well," said Chester to cover his self-conscious cough. Hans was going to *kill* him at this rate with all his little niceties. "It's not like Ethel will ever listen to me. She's all about profit, so she wants the cheapest crap to sell at the highest price." He rolled his eyes. "Except for that bloody charity tin. I mean, don't get me wrong, I'm happy that she apparently *does* have some kind of heart, and I give to it happily. But I wish she'd stop teasing us with Christmas bonuses every year, only to basically bully us all into giving all the money to the charity."

Hans frowned. "How's she doing that?"

Chester sighed. "Sneakily. One year, a guy refused, and then in the new year, mysteriously Ethel accused him of stealing from the till. There wasn't any real proof, but he still lost his job. It's like an unwritten rule she has that we all have to comply with."

It sounded so pathetic out loud, and Chester was embarrassed that he couldn't seem to do more to fix the shop than he was. But when customers still shopped there, he didn't really have a leg to stand on to implement change.

"So," he said, switching the subject from his exasperating job situation. "How are we going to explain the long-distance thing if anyone asks? If we're dating, we'd probably have talked about that."

Okay, so…yeah. He might have had ulterior motives for asking that. He wanted to see if Hans had thought that through. And if they came up with a hypothetical answer, maybe Chester could daydream about putting it into practice.

But Hans's face fell. "Uh. Yeah, that's a good point." He chewed his lip and frowned, looking down at the floor. "I dunno. Maybe we say that we're just going to see how it goes? Honestly, I couldn't keep a relationship going in London, so I've got no idea."

That hadn't been the answer Chester had been hoping for. But what had he been expecting, really? For Hans to admit that he had a pair of ruby red slippers under his bed and that he'd just click his heels three times whenever he wanted to come visit?

"Sure, that sounds like a good enough answer," said Chester, mustering up as much cheeriness as he could. "They probably won't ask anyway, but it's good to be prepared."

"Totally," said Hans.

Chester refused to let himself be disappointed that they hadn't come up with a solution to their location issue on the spot. He was determined to enjoy his evening with his best friend, so that was what he would do.

They'd wandered away from the market now and had gone down the side street where Chester had parked his ancient, bright orange Mini Cooper. The thing was about fifty years old, he swore. But his nana had given it to him after he'd passed his driving test, and it was pretty much his most prized possession.

When it started. If it started.

Watching Hans try and fold himself into the clapped-out classic Mini was kind of funny, only because Hans was laughing, too. "Oh my god, this is a clown car!" he teased Chester. "Did you specifically get the most anti-me banger you could find?"

Chester eyed him warmly as he slid into the driver's seat.

"Yeah…I always knew you'd be back one day, and I wanted to make sure I gave you a hard time when you did."

A dark look flashed across Hans's face, and Chester wished he could take the joke back. He bit his lip and reached across to squeeze Hans's thigh.

"Sorry, that was bad taste," Chester said as their eyes met. He exhaled, wishing that they weren't dancing around each other in so many different ways. "I missed you, but I'm so glad you're here now and we're getting up to trouble again. That's it. That's all that matters."

Hans perked up. "Yeah, you're right," he said, nodding. "This right here and now is what matters. Regrets are pointless."

"Unless you learn from them," said Chester, still clinging on to that cruel hope that was lingering in his heart. "Like… not texting your best friend for years because you're afraid he's moved on from you. That's one I plan on learning from."

The look they shared practically sparked with longing and tension, but Chester had no way to know if that was just how he was feeling and he was imagining it on Hans's part. So he slipped his hand back off Hans's leather-clad thigh and started the Mini's engine. Mercifully, it started first time for once.

"Uh, what's the postcode?" Chester asked as he got his phone out to activate the navigation app.

He'd never been to Hans's enormous family home, but even if he had, he wasn't going to remember an address from a decade ago. Apparently, Hans didn't even remember it himself. Chester watched as he frowned and retrieved his own phone, jabbing at it and scrolling down the screen until he found what they needed.

For the next few minutes, Chester focused on setting up his phone to direct them to the house, then on safely easing the car's tyres over the freshly fallen snow. The heater sputtered valiantly at them, trying to puff some warm air their way. At least the lights weren't on the blink tonight.

Chester had always kind of known that the Jagers' estate and home was outside of the village. Both Hans's mum and dad were from old money, and their families were both independently wealthy. But he was a little concerned when the SatNav started taking them into the middle of the forest. "Uh…" he began to question if this was the right way.

"I promise I won't stop texting you this time," Hans blurted, cutting off Chester's query.

What Chester really wanted to do was swing and face Hans, then search his face, asking if he really meant that. An ember of hope flared to life inside Chester's heart, wanting to believe that Hans wouldn't just vanish from his world again like he had before.

But he couldn't tear his eyes from the road. Now that they'd left the village, a freezing fog had enveloped the night, and Chester would have been lying if he said he wasn't a little worried.

"I, uh," he said, biting his lip as his heart rate picked up. It was like they'd been dropped into pea soup. The fog was kind of beautiful, glowing in the moonlight reflected off the fallen snow, but in the space of about ten seconds, Chester had gone from driving normally to slowing right down to a crawl. "Yes, Hans, I…me too, I just…"

Chester shivered, the coldness seeping into the car despite the heater's best efforts. He glanced at the directions from his phone clamped to a holder that was suckered to the windscreen. They were still a seventeen-minute drive from the house. It really was out in the middle of nowhere, surrounded by acres of woodland.

Chester recalled that the estate ran in the family from Hans's mother's side, and that was one of the reasons she had ridden her horses around the grounds with such confidence, as she'd known the woods inside and out since childhood.

Until the accident.

Did that mean one day this property would fall to Hans or Greta? Or both? Or would Miriam even allow that?

Chester shook his head. He could mull over all of this during what was bound to be their very awkward dinner. There were already verging on being late, but Chester hadn't factored in the risk of sudden freezing fog hindering their drive. He forced down his anxiety over making a bad impression to Hans's family and focused solely on driving safely.

Or at least, that was what he tried to do.

"It's okay. We don't need to talk about it," mumbled Hans, sounded wretched.

"No!" Chester blurted out as he navigated a corner at a snail's pace, but still feeling like he was about to tip over the crest of a rollercoaster. "It's not that I don't want to talk about it. I do! It's just that the weather's atrocious and I'm just trying to drive safely." He gritted his teeth, unable to stop his fears from starting to spill out. "I love that you're back, Hans, but for how long? I know we're just pretending right now, but I feel…"

The words died in his throat.

About the same time that the engine also died, jerking the car to a halt and flickering the headlamps off with it.

8

HANS

"WHAT'S GOING ON?" HANS ASKED.

Chester licked his lips, his throat bobbing as he swallowed. "I think the fog got into the engine," he whispered. "It's happened to me once before." He bit his lip and put the car back in neutral, then tried turning the keys. The ignition clicked, and the starter turned over, but nothing caught.

"Fuck," Hans said. He glanced at the map that was currently being displayed on Chester's phone. They were still pretty far from home.

'Home'. *That's not the right word,* thought Hans ruefully. Not since his mum had died. 'The house he'd grown up in' was a more apt description these days.

Chester shook himself and suddenly twisted the keys back, then pulled them out from the ignition. "We need to get out of the car, now," he said as he hastily freed his phone from the display holder and grabbed his bag from the backseat. "We could get smashed into by anyone coming around the corner too fast."

Hans frowned and reached for his door handle. "Shit, yeah. I wouldn't have thought about that."

It was freezing outside. Way colder than it had been at the market. He gasped in a lungful of air that made him cough, then hastily shut the car's passenger door.

Chester was already busy locking the doors, then popping the boot to retrieve the reflective red hazard triangle to prop up against the Mini's back wheel. Hopefully, that would stop anyone from crashing into it. But Hans still didn't feel like sitting inside the vehicle, just in case.

A horrible thought flooded through him.

What if he'd only just got Chester back, only to lose him to a car crash or hypothermia?

No. No, Hans wouldn't let that happen. He'd give Chester all his clothes to keep him warm if he had to.

"Should we call roadside assistance?" Hans asked, only to look over and see Chester waggle the phone that was pressed against his ear.

"Already on it," he said. His teeth were chattering, and his body was visibly trembling. At least he had his hat and gloves on, but he was so much smaller than Hans he was bound to still be losing more body heat.

Right, time for Hans to do his job and keep his best friend warm. He strode over and enveloped Chester from behind, wrapping his big arms around Chester's slim, shivering frame. Immediately, he felt his friend relax against him. Hans could just about hear the hold music coming through the phone.

"Warmer?" Hans asked. *God.* It felt so right hugging Chester. It was as if they were really boyfriends and it was the most natural thing in the world for Hans to snuggle with Chester like this. They'd always been pretty physical with each other as teenagers. Playfully shoving and grabbing each other as much as they'd hugged and leaned against each other. Why did things have to be so complicated now?

Chester sighed, no longer quivering, and fitting perfectly against Hans's chest. "Much better, thank you," he said.

He glanced over his shoulder, and they locked eyes, and all Hans could think was how easy it would be to lean down and kiss Chester in that moment. In fact…had Chester just inched a fraction closer to Hans? Were their mouths really only millimetres apart? What if Hans were just to…?

"Hi! Yes, hello!" Chester blurted as someone picked up the call. Hans snapped his head back, cursing himself. He hadn't come over to hug Chester to try it *on* with him. That was creepy. He was just trying to protect him from the elements.

No more kissing thoughts, Hans scolded himself.

He couldn't quite make out the words on the other end of the call, but he could tell from Chester's responses that it wasn't good news. "Okay." Pause. "Yes, I understand." Another pause. "No, that'll be fine. We'll manage. Okay, thank you," he said heavily before closing the call.

"What is it?" Hans asked.

Chester shook his head as he pocketed his phone, then clung to Hans's arms. The fog swirled around them like a living thing, clinging to their breath and seeping into their clothes, right down to their bones. "They can't get anyone out until the morning. The dispatcher said they had a four hundred percent increase in calls in the past couple of hours. Apparently, the fog is everywhere and they're stretched too thin. I thought we could probably walk to your house from here, so she's booked us in for the morning."

Hans clenched his jaw, trying not to let his panic show. "Okay," he said slowly. "You know it's pretty far, though?"

Chester nodded and sighed. "She basically said there was no hope of a tow tonight, so I was being optimistic."

Hans chewed on his lip. "I definitely don't want to call my

family and ask anyone to come get us. That would just endanger them, too."

"Agreed," said Chester. Damn it. He was already shivering again despite Hans's body heat.

What were they going to do? They were *miles* from the house, and Chester knew it. They'd both seen the map…wait, the map.

Hans got his phone out and brought up their current location. Luckily, the internet was only being a bit slow. They could have no signal at all and be really shafted.

"Look," he said, showing Chester the screen. "We're here, and the road *would* be seventeen more miles because the woods are also protected heathland, so the road has to go all the way around them. But look." He zoomed out just a little and showed Chester the property. "We're actually not that far from the house as the crow flies. We could walk it in a couple of hours or less, I bet."

Chester blinked, then looked back at Hans. The fear was clear on his face. "Walk *through* the woods…at night…in freezing fog?"

Hans licked his lips. "Yeah, when you put it like that, it doesn't sound great. But we can't stay here until morning."

Chester dropped his head and was quiet for a minute. Luckily, the road was empty, and there hadn't been another car go past them yet. In fact, as the road pretty much only led to Hans's family estate, the chances of another vehicle were extremely small. So he didn't fancy waiting around trying to thumb a lift, either. But that did mean that there was less of a chance that Chester's car would get hit, even with the reflective triangle.

Hans looked at the map, assessing their options again, when he realised with a jolt he knew where they were.

It was the bend where his mum had died.

His shiver was nothing to do with the cold. He felt like

he'd walked over her grave without realising. Hans had always wondered if it had been a car that spooked Peanut Butter that day because his mum had been found so close to the road. But despite him being quite a young horse, his mum had been riding her entire life and would have been able to control him if it had just been a passing vehicle, Hans was sure. So that day remained a mystery.

This wasn't the time to be ruminating on that old wound, though. Despite his size, he was starting to get cold. He really wished he had a hat and gloves.

"Right, shall we try and make it to the house?" he asked.

"Yeah, I guess we should try," Chester said. "In which case…"

He pulled away from Hans's embrace, and immediately Hans wanted to protest. He realised he didn't have any right to simply because he was enjoying it, but he was worried about Chester's safety. "You'll get cold," he said, hoping he wasn't pouting.

Chester laughed, his breath curling out as smoke. But the sound reassured Hans that Chester hadn't pulled away because he was uncomfortable. Hopefully. "That's what I'm doing," he said as he popped the boot again. "I think I've got…ah! Here we go. A spare hat and gloves for you, and a torch, so we don't drain our phone batteries."

Hans blinked as Chester locked the car again. It was as if he'd heard Hans's thoughts. Bloody hell, he'd forgotten just how much he loved Chester taking care of him. It was like they were so in sync Chester could just sense what Hans needed. Hans wished he could do something like that for his friend in return.

"Wow. That's so incredibly prepared," he said, impressed. "Thank you."

He stilled as Chester didn't pass him the hat. He pulled it on Hans's head himself. Hans's heart flipped at such an intimate act. He couldn't remember anyone dressing him since his mum had when he'd been a small child. He realised a lump had risen in his throat, and his pulse was racing. Chester's hands were still either side of his face, tugging on the bobble hat to get it just right.

Their faces were inches apart again, their cloudy breaths mingling together.

Chester's gaze flicked from the hat to meet Hans's eyes, and for a second he also froze. Then he laughed and stepped back, handing Hans the gloves. "There you go," he said with a cough. "That should help a lot. And when we get walking, we'll heat up." He clicked the torch on, and its beam pierced through the fog. "Lead the way."

Hans wasn't sure if he was disappointed or confused. He thought they might have almost kissed in the dark back at the market, as well as when they'd been waiting for the phone call to connect just now. Combined with this, was that three almost kisses in the space of half an hour? Or was he completely imagining things?

Regardless, this wasn't the moment to stand around and mull it over. It was too cold, and they had a long walk ahead of them. He glanced at his phone and assessed which direction to point them in as they entered the woods.

"This way."

Chester sighed as he crossed the road with Hans. "This isn't exactly the evening I'd been hoping for," he said.

Hans huffed and moved to take Chester's hand, leading him through the tree line across the road. He wasn't sure if holding his hand again complicated things further, but he wanted to keep Chester close in the dark, so decided not to dwell on it.

"Tell me about it," Hans grumbled. "I was dreading dinner, but even that seems preferable now. We should just have stayed at the damn market and had some proper food there. At least that way we wouldn't be cold *and* hungry. Lucky we had those roasted chestnuts, I guess."

He bit his lip, wondering if Chester remembered that they'd shared a bag of those before, when they'd visited the market as teenagers.

Chester didn't give any indication either way. "They were yummy," he did agree, though. "I've still got those candy canes if we get desperate," he said with a weak chuckle.

Hans tried not to be disappointed. He'd have to be a bit braver with his feelings than that and not give Chester some cryptic sign that he had to decipher. Something like asking 'Hey, did we almost just kiss? Because I might like that' rather than 'I'm going to recreate something we did when we were young because I want to know if you *like me* like me without having to ask outright'.

He might be twenty-eight, but in some ways, he still felt like that awkward bloody teenager.

"Don't joke," he said darkly, continuing the conversation. "It might come to that. I'm a very grouchy boy when I can't eat. Oh, shit. Speaking of which, I better call Greta so she can let everyone know we're going to be late for dinner…or just miss it altogether."

He sighed, using his free hand to press the phone to his ear. He'd noticed that Chester had let his hand be held with no protest or fuss, and Hans couldn't help but feel hopeful that was a good sign.

"Miriam's either going to be happy that she'll have two fewer queers in the house," Hans said to Chester as he waited for the call to his sister to connect, "or mega-pissed that we ruined her special fancy meal."

"I bet she'll find a way to be both," Chester said with a scoff as they made their way deeper into the forest.

It was possibly slightly warmer with the density of the foliage, but it was also darker, with only the single beam of torchlight to guide them. They should probably turn it off and try and let their eyes adjust to the gloom, but Hans really didn't fancy that. He'd have been lying if he said he wasn't a little freaked out, but he had to be strong for Chester. He'd promised to take care of his friend, and that was what he was going to do.

"Hey, bro," said Greta cheerfully as she finally answered the phone. "You dead yet?"

"Har har," said Hans in a deadpan tone. That was one of her favourite greetings. "Close, but not quite."

"Oh, shit," said Greta, immediately serious. "I was kidding. What happened?"

Hans shook his head, even though Greta couldn't see him. "We're okay. But Chester's car completely broke down in the fog. We've had to abandon it and are now walking through the grounds to get to the house. I reckon we're a couple of hours away."

Predictably, Greta wanted to come to their rescue. "I'll come get you," she said immediately before swearing. "Fuck, I've already had a glass of wine, though, and it's Dad's *really* good French stuff, so it's gone straight to my head. I could ask him-"

"No, seriously," Hans said. "I don't want any of you out in this fog. It's dangerous. We're warmer now we're walking, and we've got our phones for navigation. Just tell Dad and Miriam we're really sorry about dinner and that we'll get there when we can."

Greta wasn't happy, but she grumbled that she would and threatened Hans that if he didn't send her regular proof that they were still alive, she'd come and find them and kill him herself. He just laughed and told her he loved her, too, then closed the call.

Before pocketing his phone, he checked it to make sure they were still headed in the right direction. Luckily, it had been fully charged when they'd left London, and he'd hardly used it all day as he'd been incapacitated on the back of Greta's bike. Between him and Chester, they should hopefully have enough charge to get them all the way to the house.

If the shadows didn't get them first.

Hans knew he had to be brave, but damn, it was fucking *creepy* in here. Every rustle of leaves or swirl of fog had him on edge, and even worse, the easy conversation they'd been enjoying before had dried up. Of course they were concentrating on traipsing through the woods and not getting eaten by wolves, but in the near silence, Hans's insecurities were getting the better of him.

Everything had been going so well at the market after the rest of his family had left. He and Chester had been having such a nice time. It had almost felt like a real date, and he'd felt okay about this pretending to be boyfriends malarkey.

But then Hans had gone and made it weird in the car by reminding Chester of how Hans had just let their incredibly important friendship fizzle out because he'd been too afraid. Chester probably didn't fancy him, no matter what Hans's stupid heart was hoping. As much as he wanted it to be something more, the hand-holding was purely practical to keep them together and not slip on their arses.

Then what about the almost kisses?

He sighed. Just because they were both gay and Hans had finally found the courage to come out didn't mean their friendship was going to morph into something else. It hadn't even been a real friendship for years. Just a memory. He was probably just imagining those almost kisses.

But that didn't stop him from yearning for Chester with every fibre of his being. Their connected hands felt like they were pulsing from the electricity that was tingling between them. As they walked, he kept glancing back to make sure

Chester was right behind him, and every glimpse just seemed to confirm what Hans's heart already knew.

Chester had been his best friend when they were teenagers because Hans had loved him. And not only was that love still there, but it was now stronger and keener because want and desire were thrumming on top as well. Chester was Hans's perfect puzzle piece, the missing link that made him better because he just adored this sweet, clever, diligent, thoughtful man.

But maybe Chester didn't feel the same, and Hans would have to find a way to be okay with that. Certainly from the stony expression on his face and the tension in his body, he wasn't happy.

"I'm so sorry," Hans said after he couldn't bear it any longer, pulling his hand free. It felt too complicated to keep them linked just then.

Chester blinked like he was coming out of a trance. "What?" he said incredulously, his eyebrows rising. He stopped, so Hans did as well so he could turn and face him. "Why would you be sorry? *I'm* sorry! It's my car that stranded us and ruined our night." He clenched his jaw and looked away, his expression bitter. "We've only got one evening together, and my old banger spoiled it all."

Hans blinked, his heart aching for how upset Chester was. "No, *no*," he said, stepping closer. "*I'm* sorry. I had to leave home all those years ago, and the one time I've been able to come back, we've had to mess around, pretending to be boyfriends instead of just remembering to be friends and enjoy each other's company. We've had to rehearse answers and lie, and it's just all a load of *bollocks*. I don't like you being cold or scared or anything like that. But any time I get to spend with you feels like an early Christmas present."

He took several deep breaths, the condensation clouding

up the air in front of him as thickly as the fog that was still hanging around them like an unwanted spectre.

Chester opened and closed his mouth a couple of times. "Hans, I…" He shook his head, like he wasn't sure what to say. Then he bit his lip and nodded like he'd decided something. "I wish you were here for more than just one night."

That struck Hans right in his chest. Chester wanted him to stay?

But he couldn't.

It wasn't that he didn't want to. He'd tried to convince himself over the years that he'd been lucky to escape such a small, boring town. But the moment he'd returned, he'd realised how untrue that was. He loved Gingerbread. He loved the people, and the pace of life, and the beauty.

But the town didn't want him back. Besides, he didn't *deserve* to be allowed to come back. If it hadn't been for him and Greta, their mum would never have been out riding in that moment. She wouldn't have been angry, so she would have been able to control her horse instead of letting him buck her into that tree. She would still be alive and married to Hans's dad, and Hans would never have had to leave home.

Leave Chester.

But that was his deepest shame, and there was nothing he could do to change it. He'd never even talked about it all with Chester, because he'd been so afraid to see that same look of disappointment on his face as Hans had seen around town. So, no. He couldn't stay for more than one night.

"I wish I could, too," he said sadly. He ached for Chester, but maybe it just wasn't meant to be. "But maybe you could come visit me in London sometime?"

Even as he spoke the words, he knew it wouldn't be enough. He didn't want a faraway friend. He wanted his best friend back in his life every day. Anything else would just be dangling temptation in front of his face, and Hans had never been very good with temptation. He had to remove it completely. Otherwise, he would always give in.

And, *fuck* he wanted to give in to Chester.

Who was shivering.

"Shit, let's get moving again, yeah," said Hans. He rubbed Chester's arms and hugged him for a moment, trying to warm him up again. "We can't have you freezing to death!"

For a second, Chester leaned into the embrace and sighed. Then he nodded and pulled away. "No, no freezing to death," he agreed as he began walking again, swinging the torch to illuminate the sort-of path they were on. "And yeah, sure, maybe I could brave London sometime. That might be nice." He didn't really sound convinced, though.

Hans bit his lip, his thoughts running away as they began their journey again. There wasn't really anything tying him to London aside from Greta, and she had loads of friends anyway. Hans didn't have to stay there. He had no money to his name, but rent was slightly cheaper outside of London. Could he try and move to a town or village closer to Gingerbread? But that was pointless if he'd already blown it with Chester by not being here for ten years.

Urgh, Hans's head was such a mess. His throat clamped up as he trailed behind his friend deeper into the forest. Here he was planning on moving house mere hours after reuniting with Chester. He was hopeless. How had he not realised his feelings when he'd been younger, when they might have had a chance to do something about it? Had too much time passed now?

He didn't know how Chester felt in any case, so he needed to get over himself and *ask* him before he started making grand plans. He'd held back in the past for fear of ruining their friendship. But that damage was already done, so what did he really have to lose now?

Not until they got somewhere warm, though. His cheeks were burning, and his teeth chattered from being out in the elements for so long. He was frozen inside and out, and his feet were aching from slipping through the mud and over the slick tree roots emerging from the ground.

"How are you doing?" he asked Chester. Because if he was cold, Chester must be worse. How were they going to make it all the way to the house? They'd only been walking maybe half an hour. They probably had another hour to go, at least.

Chester didn't answer for a moment. Then he turned to face Hans again. "I could do with a hug," he said weakly. Even in the dim light, Hans could see his lips were blue and he was trembling from head to toe.

"Oh, baby! Come here!" Hans didn't hesitate to throw his arms around him. He didn't care he'd said 'baby'. There were more important things to worry about right then, and by the way Chester snuggled against him, he didn't seem to mind in any case.

"Thanks, big guy," he mumbled against Hans's chest. Hans rubbed his back and arms and pressed his cold cheek against Chester's damp beanie hat. He tried to use his whole body to warm up his friend, but of course that meant certain intimate areas were now right against each other too, and Hans bit his cold lip hard to try not to allow his cock to do anything inappropriate.

He would have given anything to make Chester warm, however, and all he had was his body. So that would have to do.

But suddenly he felt another shiver that wasn't anything to do with the cold. Just like before, when he'd realised they'd been at the site on the road of his mum's death. Like he was walking over her grave – or someone was walking over *his* grave. However, it wasn't really a bad or creepy feeling, just as if they weren't quite *alone*.

And that was when he saw the arrow.

It took him a second to appreciate what he was seeing in the dark, but it was definitely there, and memories flooded Hans as well as a big balloon of hope.

"Chester, look!" he said excitedly. He pointed at the engraving, and Chester swung the torch beam around until he could see what Hans was pointing at.

"What's that?" he asked, curious.

Thanks to Hans, Chester's teeth were no longer chattering, at least. So Hans didn't let him go as he moved them closer to inspect the carving. He reached up and rubbed the bark, feeling the engraving there through his glove. It was slightly weather-worn, but there was very clearly an arrow carved into the wood. Hans recognised it from his childhood, and his cold skin tingled with a sense of belonging he hadn't felt for fifteen years.

"It's a sign," he said, meaning that in both senses of the word.

Strangeness welled up inside him, warming him from the cold. It honestly felt in that moment like his mum was reaching out from the beyond and pointing the way, helping out her lost child and his love.

Hans indicated the arrow engraved into the tree right in front of them. It was pointing left, the way they'd been walking. "My grandnan made these markings when she was a girl," said Hans, tracing his gloved fingers over the deep grooves. "Then my mum showed Greta and me when we were little. I'd completely forgotten about them."

Chester touched the arrow as well, then looked the way it was pointing. "What is it, though? Where does it lead?" he asked.

Hans sighed. "I don't know if it's still standing. But it

might be somewhere warm. And if not, these arrows will eventually take us home, so they're probably more reliable to follow than the map, if nothing else."

Chester turned and looked up at Hans, his cheeks red and his blue eyes wide with fondness. "Are we going on an adventure?"

Relief rushed through Hans. Chester had always managed to distract Hans from his sadness with some silly, hare-brained adventure when they'd been young. This was truly Hans's best friend, and there was hope that things weren't completely ruined between them.

For now, they had a purpose once more. "Yeah," he said, nodding as a smile crept onto his face. "A little adventure. If you trust me?"

Chester scoffed, as if that was even in question. "Of course I do." Then his face lit up. "Double-dare super-promise!"

Hans's mouth dropped open. "Double-dare super-promise. I haven't heard that in ten *years,*" he marvelled as he shook his head. "I'd completely forgotten about that. We used to say it all the time!"

Chester beamed, wriggling happily against Hans. "I'd forgotten, too. I haven't had anyone to say it to until now." He laughed and gave Hans a squeeze. "It's good to have my adventure partner back."

Hans's heart felt like it might burst right out of his chest from longing, and as they looked at each other, the urge to lean down and kiss Chester was almost too hard to ignore.

But Hans remained a gentleman.

"Shall we see where the trail leads?" he asked, jutting his chin at the decades' old grooves in the tree. Of course, Hans knew where he *hoped* it would lead. They just had to see if anything much had changed in the thirteen or so years since Hans had last followed the arrows.

Chester bit his lip and grinned. "I'd love that," he said eagerly. "Maybe this evening won't be a total disaster, after all."

As far as Hans was concerned, it couldn't be a disaster if they got to spend time together again. But hopefully, they might be able to stop and get warm for a little while before trekking to the house, and if Chester was taken care of, then Hans was happy.

If that was all he could do just then, he'd take it in a heartbeat. He could sort his feelings and his potentially broken heart out later when he was back in London. For now, they were together and the night wasn't over yet. So Hans was going to do his best to save it.

Like Chester had always saved him.

9

CHESTER

"THERE," SAID CHESTER, POINTING EAGERLY AS HE SPOTTED the next marker up ahead.

He was still bone cold, shivering, and warring with his feelings about Hans, but there was nothing like being on a little excursion with his best friend again for a good distraction. Sure, it helped that the trail might lead them 'somewhere warm', but the thrill of searching for the arrows was giving Chester some much-needed adrenaline that was warming him up right now.

That and Hans's regular teddy bear cuddles that Chester really couldn't get enough of.

Hans squeezed his hand and picked up the pace a little. Chester couldn't believe they were still holding hands. Hans had mentioned something about not wanting Chester to fall over in the dark, but Chester had to question if it wasn't something more. Something to get excited about.

"Well done," Hans said as they got up close to the marker Chester had seen. "I hardly ever followed the arrows from this direction. They're all over the estate's grounds, but Greta and I only really ever used the ones going away from the house."

Chester smiled at his best friend's enthusiasm. Chester still had no idea what they were forging ahead towards, but that was part of the fun: trusting that Hans was leading them the right way, and that Chester wouldn't be disappointed when they got there. Or, if time had ravaged whatever they were looking for, that Hans would push on and they'd follow the arrows to the safety of his house.

As much as Chester still loved fussing over Hans after all these years, he was also enjoying this new, older version of his best friend, who was more confident at taking care of Chester, too. The cuddles and hand-holding and decision-making were all very attractive, Chester couldn't lie.

"Oh, wow," said Hans softly, his breath curling in the night air. "I think this might be it." The fog clung to the trees all around them, but the torchlight gave them a little illumination as they approached *something* up ahead.

At first, all Chester could make out was a mound of earth in front of them. It wasn't very high, but it was noticeable as there were no trees growing on this patch. There were plenty of branches that had grown above, like the other trees had stretched to try and close the gap in the canopy, but the mound was in a neat little clearing of its own.

Over it grew a mix of trailing ivy, pale green moss that seemed to glow in the faint moonlight, blades of grass, and pretty little yellow flowers that were poking proudly out of the soil. It was amazing the small blooms could survive in winter, and Chester admired their spirit. Everything was dusted with only a light sprinkle of snow as the canopy above had mostly protected the ground.

And then Chester saw the door.

He gasped as he and Hans moved around the what had to be

the front of the mound, pointing the torch at the entranceway. Half a dozen steep steps led down to a wooden door that you could easily miss if you weren't specifically looking for it, especially in the dark. Around the frame was corrugated tin, making a tiny rounded archway around the door.

Chester's eyebrows shot up. "It's an Anderson shelter," he said in awe.

Hans nodded, his eyes blinking rapidly for a few seconds as Chester guessed he fought back tears. His emotions always ran so close to the surface, and Chester loved that about him.

He loved everything about his teddy bear, he realised.

"My Grandnan's family put this in during the war," Hans explained, hugging Chester to him again for warmth. It was like the best security blanket ever. "They had others near the house that were removed before I was even born, but they left this one. It was for anyone caught out in the woods if an air raid struck." He rubbed Chester's arms. "My mum used it as her playhouse growing up, and then Greta and I used to muck about in it. I bet it's filled with spiders now, but seeing as we found the arrows, I thought it might be the perfect port in a storm. Or at least nice to take a little detour down memory lane."

He took a deep, shuddery breath that was raw with sadness. It made Chester want to pepper kisses all over his face.

"Can we go inside?" Chester whispered in the quiet of the night.

Hans laughed. "I dunno," he said, sniffing and laughing again, like he was shaking off his melancholy. "I hope so. It's probably a wreck now. I doubt anyone's been out here since Greta and I were kids. But maybe we could try and warm up a bit before venturing out again?" He paused, and Chester looked up to see him biting his lip. "I always wanted to show you this when we were kids, but..."

But Chester had never been to Hans's house. He'd always assumed that was Hans's way of keeping Chester separate from the death of his mum, who he knew had died somewhere in this forest when her horse had spooked and thrown her into a tree, killing her instantly. Chester had tried to understand not being invited as best he could as a child, but it made more sense as an adult. It was more likely that Miriam, who had moved in so quickly after the accident, wouldn't have been a welcome host. She hadn't even wanted Hans or Greta around, so why would she want any of their friends? Horrid woman.

Chester rubbed his hand over Hans's. "I'm so glad to see it now," he said. "Come on. I'm not afraid of a few spiders. Let's take a closer look."

He was totally lying, of course. He was dreadfully afraid of spiders, but for Hans, he would put on a brave face. They let go of each other and approached the stairs. Hans went first, gingerly tapping on the first one with his boot. "I wouldn't be surprised if this place was rotted through," he muttered to himself.

But Chester squeezed his hand and stopped him from descending any further. "Are you sure about that?" he asked, pointing.

Now they'd moved closer, Chester could see with his torch through the fog around the other side of the mound.

Where someone had installed solar panels.

Hans frowned at the strange sight, opening and closing his mouth. "Well…those can't get much sunlight down there, can they?" he said in confusion.

Chester laughed gently. That was so typical of Hans to ask the practical questions. "You'd be surprised what power those things can generate and store," he said. "The point is, if someone's installed them, they must be using this hideaway sort of regularly."

Hans chewed his lip and looked back at Chester in concern. "You don't think someone's been in here that shouldn't have been, do you?"

The pain was clear in his voice, and Chester really hoped not. This was obviously an important connection to his mum for Hans.

"Shall we check if the door is locked?" Chester suggested. There was no point in speculating when they could find out for themselves.

Hans nodded. "Good idea."

He turned and began making his way carefully down the steps into the gloom of the doorway. Chester's suspicions that the shelter was not abandoned were further confirmed by the small tub of winter-blooming pansies by the front door. Their yellow, white, and purple heads seemed to bob and wave at Hans and Chester as they approached, making Chester smile. Someone had to have planted them this year, and they didn't look overgrown with weeds.

From behind Hans's bulk, Chester watched as Hans reached forwards and tried the door handle. It was indeed locked. But Hans didn't look at Chester in disappointment. In fact, he immediately turned to the flower pot and tilted it up slightly.

Underneath was a key.

"Huh, I didn't actually think that would still be there," Hans marvelled. His breath swirled as he picked up the key, settled the pot again, and stood back up. He showed the grubby metal to Chester. "What do you reckon," Hans asked, raising his eyebrows as half a smile crept onto his face. "You ready to face the spiders?"

Chester was so cold his joints were aching, and he thought he was going to rattle apart from shivering. He didn't care if someone else had now claimed the shelter for themselves and he and Hans were trespassing. This was the Jagers' land, and this shelter was designed for emergencies.

"Hell, yeah," he said.

Hans brushed the dirt off the key and slotted it into the lock. Chester's first surprise was that it did indeed fit. The second was that it turned and clicked, allowing them entrance inside.

A flutter of nerves travelled through Chester's belly along with a little burst of excitement. There was every chance this was going to be somebody's dank tool shed, but on the other hand, it had once been Hans's playhouse, passed down through the last two generations on his mother's side. This was precious history, and Hans was sharing it with Chester.

That had to count for something, didn't it?

As the door swung inwards, Chester lifted the torch and pointed it over Hans's shoulder, illuminating the small underground bunker.

Or…not so small.

Chester gasped and felt his eyes go wide. Every kid in Britain studied the Second World War at school at some point, and Chester was well aware that Anderson shelters had been a standard tin can that could just about squeeze six people inside. They were designed to be easy to make and just to shelter people until the bombs stopped falling.

This was not that.

Hans shook his head, probably in disbelief as he stepped onto the welcome mat and scrubbed his muddy boots over it. Then he reached over to his left and flicked on a light switch.

Chester's theory about the solar panels and a caring occupant was looking more and more likely.

The space had obviously been extended and was now about the size of Chester's lounge, kitchen, and bedroom combined. The floor was carpeted, there was a proper roof, and the walls were woodchip panelled. Hanging from the ceiling were two pendants with simple lampshades, bathing the room in a warm, buttery yellow glow.

The air was damp and earthy, but not in a decaying way. Chester's eyes widened as he took in the rest of the bunker. This place was clearly well loved, and that made him so happy for Hans. It would have been awful to discover that his mum's special place had been left to rot or taken over by squatters, but that definitely wasn't the case here. The space was filled with homely touches, and Chester clicked off the torch then rested his hand on Hans's arm as they both looked about.

To the left of the room was an old-looking but perfectly serviceable three-seater couch with a couple of chunky crocheted blankets draped over the top. Several cushions with various doggie designs were scattered along it, and someone had left a spy thriller novel resting on the arm, the bookmark showing that the reader was halfway through the story.

A shiny red and surprisingly small generator was resting in one of the right-hand corners. Chester didn't know much about camping, but he guessed it was powered by petrol or something. It had all kinds of shaped outlets for different gismos, but currently plugged into it were a fairly larger space heater, a kettle that was resting on a free-standing counter with two cupboards underneath, and a phone charger. Chester couldn't believe their luck. Using the map app took up a lot of battery, but now they might be able to top up their phones before they left. Crazy.

A bookcase was situated opposite the sofa. It was stacked with books as one might expect, but also glass decanters of what looked like whiskey, a collection of snow globes and china ornaments, and on the bottom shelf, an entire row of old vinyl records. A wine rack stood beside a camp stove, filled with bottles of various kinds of red, and a dog basket was snuggled into another corner with a few chew toys lying inside it.

And everywhere – on every little coffee table, shelf, countertop, and hung on the walls – there were framed photographs.

This was not an abandoned spider hole. This was somebody's sanctuary. And Chester had a pretty good idea who it belonged to.

10

CHESTER

CHESTER SNAPPED OUT OF HIS DAZED STATE AND FINALLY turned to shut the door behind them, keeping some of the chill out, even if the hideaway was still pretty cold. At least the overhead lights cast the room in a soft glow, giving Chester the impression that a fire was crackling merrily away in a hearth.

Chester moved back to look at his friend. Hans had his hand over his mouth, turning slowly to take the whole place in. He lowered his hand, shaking his head.

"This is my dad's," he said softly as his eyes glistened with unshed tears. Chester had thought as much. "Those are his records. That's his favourite Scotch whisky. Mum always bought it for him for Christmas along with – ha!" He moved over to a glass jar on the countertop where a few condiments were also sitting. Working in a sweet shop, Chester recognised the contents of the jar immediately. "Liquorice Allsorts! Ha. We all hated them, but they're Dad's favourites. And look!"

He dashed over towards a square briefcase-looking object

on the other end of the counter with a crank sticking out of the side. He clicked a couple of clasps on the sides and eased open the gleaming leather lid, beaming down at the contents inside. It was a portable, wind-up record player. Chester had never seen one in real life. He barely remembered cassette tapes and CDs, let alone actual vinyl records.

Hans sniffed, and Chester was immediately on alert. This was bound to be very emotional for him after an already long and tiring day. Chester bit his lip as he came and stood by Hans, placing his hand on the cold leather sleeve of his biker jacket.

"Are you okay?" Chester asked softly.

Hans sniffed again and reached for one of the dozens of framed photos. This one was free-standing by the record player, and Chester realised the picture was of a very young Hans and Greta at the beach with their dad and a woman who had to have been their mum. She had such a warm, smiling face with bright eyes and windswept blonde, curly hair. She looked like she didn't have a care in the world besides the laughing children wriggling in her arms.

Hans choked back a sob, but quickly looked to Chester with a wet smile. "I'm happy," he said urgently like he didn't want Chester to misunderstand his reaction. "These are happy tears, I swear. I thought...I thought my dad hated Greta and me. That if he could move on to Miriam so quickly, then he'd never loved our mum. That he was glad to let us all go. But..."

He trailed off and looked around the obviously well-cared for and frequently visited space.

Chester rubbed his arm, his heart full of love and happiness for his best friend. "I think it's pretty obvious that your dad comes here to be here with you. All of you. As a family."

Hans nodded, still looking around like he couldn't quite believe it. There was no trace of Miriam anywhere, but Chester kept his thoughts on that to himself, not wanting to spoil the moment. He couldn't help but wonder, though, if Johan came down here so often to *escape* his second wife. And if he was missing his kids so much, why did he never contact them?

Speaking of which. "Hey, look at that," he said, pointing at a corkboard that was mounted on the wall to the right of them.

It was filled with birthday, Christmas, and Father's Day cards, all pinned on top of one another so the cork was barely visible anymore. As he and Hans looked closer, some of them had clearly been ripped in half, then carefully taped back together, and one looked to have been dried off after getting coffee or something on it.

Again, Chester kept his thoughts to himself. But if he had to guess, he would have said that maybe Hans's step-mother had tried to get rid of a few of these cards, but his father had rescued the remains and brought them back to life.

"Why didn't he ever *talk* to us?" Hans whispered, touching one of the cards with football and beer on the front. The standard kind of 'Dad' card that Chester hadn't ever been old enough to buy himself for his father before he'd passed. "Do you think he still loves us, deep down?"

He turned to Chester with raw hope etched all over his face. It almost broke Chester's heart. "Definitely," he said, grasping both of Hans's elbows and looking up at him. "And I don't know why he didn't try to reconnect before now. Maybe he felt he couldn't? But I think this is proof that he's thought about you all a lot in the past decade. You saw how happy he was to see you and your sister tonight! I think...I think there's a lot more going on here than we know."

Hans nodded, his gaze roaming around the bunker until it met Chester's, lingering…

Chester's breath caught in his throat. It was like they were in a trance, unable to look away from each other in the soft lamplight. But Hans was vulnerable in that moment, and Chester wasn't going to do something crazy.

Like how he'd almost kissed Hans at the market. And by the broken-down car. And in the woods.

So he cleared his throat and gave a soft laugh as he stepped away. "I have a silly idea," he said, rubbing the back of his neck.

"I bet it's not," said Hans fondly, making Chester's heart flip.

"Well, um," he began, glancing around the place. "It's warm here. Or, I mean, it's not really." They both laughed, their breath just visible in front of them. "But it's warmer than outside, and there's a heater. And…" He moved to open one of the cupboards to find it filled with cans and boxes of food. "Yes! There are things to eat and booze and blankets…"

He bit his lip, then took the plunge. There was a very real chance that this could be the only evening he'd ever get alone with Hans Jager after tonight.

"There's no awful step-mother breathing down our necks or family drama. Why don't we hunker down here for the night? We can try and make it back to the car in the morning to meet the repair person, then drive to your house to face the music."

He watched Hans carefully, waiting for him to tell him that was a stupid idea, that they should keep going, that they could still make dinner if they tried…

That spending a night alone together was a terrible idea…

And then Hans's face broke into a gorgeous smile. "Now *that* sounds like an adventure," he said with a rich, warm laugh that seeped gloriously into Chester's bones. "Brilliant. I love it. Let me text Greta so she doesn't kill me, and they can go ahead and eat without us. They've waited long enough." He snorted as he got out his phone, glancing at the dog bed. "Dodger might even get some of our food if it can't be saved," he said, sounding gleeful. "Oh?" he added as he looked at his phone screen. "Well, I never."

"Everything okay?" Chester asked tentatively.

Hans shook his head and chuckled. "Greta sent me a message ten minutes ago, saying that Dad told her to tell us to look for the arrows and find our way to the shelter. She added a lot of question marks and confused and thinky faces, so I guess he didn't tell her he's been coming here. Maybe it's a secret from Miriam?"

"Maybe," Chester said warmly. He was pretty sure that was obvious, but Hans needed to sort through this family stuff in his own time.

"All right," said Hans as he quickly tapped on his screen. "I've told her that we're already here and bunking down for the night, so not to worry or wait up. Sent! Okay. I need to, um, visit the little boy's room outside. I assume there's nothing around here?" He glanced about, and Chester shook his head.

"Your dad did a great job converting this place," he said with a smile, "but I think indoor plumbing is even beyond him."

Hans saluted. "No worries. Back in a jiffy."

Chester tried not to get too giddy as he was left alone for a minute, but this was like a dream. He was hidden away in a cosy secret bunker with the love of his life. Yes, he *knew* that Hans's life was in flux and they lived far away from each other and that Hans might still just think of him as his childhood best friend. But at least the night wasn't totally ruined, and they were going to get to spend some time together after all.

Chester dropped his bag to the floor but kept his coat on for the time being. As he crouched down to get the generator going to power the heater, he couldn't help but bite his lip and fantasise for just a second that something more, something magical *might* happen tonight.

But that was getting ahead of himself.

As Hans was still outside relieving himself, Chester began searching through the cupboards under the counter, already feeling the first ebb of warmth coming from the heater. He was impressed at how well stocked this little place was.

"Come see," he said excitedly as Hans came back inside, hastily shutting the door behind him. There was a draught excluder shaped like a sausage dog that Hans placed along the crack, and the faint but chilly breeze disappeared right away. Chester smiled as Hans ambled over to him. "There are a couple of pots we can use on the camp stove, and some big bottles of water for the kettle. There are loads of canned stuff and instant noodles and a few bags of honey-roasted nuts."

"A feast!" Hans declared.

He stood and twirled around, which was pretty adorable, considering his size. He picked up one of the blankets and draped it over Chester's shoulders, then did the same for himself with the other one. They were thick and a little cumbersome, but Chester was already feeling so much better than he had been out in the forest he didn't care.

"Will your dad mind?" he asked, gesturing to the store cupboard they were about to raid. There was plenty, but Chester wanted to make sure before they dove in.

Hans shook his head. "Not if he told Greta to tell us to look for this place. I say we make ourselves at home."

Chester didn't need telling twice.

Within minutes, they had food on the go, a bottle of red wine opened and two glasses poured, and Hans picked out an old Elton John album to play. Chester had never listened to a vinyl before, but the sounds were surprisingly rich and deep, and the little crackles added a huge amount of charm to it.

As the bunker warmed up, it smelled more earthy and woody, but Chester kind of liked it. After a while they felt comfortable enough to take off their jackets, and Hans's heavy musk from a day of wearing biker leathers drifted through the air, adding to the other scents and making Chester's mouth water.

Fuck. He was so cute as he danced around with the colourful crocheted blanket swishing behind him like a cape. He sang along to Elton and sipped his wine, his cheeks rosy and his smile big. Chester could have watched him all evening.

"This is already the best night I've had in a long time," Hans announced as the kettle began to bubble.

Chester was sure that Miriam had organised something extremely fancy back at the house for dinner, but Chester had to agree that Johan's man cave offerings felt like a banquet. They cooked up vegetable soup with instant noodles and tinned hot dog sausages, all topped off with the sweet but salty nuts as a side.

Chester hummed as they snuggled into the old, slightly worn but perfectly comfy sofa, their plates filled to the brim with hot food. Chester was damned hungry, so Hans must have been starving, and for a while, they ate happily without needed to say anything as Elton kept them company.

The wine was going to Chester's head, but he didn't care. He certainly wasn't going to be driving anywhere tonight, and it was helping him to relax. He wanted to enjoy Hans's company in the here and now, not be fretting about tomorrow. As he took another sip, he could feel his worries slipping away.

Apparently, he wasn't the only one.

"There's no one else like you, Chester," said Hans.

He'd placed his empty plate down on the table and was snuggled into the corner of the sofa with the blanket draped around his shoulders and his red wine glass dangling between his fingers. He sighed and tilted his head as he looked at Chester.

It was a bit too much. Chester wanted to lean into it, to bask in Hans's warm glow of appreciation. But that way led to danger. Chester had promised himself that he wouldn't ruin tonight by doing anything stupid, but it was a little difficult when Hans was looking at him all dreamily.

Chester laughed and sipped his own wine. They'd opened a second bottle, and he was feeling very content after a couple of glasses of Mr Jager's 'good stuff'. No wonder Greta hadn't wanted to drive.

"There's definitely no one like you, teddy bear," he said.

Then he froze.

Wrong nickname! He screamed at himself. He'd meant to say 'big guy' – that was what he called Hans out loud. Teddy bear was his private, inside brain name!

He risked sliding his gaze back over to Hans, and was mortified to find his eyes wide and dancing with mirth, as well as a smile creeping onto his face.

"Sorry, that was, uh," Chester blurted with no idea of what he was trying to say. "I don't know…I mean…uh…"

Hans burst out laughing. "Holy fuck, I'm your teddy bear? Really?"

He sounded delighted, but was he just mocking Chester? No, that wasn't like him at all. Besides, he *had* called Chester 'baby' in the woods, hadn't he? Chester knew that it was because he had been worried about Chester being cold, so it might have just been a word that had slipped out in sympathy. But there was definitely a difference between that and 'teddy bear', for crying out loud. He was horrified.

Chester closed his eyes and willed the burning sensation

to ease from his cheeks. But the bunker was quite warm from the electric heater now, and Chester had been enveloped in the blanket whilst eating, so his core temperature was too hot to calm down. He shrugged off his blanket, but it didn't do much. So he just took another gulp of wine.

When he glanced over at Hans, his face had fallen, and Chester felt even worse. But before he could speak up, Hans beat him to it.

"No, don't be sad," Hans said, shifting closer on the sofa and touching Chester's knee. "I like being your teddy bear. That's the sweetest nickname."

Chester's legs were crossed under him, so he couldn't move away without looking totally obvious. But honestly… he didn't want to move away. He really, *really* liked the feeling of Hans's large hand resting on his knee, his thumb gently stroking the inside of Chester's thigh.

It really wasn't a sexual move, but Chester's cock responded immediately, throbbing in his jeans. He bloody *loved* the sensation of Hans touching him.

He wanted more.

Instead, he put down his wine. "Maybe I need some water," he said.

Hans moved immediately, placing his own wine glass on the table and taking his hand away from Chester's leg. He felt the loss keenly, but it was probably for the best. Hans jumped up to crack open one of the fresh bottles of water and poured Chester a glass. "Here," he said eagerly, sitting back onto the couch and pressing the drink into Chester's hands with a happy smile.

Chester's heart threatened to crack. Hans wasn't just a teddy bear. He was a puppy, so eager to please and be praised and loved.

He hadn't been loved nearly enough in his life.

Chester downed his water, and it immediately refreshed

his mind just a little. He wanted to make sure if he was going to show Hans a little bit of (hopefully safe and purely friendly) love, that he was in his right mind and didn't cross any lines.

He placed the empty glass down by his wine, then offered his hand out. "Will you dance with me?" he asked.

Just as the bloody song finished.

But it turned out that Elton had his back. Instead of a sad song, 'I'm Still Standing' blared to life. It was Chester's favourite 'fuck you' break-up song, and all his caution vanished in an instant as he jumped to life – literally.

He sprang to his feet, grinning from ear to ear as he pulled Hans with him. "I love this song!" he shouted like an excitable teenager.

Hans allowed himself to be pulled to his feet, his blanket falling from his shoulders, too. He spun Chester away from the table into the small space in the kitchen where they could move. "I know you do, sweetie," he said with the deepest affection. "Why do you think I put his greatest hits on?"

Chester's heart flipped. Hans had remembered that? *And* he'd just called him 'sweetie', and it definitely hadn't been because he was worried about Chester being cold. It had been from pure affection that made Chester's heart sing even louder than Elton.

He couldn't help but be fuelled by happiness and hope as they started throwing themselves around like maniacs, laughing like fools. *I love you, Hans Jager,* he thought, managing to keep that to himself at least.

They danced until the song finished and then just kept going, giddy and sweaty and utterly without a care in the world. Chester felt like he'd been holding his breath for ten years and had finally let it go. The next song started, and they only paused to swig their wine. The music was loud, and Chester didn't feel the need to say anything other than singing along to the lyrics he knew. He was so comfortable and at ease, like he always used to be around Hans.

And then the next song began. The first few notes of the piano started, and both Chester and Hans's exuberance came naturally to a near stop, and they swayed on the spot, breathing heavily and giggling sporadically as they looked at each other.

It was 'Your Song'. Arguably Elton's most romantic hit (or at least Chester thought so). He laughed again, feeling a little fluster creeping in. So he turned and took another gulp of wine, knowing it wouldn't hydrate him but hoping it would help his suddenly dry throat all the same.

Hans's fingers slipped over Chester's shoulder, his skin burning hot through Chester's jumper. Chester's breath hitched as he placed his wine glass down, looking over his shoulder, feeling like his heart was about to stop.

Hans wet his lips, his pink tongue tantalising as it darted out. "Will you dance with me?" he asked, repeating Chester's words back to him.

Chester felt a little faint. He tried telling himself that this was what best friends did. But as he nodded, Hans slipped his other hand around Chester's waist and pulled him close as they began to gently rock from side-to-side.

Chester wasn't sure what to do with his hands, but eventually, he settled on placing them very carefully and delicately on Hans's lower back. He did his best not to lean too intimately into their embrace, but it was a little difficult when Hans was hugging him tight and resting his cheek on the top of Chester's head. He'd taken his beanie hat off, and he could feel the warmth of Hans's skin through his hair.

They'd never been quite this close before.

What was going on? Was Hans vulnerable from drinking? Should Chester pull away? This was only going to cause confusion and heartache.

Right?

"We can stop if you want to stop," Hans said, his voice rumbling above Chester.

Before Chester's brain could catch up, his fingers instinctively curled around the material of Hans's T-shirt and into the flesh of his back. "No," was all he could say, turning his face into Hans's soft chest.

Chester could feel the strength within from all that time Hans spent at the gym, but he was immensely glad that Hans wasn't super buff. Chester adored how cuddly he was, and they continued swaying blissfully to the music for a little longer. Chester inhaled Hans's unique scent, feeling dizzy from it. Hans smelled like leather, musk, and sweetness. Like apple cider after a hard day's work.

Like home.

"Don't leave."

It took a moment for Chester to realise that he'd been the one to speak.

Hans looked down at him sadly, and their eyes met. "I don't want to," he said softly. He let Chester's shoulder go to brush the backs of his fingers against Chester's cheek. Chester shivered, although he was toasty warm.

This was really happening.

Chester's heart was banging against his ribcage, and he couldn't seem to take a full breath into his lungs. His cock was still half-hard and pressing against the denim fabric of his jeans, and he could taste Hans's delicious scent on his tongue, mixing with the rich wine.

He blinked up at Hans. "Then don't leave," he rasped.

Hans bit his lip, his eyes drifting down to Chester's mouth. "I'm here right now," he murmured. "And I'll stay by your side until I'm dragged away. Will that do?"

Chester could have cried. He hated this limbo. But he had

just enough wine swirling through his veins that he let go of his frustration and doubt about the future.

Instead, he rose to his tiptoes and, after what felt like a lifetime of waiting, crashed his lips against Hans's plump, sweet mouth.

11

HANS

Chester tasted like sugar and spice and all things nice.

Hans was kissing him back and running his hand through Chester's hair – thick and dark like good chocolate – before his first doubt hit him.

Was this going to ruin everything? They'd only just got their friendship back. Had he made a mistake by asking Chester to dance?

Then Chester's hand slipped down to cup Hans's arse cheek, and Hans knew this was no mistake.

They'd deal with tomorrow when it came.

Right now, some kind of dream was coming true.

Hans moaned and copied Chester with the hand not tangled in his hair. His bum felt pert and meaty through his jeans, surprising Hans. Come to think of it, his chest against Hans's was kind of hard and bumpy, too.

"Are you ripped?" Hans blurted out as he broke off the kiss and began eagerly pawing at Chester's jumper.

Chester laughed loudly and stilled Hans's hands with his own. "Hans…if you're really sure about doing this, I'll show you everything. Even if…if it's just for one night. But you have to promise me that you won't shut me out again. Even if we're just friends. You really…*really* matter to me."

Hans's heart felt like it was going to explode out of his chest. He dropped Chester's jumper and lifted his hands to cup either side of Chester's face. "You matter more than anything to me," he murmured, searching Chester's stunning blue eyes, trying to convey the truth of how he was feeling with all his heart. "I don't know what the future holds, but I mean it. You're everything, and I was a fucking idiot to have ever let you drift away." He licked his lips. "Can we have tonight and worry about tomorrow when it comes?"

Maybe it'll be okay.

"Tonight," Chester agreed. He leaned in like he was worried about breaking Hans, pressing their lips carefully together. "Let's just have tonight."

Hans had shagged quite a lot of blokes. He'd always had a nice time with his girlfriends before that, because he'd always taken the time to really get to know them, so it had felt comfortable enough.

But then he'd discovered what it was like to have a man strip him down and fuck him senseless, and there had been no going back. There was nothing like feeling a hard cock pressed against him or smelling a distinctive, pungent man musk.

But it was like Hans was having a third revelation in his sexual evolution. Chester was like *nobody* else. He was so familiar, like a favourite pair of jeans, worn in and soft from years of loving wear. And yet he was also totally brand new and shiny, like a toy Hans had been looking at for half his life and had only just got the courage to get out of the box.

He tasted so sweet from the wine and honey-roasted nuts. Hans lapped at the sugar on his lips and tongue, groaning as Chester deepened the kiss, exploring Hans as much as he wanted to explore Chester.

Somehow, their feet were taking them back towards the couch, and a part of Hans's mind noticed that the record had finished playing, leaving them in quietness. That was okay. He didn't need anything else but Chester. After so many missing years, so many opportunities they never had the chance to take, Hans didn't want anything to distract him from the fact that he was kissing his best friend.

And it was *amazing*.

Chester fit so perfectly against Hans it was like they'd been moulded to fit that way. And the way he commandingly pushed and tugged at Hans as they stumbled into the sofa was seriously pressing all of Hans's buttons.

It had taken him a long time to realise he liked his guys bossy. Even longer to accept that was perfectly okay and didn't make him weak or something stupid like that. Still, Hans had told himself he was going to look after Chester that night.

As the backs of his knees hit the sofa, Hans broke their kiss again and pawed awkwardly at Chester's arms, feeling his cheeks heating up. "I should," he mumbled. "I mean… would you like to…uh…we could…?"

"I would like to take charge," Chester said clearly and kindly, cupping the side of Hans's bristly chin.

Whoosh. There went all the air from Hans's lungs and the blood to his cock. He was *painfully* hard in a matter of seconds, and he just stared at Chester for a second, breathing heavily.

Chester's expression dropped just a little, and he licked his lips as he lowered his eyes. "If you're not into that-"

"Yes!" Hans blurted. "Yes, please. Pretty please with a cherry on top. Please, Chester. That sounds heavenly. I'm all yours. I love it when you take care of me, *so* much. I'm melted chocolate for you, I promise."

A fire lit back in Chester as he looked up, meeting Hans's

eyes with a smouldering gaze. "Do you double-dare *super-promise*?" he asked playfully.

For a second, Hans didn't know how to convey how much he wanted this. Then he surged forwards, pressing his lips to Chester's, whilst also grabbing his hand and putting it between Hans's legs so that Chester could feel just how ridiculously turned on he was.

"Yes," he gasped against Chester's mouth. "Double-dare super-promise. I…I want to be your teddy bear."

Chester sounded like he growled, but then he was kissing Hans too hard for him to really know anything other than how Chester's body felt so good and perfect against his own. They tumbled backwards onto the couch, which was just about big enough to take Hans lying down.

Thank fuck, because Hans wasn't going *anywhere*.

Chester wriggled on top of him, giggling as he straddled Hans's hips. Then his expression became startlingly serious. He leaned on Hans's chest with one hand, then used the other to caress up his neck and along his jaw, his fingertips leaving scorching tingling traces behind.

"I love you, you know," he murmured before his lips quirked with a tiny smile. "You always were my teddy bear."

Hans stared for as long as it took him to process the words that Chester had said. Just when it seemed the moment had stretched on too long, Hans suddenly reached up and captured Chester's hand, pressing the backs of his fingers to his mouth. Hans kissed them tenderly.

"I've always loved you, too, I think," he confessed in the secret safety of their underground bunker. It was as if the place had been forgotten by time and the real world didn't matter outside of this shelter. "But not like this," he added. "This is new. This is *amazing*."

Chester bit his lip. "I think I know what you mean," he said. He dipped low, catching Hans's mouth for a passionate kiss, sucking Hans's lower lip between his teeth and plunging his tongue inside Hans's mouth. He rolled his hips as he did, and Hans appreciated how perfectly their steal-hard cocks were lined up.

He bucked and gasped, almost flinging poor Chester to the floor.

But luckily Chester was made of sterner stuff. He gripped onto Hans's shoulders and laughed heartily as he shifted his weight over, managing to hang on enough until Hans settled back into the couch.

"Easy there, teddy bear," he said, kissing up Hans's jawline.

Hans ran his hands up and down Chester's back, gasping for air. "That rhymed," he said absently, not sure what he was even talking about.

Chester felt *this good* in his arms, and he'd neglected that for over a *decade?*

Hans was a fucking moron.

Well, no longer. He surged up and captured Chester's mouth for a kiss that tried with all his might to convey the last ten years of longing that he hadn't even been fully conscious of. He did his best to make it a kiss that Chester would never forget. Greedily, he searched for Chester's mouth, pulling him in.

Claiming him.

No matter what happened this night, Hans would leave Chester knowing that he was one of the most important people in his entire life. And undoubtedly the sexiest.

Back to his earlier investigation, Hans's hands crept their way back to the hemline of Chester's jumper as they kissed, his fingers trailing along the hot, tight skin of his abdomen. "Can I?" he murmured as his palms slipped over the rigid planes of Chester's stomach.

Chester hummed and gave Hans's lips a peck before

leaning back, allowing Hans to yank his jumper up over his head, discarding it onto the floor.

"*Fuck*," Hans cried, his hands already skimming over Chester's rock-hard abs. "How can you work in a sweet shop and look like this?"

Chester snickered and wriggled on top of Hans's hips. "I have my ways of keeping fit. Now it's your turn, come on."

Hans bit his lip as Chester reached for his T-shirt. Ethel's nasty remarks about him being a fat little boy suddenly rang in his ears. "I...I'm not ripped," he stammered, not moving to help Chester get the T-shirt off.

Chester paused in his tugging and frowned down at Hans. "Why should you be?"

Hans shrugged and felt his cheeks getting hot. *Damn it.* He didn't want to spoil this moment with Chester by letting his insecurities sneak their way in. But he'd be lying if he didn't admit that more than one guy had called him chubby in the past, and not in a kind way.

He didn't want to let Chester down.

Hans opened and closed his mouth a couple of times. "Because that's what guys like," he said lamely. He knew he had muscles underneath, but some people expected them to show when he got naked, and the flash of disappointment was always easy enough to spot on their faces.

Chester blew a very loud raspberry. Then he ran his hands up Hans's chest and leaned down to kiss his lips playfully. "I don't give a shit what other guys might think," he growled. "You're fucking gorgeous. Now, please. Fewer clothes."

Hans blinked, the wine still thrumming deliciously through his veins and making Chester's words easier to believe. Yeah, Chester was *right*. He was a sexy bear, and he knew it. Time to share that with his best friend and do some naked cuddling.

Chester squealed happily as Hans arched up and stripped off his T-shirt, leaving them both bare chested as Hans dropped back down on the soft material of the couch, pulling Chester against him. His skin was scorching hot, and if Hans was in any doubt of Chester's feelings, the way he ran his fingers through Hans's chest hair and sucked on his nipple made him feel a *lot* better.

"C'mere," Hans said, slipping his hand behind Chester's head, encouraging him to kiss Hans's mouth again. "Fuck, you taste so good."

Chester suddenly paused, pulling back a little to search Hans's eyes, a grin creeping onto his face. "I have an idea," he whispered. Then he was jumping off the couch and wagging his finger at Hans as he ran over to where he'd left his coat and bag. "Don't move!" he threatened.

Hans laughed, rubbing his chest and feeling the ghost of Chester's touch, missing him already. "I won't," he promised.

In a few seconds, Chester was strolling back over, focusing on the candy cane in his hands that he was currently stripping the plastic wrapping off. Discarding the rubbish onto the coffee table, he straddled Hans's hips once more.

Then his eyes fluttered closed as he ran the straight end of the candy cane along his tongue before moaning as he sucked on it wantonly.

"Fucking hell," Hans groaned with a shiver. He reached up to touch Chester's throat, feeling him swallowing. His naked chest was already slightly shimmery with perspiration, and his eyes blinked back open to watch Hans watching him.

"You like that?" Chester asked, naughtiness clear in his voice.

Hans's cock ached, and his balls tightened as he stared at Chester lapping his tongue over the candy cane. "I…can you do that to me?" he asked.

Chester cackled and leaned down to give Hans a tender, sugary kiss. "That's the idea, big guy," he purred, palming Hans's hard-on through his leather trousers. "But I've been waiting a long time for this, and I want to make it last."

Hans sobered for a second as he rubbed the side of Chester's neck. Their faces were close together, and the tang of the candy and wine was sweet on Chester's breath.

"How long have you been waiting?" Hans asked in a breathless voice.

Chester licked his lips as sadness wavered behind his eyes. But then he smiled brighter and flicked the candy cane over so the tip landed on Hans's lower lip. "All night," Chester said, sliding the sweet treat along Hans's tongue.

Hans wasn't exactly satisfied with that answer. He suspected there was more there than Chester was letting on. But he didn't want to ruin the moment, so he got into the spirit of things and sucked the candy cane against his cheek, running his tongue over it and moaning.

"Oh, fuck, yeah," Chester rasped, watching hungrily as Hans showed him exactly what he wanted to do with his cock as soon as he got it in his mouth. "Fuck, you're gorgeous." He dropped the candy cane onto an empty plate before crashing his mouth back down on top of Hans's, kissing him fervently as he grappled with the button and zip on Hans's leathers. "I thought I said fewer clothes?"

Hans grinned back up at him and together they both started wriggling out of their trousers. Chester's jeans were much easier for him to remove, and he hopped back up to kick them and his underwear off. Hans stalled in his efforts to get the tight leather off him, taking a moment to soak in every single detail of seeing Chester completely naked for the first time.

He was like an angel.

His skin seemed even paler with only his dark hair as

contrast. It was thick on the top of his head with just a hint of stubble, then dusted lightly over his arms and legs with a smooth chest. But his cock was standing proud and glistening from the dark thatch between his legs. Chester caught Hans staring and grinned, stroking his length and hissing as he rubbed his thumb over the slit.

"You want to try my candy cane?" he asked, looking through his dark eyelashes down at Hans.

Hans gulped and nodded. Then he remembered he was still stuck in his bloody bike leathers. They were bunched with his briefs around his thighs, so at least his cock was freed, but he didn't feel very dignified.

Chester licked his lips, though, and eyed up Hans's bouncing, weeping dick. Apparently, he didn't mind that Hans was only half-undressed still.

"Yummy," he said, dropping to his knees beside the couch.

Hans gasped and bucked as Chester devoured him down almost to the root, squeezing the base of the shaft and sending sparks flying through Hans's vision.

"Fuck!" Hans cried, running his fingers through Chester's thick hair as he began to bob and swallow around his cock. Chester's mouth was scorching hot, and his tongue was firm and strong as it rubbed against Hans's length. He gasped and twitched, trying to relax into the blow job and not shoot his load in the first few seconds like a bloody teenager.

But Chester was so very good at this, Hans had to grit his teeth and focus on his breathing so he could enjoy it without jumping the gun. As much as he regretted ten whole years of missing out on kissing and snuggling with Chester, in that moment, he had to say he was glad they'd both gone out into the world and gained experience. They weren't fumbling, awkward teenagers working out what to do with their bodies. They were grown men who knew their wants and needs and had confidence in how to please their partner.

Or at least, Chester certainly did. Now it was Hans's turn to show he did as well.

"Chester," he gasped, urging his friend – his *lover* – to lift his head and kiss him on the lips. "I want to be naked. Help me get these trousers off."

But Chester grinned as he hopped up astride Hans again. This time, though, there was nothing in the way of their cocks as they bumped together, and Hans hissed in pleasure as Chester wrapped his hand around them both. They were slippery with precum and slid together deliciously, and Chester stroked them both.

Leaning forward, Chester still had that devilish look as he nipped at Hans's lip and kissed him. "I quite like you all trussed up and at my mercy."

Hans groaned and almost came there and then. "Yeah, o-okay," he stammered, not sure what else to say. He'd never been tied up by anyone before, but in that second, he decided that he *really* liked the idea of Chester doing that to him. With him. "You're in charge."

Chester sighed and rubbed his cheek against Hans's, his stubble rasping against Hans's beard. Chester squeezed around their cocks, making Hans gasp and jerk. In response, Hans dipped his head to suck a kiss onto the side of Chester's neck.

Chester squirmed and panted, running his free hand against the short bristles at the back of Hans's neck. Suddenly, it was more than a kiss. Hans was desperate to mark Chester with something that would last beyond this night. Something he could take with him in case...

Just...something to take with him.

Hans sucked and nipped and licked the skin until it was shiny and red, then when he was satisfied, he pressed several sweet and gentle kisses to the tender skin.

Their mouths found one another again, this kiss slow and

languorous as their hips rocked sensually together. Chester's pale skin was flushed across his cheeks, down his neck, and across his chest. His dark hair was damp and falling down onto Hans's forehead.

Hans knew so many personal details about his best friend from their teenage years. But until tonight, Hans had never known what his best friend's face looked when it was contorted in pleasure. He'd had no idea what delicious, breathy little sounds he made when his cock was sliding against Hans's. And he'd certainly never have guessed that sweet, adorable Chester Wild was such a devil in the bedroom.

Or on the sofa, as it so happened.

Said sofa creaked and Chester hurriedly shimmied down Hans's body, kissing his chest as he went, then taking a quick lick of his cock as he passed. "You're right," he declared happily, wrapping his fingers around the top of Hans's trousers. "These need to go, please!" He looked very smug as Hans laughed and tried his best to help shove the material down, but the leather was determined to cling to his bulky thighs.

"Fucking hell," Hans grumbled, feeling like a flailing fish as he squirmed and Chester pulled. "This is so embarrassing."

"Not it's not. It's fun," Chester said with a breathy, carefree laugh. "I hate when sex is all serious and boring. I like to know I'm here with a *person*." He giggled. "Even if that person is currently stuck in his clothes."

Hans huffed, leaning up to catch Chester's mouth for a kiss. Then he gave up any pretence of being sexy, seeing as Chester didn't want that, and jumped up to his feet to get a better angle with which to attack the trousers.

Chester rested back against the couch, spreading his arms and legs, completely unabashed as he drank in the sight of Hans scrambling out of his leathers.

"This has got to be the worst striptease ever," Hans complained, stopping with the damn trousers around his knees so he could reach for his wine glass and take a big gulp. "Normally, they aren't this much of a bitch to get off."

But Chester just shook his head, rubbing his thumb over his lower lip with one hand and grasping his stiff shaft with the other, giving it a luxurious tug. "Nuh-uh," he said. "Best *ever*. And you stink of man so much after a day in those things it's making my mouth water. I like the leathers. Big fan."

Hans bit his lip bashfully, basking in the praise. He took a breath before sipping another mouthful of wine and setting the glass back down. Then he recommenced his efforts to get out of these bloody clothes once and for all.

Finally, mercifully, he kicked the damn things away, then stood proudly naked for Chester with his hands on his hips, his cock standing to attention like a flag pole. "Ta-da!" he announced playfully.

Chester laughed and clapped, then crooked a finger at Hans, telling him to come back to him. Hans walked over to the couch, trying to look at least a *little* bit cool and sexy. It might have worked. Chester's eyes widened, his pupils large, and his mouth dropping open. As Hans approached, he slipped his hands over Hans's hips and his lips over the tip of his cock, sucking on it like a lollipop. Hans groaned, carding his fingers through Chester's hair and letting himself buck into the hot wetness, loving how Chester tongued his slit.

Chester looked up at him with his bright blue eyes and popped off Hans's cock, his lips swollen and wet. "Lie down, beautiful," he said, his voice filled with reverence. "I've got a lot more plans for you tonight."

12

CHESTER

IN ALL OF CHESTER'S FANTASIES, HE'D NEVER IMAGINED finally being with Hans would play out like this. Getting stranded in the woods had certainly not been a part of the plan. But the adorable secret sanctuary, dinner, wine, and snogging were all much better surprises.

And now here they were, totally naked and writhing on the couch together. Chester was breathless from kissing and couldn't even remember being cold earlier, as he was so scorching hot now. His hands ran over Hans's hairy chest as they frotted and squirmed and basically just revelled in their nearness.

Hans had asked how long Chester had been wanting this. It felt too much, too raw to give an honest answer, so Chester had simply said since that afternoon. But in his heart, he knew the truth.

It felt like he'd been waiting his whole life to finally be with his best friend like this.

But he didn't want to dwell on that and make this seem like a bigger deal than it was. Hans was almost certainly going to go back to London once the business with his family was done, and Chester needed to cherish the gift of their time together in this moment.

Embrace tonight. Not worry about tomorrow.

Chester knew it would be difficult, though, because he could tell that the feel of Hans's body against his was already fucking addictive. He wanted this all the time, to have his gorgeous, cuddly teddy bear at his beck and call. How Hans could ever be self-conscious about his body was a mystery to Chester. He was strong and warm and hairy and just so bloody manly.

Even in the midst of their passion, Chester was already looking forward to snuggling up against his solid body which radiated heat, falling asleep wrapped in Hans's thick arms, then waking in the morning knowing that he was safe and loved.

Even if it was just for one night.

Hans groaned as Chester slowed his hand again, stroking their two hard and slippery cocks together leisurely. "You *tease,*" Hans grumbled with a pout. He kissed down Chester's throat and pulled his hair. "Are you ever going to let me come?"

Chester hummed and nipped Hans's bottom lip. "How do you *want* to come, beautiful?"

Hans was panting, his skin damp with perspiration and his pupils blown with lust. "Uh," he said as he pawed at Chester's back and arms. "I don't know. My brain is broken."

Chester dropped his head back and laughed. "God, I wish we had supplies so I could fuck you senseless. Although…" He bit his lip and waggled his eyebrows. "You trust me?"

Hans pressed his lips tenderly to Chester's. "Absolutely. Double-dare super-promise."

Chester chuckled warmly, feeling content down to his bones. "Brilliant. Let's have some fun, then." He reached over to the empty plate where he'd left the candy cane, bringing it to his mouth to get it good and wet.

Hans groaned. "More teasing," he whimpered.

But Chester shook his head. "You've been a good boy. Father Christmas says you're on his nice list. So now you get your present. Knees up, please!"

With his back flat on the couch, Hans grinned and did as he was told, grabbing his knees to expose his hole. Chester sighed happily, kissing his way down the inside of Hans's thigh, skirting around his hard, weeping cock (because, okay, he was a *little* bit of a tease) before nuzzling his way between Hans's cheeks so he could start lapping at his musky, hot hole.

Hans bucked and fumbled to get his fingers through Chester's hair, throwing one of his legs over the sofa back to keep it raised. "Oh, fuck, *yes*," he hissed as he tugged on him, and Chester worked his entrance with his tongue and lips, getting the ring of muscle as wet as he could. "That's...oh, fuck...don't stop."

Chester chuckled. Normally he'd agree. He loved rimming and would have happily done this as long as it took to get Hans ready for his cock, but they were both pretty desperate to come by this point, so Chester took mercy on him.

Next time, a tantalising voice whispered at the back of his mind. *Next time you'll have condoms and lube and maybe even your favourite soft leather handcuffs. Next time will be even better.*

But there was no guaranteeing there would be a next time, so Chester continued with his plan to make *this* time as special and memorable as possible. "Ready?" he murmured, peeking up to see Hans watching him over his heaving chest.

He nodded eagerly. "Yes."

Chester grinned and bit his lip. "You don't know what I'm going to do."

Hans shook his head just as enthusiastically. "Don't care. Want it all. Do it, Chester. I trust you, remember?"

That made Chester's heart ache, and he tenderly kissed the sensitive inside of Hans's thigh. "Thank you, teddy bear," he said warmly, nuzzling his cheek against Hans's ticklish leg hair.

Then he kissed his way back down to the thicker hair where his cock and balls were red and heavy. With another good lick of the candy cane to ensure it was smooth with no sharp edges yet, he rubbed the rounded tip against Hans's entrance before pushing it through the tight ring of muscle, watching gleefully as Hans's head dropped back with a moan.

Chester licked his palm and wrapped his hand around Hans's shaft, stroking him as he pumped the makeshift dildo deeper into his hole. He lapped and kissed at Hans's shiny tip, but Chester didn't want to miss devouring the sight as he played with his lover's most intimate parts. He wanted to keep the memory of the glistening candy cane sliding in and out of Hans's hole for as long as he lived.

Chester licked another bead of precum from Hans's twitching, throbbing cock. "Do you want to come like this?" he asked playfully.

"I, uh..." Hans screwed up his fists and pressed them against his closed eyes, and he laughed breathlessly. "Fucking hell. If I'm on the nice list, you're on the naughty list, Chester! I don't know. You're in charge. I want to come however you'll enjoy most."

Making sure the candy cane was eased in deep, Chester let it go, then leaned up to kiss along Hans's beardy jaw until he found his lips. Hans moaned and lowered his hands to cup either side of Chester's face as their lips moved tenderly together.

"How about like this, big guy?" Chester said as he reached

between them to grip their cocks once again. "Does the candy surprise feel good where it is?"

Hans groaned and bit Chester's lower lip, dragging it between his teeth. The slight nip of pain sent electricity zinging directly to Chester's balls. "It's good," Hans said, reaching up and massaging the globes of Chester's arse. "Not as good as your cock, but close enough."

Chester let out a guttural moan and nipped at Hans's collarbone. "Sweet baby Jesus, I want to fuck you on your hands and knees. I want to be balls deep inside you and wank you off until you come."

He was so overcome with lust he shuddered. But Hans guided their mouths back together for a gentle kiss. Even though he breathed heavily, his eyes were steady as he locked his gaze with Chester's.

"I promise you we'll do that next time," Hans said. "I don't know what tomorrow will bring, but I want everything you just described, desperately. We'll make it happen."

Chester's heart hammered in his chest as he dared to believe what Hans was saying. He nodded and licked his tingling lips, not breaking their intense connection. "We'll make it happen. Double-dare super-promise."

At that, Hans grinned, breaking the spell as he wriggled underneath Chester. "Right, let's shove this candy cane all the way up my arse, then wank ourselves silly. Sound good?"

Chester cackled as Hans got his hand between his legs and pushed the candy cane as far as it would go, wiggling it until he obviously found his prostate, judging by the way he screwed his eyes up and gasped.

"Oh, fuck. Okay. That's the spot." Hans kissed Chester's lips a few times. "Okay, go now. I don't think I'm going to last much longer."

Chester agreed with that. Time for the big finish. With Hans impaling himself on the sweet treat, Chester braced himself with his left hand and used the right to wrap around both their cocks as they thrust into the slippery tunnel he'd created. They were gushing precum now, and it couldn't be long until they both spilled everywhere.

Their kisses were hungrier now, messy and urgent as they panted, their bodies rocking so much the couch was squeaking beneath them. "Hans," Chester breathed, looking deep into his big brown eyes.

Hans gripped him with the hand not pulsing the candy cane. His fingers dug against Chester's ribcage, and Chester hoped they'd leave bruises to go with the love bite he was already proudly sporting on his neck. He wanted to be able to look in the mirror over the next few days and remind himself that this hadn't been some sugar plum dream. This was real, no matter how fleeting.

Sweat dripped from Chester onto Hans, and the aroma of their passion mixed with the warm, earthy scent of the bunker. The only sounds were their gasps and the slap and rub of skin-on-skin. Chester surged forward to kiss Hans hard. "I'm going to come," he warned, moving his hand faster over their lengths.

Hans nodded, urging Chester on. "Me, too," he grunted. "Don't stop. So good."

Chester had no intention of stopping. Even though there was a part of him that wanted this moment to last forever, he gave in to his climax, crying out as he peaked. Thick ropes of cum began spluttering over Hans's hairy chest, and within seconds Hans bellowed as he joined in, their cum mixing together as it painted them both.

Unable to hold himself up any longer, Chester collapsed on top of Hans as they both gasped for air. Hans's fingers were trailing gently along Chester's spine as Chester blinked, slowly coming back to reality.

Sure, that wasn't the craziest sex he'd had by a long shot.

But the rawness of the emotional connection had left him reeling, and he found himself clinging to Hans's shoulders like a life raft, their mess cooling between them.

"Hey, you're shivering," said Hans, concern in his voice as he pulled one of their discarded blankets over them. The candy cane clattered onto the plate again. Then Hans used both arms to hug Chester tightly and kissed his temple. "Was that okay? Are you all right?"

Shaking his head to try and get back to his senses, Chester exhaled. "That was incredible," he said, pressing his cheek to Hans's and closing his eyes. His heart was still racing, but the dizziness was fading. The threat of passing out was leaving him. "I'm good, but we should probably clean up this mess."

"In a minute," Hans grumbled, kissing against Chester's hair.

"We haven't got running water here," Chester fretted.

But Hans was having none of it. "We've got a bottle and some kitchen roll. We'll be fine. I want to just bask in this moment a while. Don't you?"

His last words were uncertain, and Chester's heart finally began listening to him.

If he had to guess, he would say that what they'd just shared meant as much to Hans as it did to him. Circumstances might be out of their control, but Chester had to hold on to that. This was special. It meant something. It wasn't a drunken mistake or an experiment. Hans had wanted to share their love as much as Chester had.

He sighed and nuzzled closer to Hans, wrapping the blanket around them and pressing a sweet kiss to his neck. "I absolutely want to bask. Sorry, I just want to take care of you."

"You did," Hans assured him. "You do."

Chester lifted his head and looked in Hans's eyes. "That

meant everything to me," he said, speaking from the bottom of his heart.

He came close to spilling his guts over being in love with his best friend for over a decade. But he didn't want to put pressure on the moment, so instead, he just smiled and gently kissed Hans's lips.

Then he smirked and glanced at their discarded dildo. "So…the candy cane was a winner?"

Hans snorted and wiggled underneath Chester, their softened cocks rubbing together. "I dunno. Have you got another one? I say we tease *you* for a while. Then we can do a fair comparison."

Chester laughed and kissed his lover tenderly. "I could be tempted by that," he said.

HANS

IN THE END, THEY DIDN'T GET TO PLAY ANY MORE WITH whatever other sweets Chester had in his bag. They'd started falling asleep last night when Chester had snapped awake and insisted that they try and clean themselves, which Hans had actually been grateful for. Dried cum was no joke with his body hair. With underwear and T-shirts on, they'd collapsed back onto the sofa with the blankets over them and the heater going and fallen into a deep sleep.

When Hans awoke that morning, though, Chester was gone.

Fear gripped his heart as he sat bolt upright, his eyes searching around the bunker. But his best friend and lover was nowhere to be seen.

Had they made a mistake? Had Chester made a run for it the second he'd woken up, desperate to get away from Hans and his regret?

Oh, shit. Was Chester lost in the forest?

Hans was up and running for the door before he even realised he didn't have any shoes or even trousers on. But just as he reached out to grab the handle, the door flung inwards, and Chester appeared. They both startled as they looked at each other. Then Chester smiled and Hans felt like he could breathe again.

Chester waved his phone and stepped forward, closing the door behind him. Hans shivered and thanked him, already hurrying back to grab a blanket to wrap around himself to ward off the chill. Chester was dressed again, down to his gloves and hat.

"Sorry," he said, still shivering a little despite his clothes. "The recovery services people called, and I didn't want to wake you, so I dressed and called them back outside. They've booked us in to come look at my car. They should get there in about an hour."

"Oh," said Hans, suddenly conflicted. He was glad help was on the way, but he'd be lying if he hadn't been hoping for a little more time to themselves this morning.

Suddenly, he was wishing they hadn't succumbed to sleep after all. Was that the only chance he was going to get to be with Chester like that?

"Well, that's, uh, that's good, isn't it?" he stammered.

Chester nodded and rubbed his arms, looking around the bunker. There was something uncertain about him. "Definitely. But, uh, we should probably head back to meet them as soon as possible."

Hans couldn't help the disappointment that filled him. As they'd been falling asleep last night, he'd thought about waking up next to Chester and how sweet that would be. He'd promised himself that there wouldn't be any weirdness.

It was feeling weird.

"Right, yeah," said Hans, nodding and reaching for his leather trousers where they'd been thrown on the floor. He *really* hoped they'd be easier to get on than they had been to take off. He didn't fancy hopping around like an idiot in that moment. "We should probably leave this place in the state we found it, or at least attempt to."

He turned around, having rescued his inside-out trousers, and found himself getting enveloped by Chester's arms.

Hans sighed, leaning into the hug.

"I just wanted to make sure we're okay," said Chester, looking up from where his cheek was resting on Hans's chest.

Hans felt himself relax a little as he dropped his trousers and rubbed Chester's back. "Absolutely," he said with feeling. "I just wish we didn't have to rush off. I wish I could make you breakfast and snuggle all morning."

Chester bit his lip, his blue eyes wide. "Next time, maybe?" he whispered.

There was a hint of hesitation in his voice, but then he smiled and stood on his tiptoes to give Hans a quick kiss on the lips.

"Next time," Hans promised firmly before letting him go. It was as if he was determined to will a next time into existence just by repeating it out loud.

In no time it was all hands on deck, though, and Hans was too busy tidying to dwell too much on what the future might hold for this fragile feeling. He felt like he was protecting this flicker of love from the howling winds that were waiting for them just outside the door.

As it turned out, the weather had completely turned from the night before, and there were no howling winds as they stepped back into the forest. Apparently, the fog had lifted as quickly as it had come the previous evening. It was as if they were entering a completely different world.

In some ways, Hans felt like they were.

Hans gave the bunker one last scan to make sure it was in good condition for his dad, with all their rubbish wrapped up and doubled-bagged in Chester's backpack. Then he locked the door and slipped the key back where they'd found it under the plant pot.

Making his way back up the bunker's steps, Hans breathed in deeply and closed his eyes to feel the sun on his face. It was still cold, but the air had lost its vicious bitter bite, hopefully meaning that the walk back to Chester's car would be much more pleasant. In fact, they held hands again the whole walk, and there was no pretence about it being for 'safety' or anything. It was just because they both wanted to, much to Hans's delight.

They didn't talk about their situation. Not their future or what last night meant, in any case. They reminisced about the past and told stories from work. Easy chit-chat that didn't leave them feeling too bogged down as they followed the arrows backwards towards Chester's abandoned car.

Or at least in that general direction.

The story Hans was telling (about the batch of cinnamon swirls he'd been baking last month, which had caught on fire) died on his lips as they finally emerged onto the road to find that Chester's car was nowhere to be seen. Hans frowned and looked up and down the long stretch, but it curved off both to the left and right, so they couldn't see that far. Hans didn't recognise it like he had the stretch where his mum had died.

"We were walking for quite a while before we found the arrows yesterday," said Chester with a frown. "I bet we started further along the road than this. The question is, in which direction…"

He let go of Hans's hand as he got his phone out, presumably to try and get their bearings. Hans knew they needed to focus, but he couldn't deny the way he missed the contact between them immediately.

Chester laughed darkly. "I mean, there's always the

chance that someone has nicked my car altogether, but let's stay hopeful, yeah?"

"Definitely," said Hans firmly. "I know I've been away a while, but people in this town were always a good sort. I'm sure no one would take it or damage it on purpose." Chester blinked at him. "What?"

Chester shook his head. "It's just a change to hear you say something nice about the village." He squeezed Hans's arm. "You're right. It *is* a good place. I'm sure we're just on the wrong bit of road is all."

Hans bit his lip. Maybe now was the moment to explain to Chester how he couldn't stay in a place where everyone knew that he'd been the reason that his mum had died. Nobody had wanted him and Greta around after that, and Hans knew it. He'd seen it in their eyes, and apparently, that was what everyone said about them, a fact Miriam was quick to remind them every chance she got.

Not when their dad was around, of course. At least she had the decency not to bring up his first wife's death in front of him and his kids. But she'd always say it in a pitying way, like it must have been so hard for the kids to be known as the local town murderers.

But Hans didn't want to go into that now, not when Chester had *never* blamed Hans and Greta the way other people had, even though he must have thought it. Hans wasn't brave enough to face that demon in that moment, not when they'd had such a perfect evening. So he let the moment slide.

Besides, Chester was right. Gingerbread was a community. Surely no one would have messed with his car, especially not at Christmas, the season of goodwill.

Hans squinted as he looked back at the road again, trying to recall if they were closer or further away from the house. But it had been ten years since he was last here, and he'd never once walked this road, only been driven along it. He couldn't tell.

Luckily, Chester was savvier than that. "Ah! Okay." He nodded as he stared and pointed at his screen, then turned this way and that. "We walked from that bend last night, I'm sure, as we looked at the map so much. And now we're here, so…that means we walk"- he spun again, getting the arrow on his phone pointing the correct way -"this way!"

Hans laughed, following as Chester began to move. A happy Chester made him happy. "Thank goodness for that. Is the repair company waiting for us already?"

Chester's thumb moved over the screen. "Looks like they're going to be another ten minutes," he said confidently, putting his phone away. "We should hopefully meet them just as they arrive. That's a bit of luck for once."

Hans nodded in agreement, but his breath caught and his head snapped down as Chester slipped his hand back into Hans's, like it was the most natural thing in the world. Hans bit his lip, watching their entwined fingers swing back and forth.

"I like this," he blurted out.

Chester looked over at him, then down to their hands. He smiled with a sigh as he met Hans's gaze again. "Me, too."

That felt enough for now. Hans didn't know how, but he wasn't going to leave Chester again. Not after last night. It felt like this was the way it had always meant to be between them.

Sure, he couldn't come back to Gingerbread, but his thoughts came back to the fact that there were plenty of nearby towns that he could maybe find a place to rent and maybe a job? He just wished he had some savings to make a leap like that. Again, he found himself struggling not to resent the fact that his dad had cut him and Greta off from any allowance and not paid for further education like they'd discussed.

But Hans was done dwelling on the past, and it might be hard to stand on his own two feet, but for Chester, he'd do it. There was hope, even if he didn't know what the future might look like.

Hans was saved from falling too far down the rabbit hole of his thoughts as they rounded another bend and Chester's banged-up orange Mini Cooper appeared in the distance. From what they could see, it appeared like the car was unscathed after its night out in the cold and that the recovery vehicle hadn't arrived yet.

"Oh, thank god," said Chester with an anxious laugh, his breath misting in front of him in the cold morning air. "I was trying to keep my hopes up, but the universe can be a dick. That's a relief!"

Hans lifted their linked hands and risked pressing a kiss to the back of Chester's gloved hand. "Hopefully, they can get it fixed soon, and we'll be on our way."

Chester hummed, and Hans was dying to know what he was thinking, but at that moment the recovery tow truck came into view, and they rushed to meet them by the car.

Hans knew far more about choux pastry than he did car engines, so he let Chester talk with the mechanic whilst he texted Greta to give her an update. It seemed like the only way she'd got through the night before was to drink herself silly, so she was feeling a bit worse for wear now. Not so bad that she wasn't fishing for details of Hans and Chester's night together, though. Hans shook his head as he simply texted her back, insisting that they'd had a surprisingly nice time given the circumstances.

He wouldn't kiss and tell. What he'd shared with Chester was too special for that.

"Right, that ought to fix it," said the middle-aged bloke

who'd been tinkering under the bonnet of the Mini as he'd given the battery a jump-start. He nodded at Chester, who was sat in the driver's seat. "Give that a try."

As the engine flared to life and Chester's face broke into a huge grin, relief washed through Hans. But then he realised that meant that his and Chester's private moment together was probably coming to an end, and he had to work to keep his expression happy.

At least Chester's car was okay, and he wouldn't have to worry about replacing it. That was absolutely a good thing. It wasn't as if Ethel would let him keep his Christmas bonus for once and he'd have some extra cash for repairs or even a new car. From what the mechanic was saying, his call-out was covered by Chester's insurance, so everything was fine.

All that was left to do was to finally make their way to Hans's childhood home.

Hans couldn't say he was exactly thrilled about that as he folded himself back inside the tiny car. "Well, then," he said as Chester looked at him. Hans licked his lips and raised his eyebrows. "We've got several hours until we need to be presentable again. What do you want to do?"

It was mid-morning by now, and Greta had said that Miriam's fancy dinner had indeed been shifted to tonight. Hans was surprised that she'd been that accommodating, but from Greta's texts, he got the impression that his dad had insisted, so Miriam was going to cook them up something different tonight.

Chester inhaled, then smiled, but it didn't quite reach his eyes. "Why don't we regroup? I'm still totally fine to come to dinner, but I'd like to have a shower and change my clothes first. Also, I should probably check in on Nana as well."

Hans made sure to keep that smile on his face still, even as disappointment ran through him. He was almost panicked at the idea of letting Chester go, even if only for a few hours.

"Yeah, yeah," he managed to agree, though, nodding. "Greta has my overnight bag, so I could do that, too. Freshen up. Um…maybe you could drop me off at the house, then come back at five-ish?"

Chester's smile seemed genuine and slightly relieved. He even squeezed Hans's knee, going some way to reassuring him that all was as well as it could be. "Yes, great plan," he said. "Then we can tackle the wicked witch together."

Hans scoffed, thinking about Ethel. "Which one?" he asked. "Yours or mine?"

The joke seemed to ease their tension a little, and with that, Chester put the car in gear and began the short drive that would take them up to the house.

The driveway was long and winding, but the second they emerged from the trees to see the property, Hans felt like he'd fallen back in time. It was like a cottage and a mansion had a baby. Three stories high with a sloped slate roof and ivy growing all over the walls, it appeared very grand, Hans knew. But this had once been his home, and he tried to recall that feeling and not look on it with a stranger's eyes.

The duck pond to the right of the building was so big it almost became a small lake, and its banks were bursting with heather and more of the pansies that Hans's dad had planted outside the Anderson shelter. Snow blanketed the grass that surrounded the property, and trees from the forest they'd spent the night in rustled as if waving to greet them.

The carport to the left of the house was mercifully empty. In his later teenage years, Hans had become used to the sight of whichever of Miriam's shiny, colourful sports car was there. She always seemed to get bored as soon as she'd bullied Hans's dad into getting her the latest model, so over the years, there had been many a different Porsche or Jaguar sitting in that spot, looking completely at odds with the rest of the rustic country aesthetic. Hans hoped that the lack of car meant she was out.

He bit his lip and looked up at the house as Chester came to a halt in the driveway. A lump was threatening to form in his throat, and he suddenly felt wobbly. Like all that grief over his mum's death and Miriam's intrusion in their lives was threatening to rush back to him all at once.

Hans startled a little as Chester slipped his palm over the back of Hans's hand, giving it a rub. When their gazes met, Chester offered him a warm smile. "I can come in with you if you want?"

But Hans shook his head. "No, it's okay. I think there's actually something to be said for a hot shower and some clean clothes. Miriam doesn't need any excuse to hate me more than she does by us looking scruffy." *Or to keep me away from my dying father,* he added privately, not wanting to be too morose around Chester when he was looking so sweetly at Hans. "I mean, I think you're gorgeous, no matter what," he assured Chester.

Fuck. It felt so freeing to be able to say that out loud.

Sure enough, Chester's expression softened as he smiled, and he leaned over and gave Hans a quick but tender kiss. "You've got this," he said warmly. "And if there are any issues, Greta will take care of you until I get back to you. Okay?"

He was very much comforted by Chester's promise that he'd come back soon, and that they'd be able to squeeze a little more time together before Hans had to leave. Even if it was for dinner with his awful step-mother. So he soothed his nerves and chose to bask in the sweet parting moment.

He really wanted to kiss Chester with everything he had, to pour his love into him. But that felt like he'd be cracking something open that he couldn't close again. Not like Chester's chaste kiss just now. Instead, he squeezed Chester's hand and rubbed the back of his knuckles with his thumb.

"See you soon," said Hans.

"See you soon," Chester promised.

Standing on the front doorstep, Hans watched Chester drive away until his clapped-out orange Mini vanished beyond the tree line. It was difficult not to feel like he'd taken a piece of Hans's heart with him.

Or maybe even his whole heart entirely.

14

CHESTER

"HELLO! ANYONE HOME?"

Chester paused as he let himself into his nana's house, not wanting to barge in on her, but also not wanting to make her get up and answer the door if she was comfy. Sure enough, her cheerful call of "In here!" came from the living room.

Chester closed the front door of her small terraced house and toed off his wet trainers. The sky was bright blue outside, but the slush of the previous snow still lingered, and he didn't want to traipse it over Nana's clean carpets.

"Chester, love!" she cried when he entered the living room.

She looked so cosy in her favourite chair. She was all wrapped up in the snowflake-decorated blanket Chester had bought her a few years ago. Her feet were clad in fluffy cream-and-burgundy slippers that were sticking out of the end. She had her legs propped up on a pouffe and a cup of tea balanced on her lap. The television was playing one of the daytime gameshows that she loved shouting at so much.

"I wasn't expecting you today, darling." Nana indicated the couch that was occupied by her three cats: Toffee,

Liquorice, and Marmalade. "Take a seat. The girls won't mind!"

The cats all looked up at Chester with their tails swishing dangerously, and he quickly surmised that the girls would definitely mind. So instead, he perched himself on the sofa arm closest to his nana. "I bought you your sudoku," he said, offering her the latest book that he'd picked up from the newsagents.

He figured it was probably best to have an excuse for swinging by, rather than skipping right ahead to blurting out 'I had sex with my best friend and now I don't know what the hell to do'.

"Oh, excellent," said Nana, reaching eagerly for the puzzle book he was holding out for her. "Got to keep the old noggin ticking along, haven't you?" She peered over her gold-framed glasses, the huge eighties-style he remembered her wearing his whole life. They were secured around her neck with a colourful length of beads that clacked together as she leaned closer to him. "You look peaky. You weren't stuck out in that storm, were you? Let me make you some hot honey, lemon, and ginger."

Chester hurriedly waved his hands as she threatened to get up from her chair. "No, no. I'm fine, Nana." He grinned. "I wouldn't mind making some regular tea, though. You want a fresh one?"

Nana considered the cup that was resting in the saucer gripped between her arthritic fingers, then suddenly downed the rest of it in one big gulp. "Oh, go on, then, love. Bring us back some of those choccy bics to dunk in as well. There's a good lad."

Chester stood and gave her a one-armed hug. "It's good to see you, Nana."

She leaned back and swatted his arm. "You were only here a few days ago. You don't need to worry so much about me. I'm *fine* with my puzzles and my telly. Next door's little girls are always in and out, too, showing me their schoolwork. And my lady came and did my hair on Thursday. Look!" She preened for him, showing off her short silver crop with a tinge of purple through it. "The girls said I was 'lit'. Dunno what that means, but it made me feel cool."

Chester grinned and nodded. "Very chic, Nana. I know you're all good here, but maybe *I* missed you a little."

Once again, his nana peered over her glasses at him. This time, though, she frowned. "Uh-oh," she said. "You better get the *really* good biscuits and come tell your old nana all about it."

Chester sighed and went to protest before changing his mind. A heart-to-heart was exactly what he'd been hoping for, and there was no sense in denying it. "Okay, give me a sec," he told her.

It had only been about an hour and a half since he'd dropped Hans at his family's home, and Chester was already feeling bereft. He'd managed a shower as planned, but then he'd got cold standing naked in his tiny bathroom, examining the love bite and finger bruises that Hans had left behind after their surprising, messy, perfect night of passion.

His heart was already feeling hollow, and Hans hadn't even left town yet.

Realising he couldn't stay in the bathroom, he'd finally got dressed into fresh clothes and decided to go visit his nana like he'd said. When he'd mentioned that to Hans, it had just been an excuse to have some time with his own thoughts and maybe work out how he was going to protect his poor heart. But then he'd quickly worked out that being left alone with his own thoughts was a rubbish idea, and jumped in his (still working) car to pop over to his nana's.

As the kettle boiled in her cluttered but extremely well-loved kitchen, he bit his lip and put teabags in two mugs.

Now he was here, he wasn't sure he was brave enough to open this can of worms. Right now, it was just between him and Hans. Telling Nana would make it real – which could be the best thing ever. Since he was a teenager, he'd wanted to see if his feelings were shared by Hans. Last night absolutely seemed to have proven they were.

Except, for the past ten years, Hans had faded to a perfect – if slightly melancholy – memory for Chester, safe from being spoiled. Now this thing between them was real and hard and concrete, and that meant it could easily be shattered into a million pieces.

Chester sighed, fetching the milk from the fridge. Why couldn't it just be simple?

Because life never was.

"Two cups of tea and the good chocolate biscuits," he announced as he came back into the living room.

He handed his nana her cup and saucer and settled himself down with his favourite mug. Luckily, the evil trio of cats had dispersed, so he could safely sit on the couch, although he kept his wits about him in case of any ankle swiping.

"Right, what's up?" Nana asked as she dunked her biccy in the strong, sugary tea, then offered Chester the packet. Despite wolfing down a sandwich back at home, he felt ravenous again, so he helped himself.

Nana had turned the volume down on the telly, so Chester knew she was serious about helping him with his problem, whatever it might be. But he shook his head and smiled as he dunked his own biscuit. "Nothing," he said with a laugh that came out a little more nervous than he'd intended. He didn't really know where to start, so he stalled. "Can't I just pop round and see my favourite nana?"

She took a bite of her dangerously soggy biscuit, saving the wet half before it fell in her tea, then arched an eyebrow at him. She'd stopped bothering with most of her make-up years ago, but she always drew on her eyebrows and used her pink lippy, so the effect was even more accentuated.

"I wasn't born yesterday," she said with a grin, wagging the half-eaten biccy at him. "Come on. Is it that old cow Ethel again? I keep telling you that you should get another job."

Chester sighed, not bothering to go into how much he loved his job *aside* from his miserable boss again. They'd had that conversation too many times already.

"No, honestly, it's nothing bad," he said, not sure who he was trying to convince more: his nana or himself. "It's just… well, do you remember Hans Jager?"

Nana's face lit up like New Year's Eve. "Oh my goodness, he was *such* a sweet boy. Of course I remember your old best pal, Hans! How could I not?"

Chester smiled, warmth spreading his chest. He loved hearing Nana speak so fondly about his long-time love.

"Well, he came back to Gingerbread last night," Chester continued, trying not to sound too shy. But inside, he was squirming like he was seventeen again and desperately pretending that he didn't have a massive crush on his best friend. "He walked right into the sweet shop."

"No, he never!" Nana exclaimed. She nudged his knee, a devilish look in her eyes. "All grown up, hey? I bet he's proper handsome now!"

Chester spluttered and coughed. "Well, I, uh…so, he and Greta are both back. Apparently, their dad isn't very well."

That made Nana frown. "Mr Jager is unwell? He popped by the Women's Institute meeting a few weeks ago when I was there, and he seemed fine."

Chester shrugged. "I don't know the details, but it must be serious for Miriam to allow the twins back into town."

At that, Nana scoffed so hard she almost slopped her tea.

She scowled as she took a big gulp, then shot a piercing look at Chester. "That woman is *no* good. I have no idea how someone so sweet and kind as Johan Jager ended up in her thrall. I guess she does have great tits."

Chester spat his tea out so far he scared the cats into running from the room. "Nana!"

But she only shrugged, helping herself to another biscuit. "He wouldn't be the first man to find himself wooed by a floosy, and he certainly won't be the last. Anyway, I don't care about her. I care about your gorgeous young man. How long's he back home for?"

"He's not my 'young man'," Chester mumbled, trying not to blush. "And, uh, that's the thing. Probably only until tomorrow. He was supposed to leave today, but the storm last night changed his plans."

"Oh, good," said his nana as she nodded. "You've still got time, then."

Chester frowned. "Time for what?"

Nana chuckled. "To tell him that you're bonkers mad in love with him," she said as if it was obvious.

This time, Chester hastily put his tea down before he could spray it over the coffee table again. "I'm not – Nana – that's just – *what?*"

She picked up the sudoku puzzle book and slapped him over the knee hard enough that it stung slightly.

Chester's eyes widened at her. "Ow?" he said, more as a question as to why he'd just been reprimanded than from any actual pain.

"You daft donkey," she said fondly. "Don't let these glasses fool you. I see just fine. You've been in love with that boy since you were lads, and I can see it all over your face that nothing's changed. You need to *tell* him."

Chester opened and closed his mouth, feeling his throat thicken and tears well up behind his eyes. "I, uh…"

"Oh, *love*," said his nana much softer as she reached over and rubbed his knee where she'd slapped him. "It's no good seeing you like this. So sad, when I'm absolutely certain there's no need to be."

"Isn't there?" Chester said with a sniff. "He's going to leave again."

Nana winked. "Not if you give him a reason to stay, he won't. He used to look at you like you hung the bloody moon. Are you telling me that's changed?"

All Chester could do was stare at her. "He…what?"

Nana chuckled affectionately and leaned down to feed Toffee a nibble of biscuit. "I wondered if you ever really saw it. Oh, love. I'd see you boys together and it was like sunshine was bursting out of you both, the way you looked at each other." She sighed. "I was ever so confused when he left, but that's neither here nor there." She wagged a crooked finger at him. "If he was just as blind as you were back then, he wouldn't have had a clue, and *that* meant you didn't give him a reason to stay. Give him one this time!" She adjusted her blanket over her legs. "That is, if you think he's still interested?"

Chester coughed to cover up his immediate reaction as his mind was flooded with images from their erotic night before. It had easily been some of the best sex of his life, not because it had been super kinky, but because it had been such a long time coming, Chester had given up hope it would ever happen.

"Maybe?" Chester said, gingerly picking his tea up again and taking a sip.

But Nana shook her head. "Either way, you should tell him."

Chester bit his lip. "I did *sort* of tell him I loved him," he admitted. "In a friend-like way."

Whilst I sucked him off and fucked him with a candy cane, he thought, not about to admit that to his nana in a million years. But even so, he got the feeling that Nana was right. He needed to be crystal clear about what he'd meant.

Which was that he hadn't been waiting all night for them to kiss.

He'd been waiting a lifetime.

"Now, you know I love Hans," Nana began diplomatically. "But that boy has known a lot of loss and rejection. You boys used to say 'love you, dickhead' – scuse my language – every other day to each other. Did you make clear that you *really* love him?"

Chester licked his lips, not even surprised that she was on his wavelength. She always knew the right thing to say. He sighed, and he must have been acting especially pathetic, as Marmalade came and rubbed her head against his leg in a rare display of affection.

"Probably not," he admitted. He downed the last of his tea, then dragged his hand over his face. "Urgh, okay, yes. I'm even more mad about him than ever. He's fucking gorgeous-"

"Language!"

"Whoops, sorry, Nana," said Chester sheepishly, but he was on a roll. "And you're right. It's not *fair* if he doesn't know how I feel. He's never going to stay unless I tell him that's what I want, what I'd love."

Nan smiled and nodded. "There we go, that's my boy. Now, what's stopping you from going over there and telling him that right now?"

What *was* stopping him? "Well, he's with his family, and his step-mother doesn't seem to like me much…" He trailed off at his nana's ferocious glare. "On the other hand," he continued brightly, "she might already be under the impression that we're already boyfriends, so what's she going to do about it?"

"Of course you two have got some hare-brained scheme

on the go," said Nana with a cackle. "I'm not even going to ask why you're pretending to be boyfriends, because it sounds to me that there's not really much pretending going on. All right, off you trot!" She picked up the TV remote and waggled it. "There's a political round coming up, and I need to beat all these silly fools on the telly."

But Chester leaned in to hug her, even as she was turning the volume back up again. "Thank you, Nana," he said, his voice thick with emotion.

"Aww, poppet," she said, patting his back. "That's what your old nana's here for. Now, you be off. True love calls!"

Chester nodded in agreement. "Yes, it does. And about bloody time," he muttered to himself as he made his way to the front door.

15

HANS

His bedroom really hadn't changed a bit.

Well, not since he'd left at eighteen. Hans could remember when he'd been very small and the walls had been covered in Fireman Sam posters and the bedspread was spaceships and aliens. Then in his early teens, it had been a mixture of rugby players and comic book characters on the walls, with a healthy stash of porn under his bed that he'd convinced himself he'd been looking at the women and not the men.

But even before he'd been shipped off to boarding school, Miriam got her hands on the house and redecorated it to a 'more sophisticated' style, which meant stripping back any hint of personality, including in Hans's and Greta's rooms. The galling sense of betrayal and shock had caused one hell of a screaming match between her and the twins, but in the end, there hadn't been much they could do about it when they weren't home for most of the year. Anything personal they tried to add just got taken away again the moment they left, so in the end, they'd just stopped trying.

Therefore, when Hans had come home over the past

couple of years of school, it had looked like this. Purplish-blue walls and grey carpet with white skirting boards and the colours of the bedding to match. There was a lone canvas print of a painting of the ocean on the wall and a ship in a bottle on the windowsill, despite the fact that Hans had no interest in sailing and hadn't even ever seen the sea in person.

But the four walls were enough to spark nostalgia. He'd spent so many hours in here playing with toys and video games, doing homework, wanking, and crying. The décor might have completely changed, but in a way, it was still his space.

Chester had never seen this room, so the two of them didn't have any specific memories together here. But how long had Hans spent looking up at the ceiling whilst thinking about him?

He'd been a fool to not realise his feelings earlier. He should have opened his heart up to the possibility that Chester could be more than a friend. That Chester was important enough for Hans to stay in Gingerbread, no matter that the town hated him and his dad had pulled away from him, not to mention Miriam's presence in his life. Instead, Hans had fled to London and denied his sexuality for another *seven* years.

What a waste.

He'd been given another chance with Chester this weekend, but was it already too late?

He sat on the edge of the bed and looked out the window into the back garden. From here, he could just see Peanut Butter's stable and wondered who took care of him now. Hans was amazed that he was still here after all this time, and Hans felt kind of proud of his dad for continuing to look after his mum's horse after what he'd done.

It was more understanding than he'd shown Hans and

Greta, but Hans couldn't bring himself to blame an innocent horse for an accident. Besides, grief did crazy things to people, and if Hans's dad was willing to change his ways now, Hans was open to the possibility of a relationship again.

Speaking of his dad and step-mum, he was thankful that they had been out for a drive in Miriam's hateful red Porsche when he'd arrived. An extremely hungover Greta had let him in before she'd crawled back to bed to sleep some more, leaving Hans to re-explore his childhood home alone.

Well, sort of alone. Jammie Dodger had kept him company, trotting along by Hans's feet with his pink tongue lolling out and his tail wagging furiously with happiness. It was as if he knew who Hans was and was happy to have him back home where he belonged. But he actually couldn't know that. Hans was just being silly, projecting his own feelings onto the sweet puppy.

Still, he was glad to have the company, as every room in the entire house was like his bedroom. The same walls but completely different décor. Gone was all the homeliness from Hans and Greta's mum. No more chintz cushions or warm wooden furniture or snow globes. At least Hans knew those had been rescued and relocated to the Anderson shelter. But where were his mum's impressionist art prints? Their childhood photos? The lumpy pottery Hans and Greta had made in junior school? All Mum's equestrian medals and ribbons and photos?

It was as if she'd been erased.

And yet…when Hans had inspected the back garden, the notches were still in the great oak tree from where they'd measured his and Greta's height every year as they grew. The kitchen might have totally been rearranged, but Hans still remembered all the Christmas dinners they'd cooked together in that space.

It hit him quite suddenly that it didn't matter what

Miriam had tried to do. So long as Hans was still here, so were his memories. His mum lived on through him and Greta.

No wonder Miriam had wanted them out of her way as soon as she'd got that ring on her gold-digging finger.

The house had the added strangeness of being set up like Miriam had dressed the place to be photographed for a magazine spread to sell contemporary garlands and wreaths. The decorations were beautiful, no doubt. But they were all blue and black and silver and *cold cold cold.* There was nothing nostalgic or fun or homemade about any of it. It was if Miriam had managed to take everything that Hans loved about the season – family, friends, togetherness, and love – and stripped it back into something aggressive but objectively beautiful.

Much like she was.

There was a black, pointy, needleless Christmas tree in the entrance hall that looked like it had escaped Halloween, only to be draped with glass icicles. The staircases had actual sharp holly leaves entwined around the bannisters. And Hans found a completely red tree with no decorations on it in one of the spare bedrooms that genuinely made him think for several seconds a blood-soaked yeti had broken into the house.

In the end, Hans had given up on his tour around the house and had a long, hot shower (with Dodger waiting patiently right outside the door, just to make sure he didn't drown). He wasn't surprised his home was as soulless as he remembered it being. His dad had been a shell when Hans had left, and Miriam was a ghoul.

He was more torn up about where he and Chester stood, really hoping with all his heart that last night had meant as much to Chester as it had to Hans. If it did, then they would make something, *anything,* work. They'd have hope.

That was his train of thought when suddenly Dodger leaped to his feet and started woofing loudly, his tail wagging like crazy as he bolted out of the bedroom door, which Hans had left ajar. His heart sinking, Hans rose to his feet from where he'd been lying on the bed, assuming that his dad and Miriam were back from their country drive. Honestly, that woman loved that car more than she tolerated most people, Hans was sure.

He mustered his resolve and resigned himself to smiling and being polite as he approached the door. But he paused in the middle of the room. It had felt easier to brace himself for facing Dad and Miriam with Chester by his side, pretending to be his boyfriend, yet offering Hans his very real strength. Could he do this without him?

Probably. He just didn't want to.

He rolled his neck and let it crack. He'd been incredibly grateful to change into the pair of jeans and fresh T-shirt he'd packed, so at least he didn't feel scruffy anymore. He also had a shirt that he planned on throwing on for dinner that evening, but he'd save that for later. The house was at least warm despite the cold and impersonal décor. So he padded barefoot across the wooden floor of his bedroom, figuring he'd probably dawdled enough and should go down to greet Dad and Miriam.

Except he didn't even make it to the door.

It flew inwards, and there was Chester, his dark hair standing up at all angles as he panted like he'd been running.

Hans stopped in his tracks, blinking. "Hi," he said somewhat stupidly. "What are you…you're here?"

Chester bit his lip, then he closed the door and pressed his back against it. "Greta let me in and told me where to go," he said by way of an explanation. "She looked hungover."

Hans shook his head, not finding any words for a second. Chester was in a new pair of jeans that clung sinfully to his thighs and probably his arse too, and a long-sleeved T-shirt that equally showed off all the impressive muscles Hans now knew lay beneath. Part of him wanted to demand to know if Chester had worn a coat outside, as it was still very cold. But in the moment, he decided that information wasn't actually his priority.

"You're in my bedroom," said Hans, stating the obvious. Then he glanced at the clock by the bedside table, even though he already knew Chester was incredibly early. "You've got hours before dinner. Is everything all right?"

"Yeah, yes," said Chester, nodding. Then he frowned and switched to shaking his head instead. "No, actually, it's not." He took a breath, then closed the distance between them in a flash, grabbing Hans's hands with his own and bringing them up to his chest. He took another few breaths as he stared into Hans's eyes, making Hans's heart want to stop beating in anticipation. "I love you," Chester said.

"Oh," Hans said with a chuckle, almost a little disappointed. "I know that – I love you too, dickhead."

"No," Chester said urgently, giving Hans's hands a short sharp squeeze. "Not like that. I mean…yes, like that, but…" He screwed up his eyes and exhaled shakily. "You asked me last night how long I'd been waiting to kiss you. The answer is *fifteen years, Hans.*" He opened his eyes, and Hans realised with a jolt that he was tearful. "I've wanted this almost since I met you, and I never told you because I was just so damn *scared.* But I'm more scared that you'll leave again, and I have to tell you the truth so you know what last night really meant to me. I. *Love.* You. Not as a best friend. As something more. So much more."

Wow. That was a *lot* to take in.

Hans just stared as the moment stretched out, trying to unscramble his thoughts. Chester had been attracted to him romantically, sexually…this *whole* time? That was crazy!

But…wasn't it also kind of amazing? Hans hadn't known his own feelings at that age, but Chester had, and their decade apart hadn't dampened that emotion.

If anything, it felt like when they'd reconnected yesterday, everything had just got stronger between them. Surely this was the 'go' sign that Hans had been waiting for? Chester had given him permission to admit that last night hadn't been a one-off thing for Hans at *all*. In fact, he couldn't see it as anything other than the start of something incredible, something big.

"Say something," Chester whispered, and Hans realised he'd let the pause drag on far too long. Worse, Chester dropped his eyelids, and twin tears escaped down his cheeks.

"Oh, no! No, don't cry," Hans begged, brushing the wetness away with his thumb.

When Chester looked back up at him with damp lashes, his beautiful blue eyes so wide and apprehensive, Hans couldn't help but press a gentle kiss to his lips, attempting to convey all the thoughts whirring around in his head.

"I love you, too, gorgeous," he started to try and explain. "It wasn't just last night. I didn't have the right words when I was younger, but I…" He took a deep breath and gestured to the room with his hand. "It's been remodelled, but this was my room. And I spent who knows how many hours staring at this very ceiling thinking about you, and our time together, whatever mischief we'd been up to that day. And, um…" Okay, in for a penny, in for a pound. "I never admitted to myself what I was really doing, but uh, I used to, um…"

"Oh my god," said Chester, suddenly laughing breathlessly. "You didn't use to wank off thinking about me, did you?"

Hans bit his lip. "Maybe? Is that bad?"

Chester barked out a loud laugh at that. "No! It's great! Me, too!"

Hans laughed and grabbed Chester's face as he kissed him. "It wasn't just that, though," he insisted. "Not just physical. I...you're my *best* friend. I didn't even realise that there's been this huge hole in my heart since I left, and by the time I figured out my feelings might have been more than platonic, it seemed too late. I didn't want to ruin anything, so I let the damn friendship *die* instead. Chester, I'm *so* sorry. But I'm done being afraid of changing things and making it weird. Because the alternative is losing you again and I can't do that!"

"Hey, hey, it's okay," said Chester as he rubbed Hans's arms, and it was only then did Hans realise how worked up he'd got himself. Chester smiled at him and pressed another sweet kiss to Hans's lips. "I know you've got family stuff going on that you can't control," Chester continued, "and there's a pretty big location issue. But...I'm in." He swallowed and cupped his hand to the side of Hans's face. "Nothing's been ruined. I promise. I want you with my whole heart. I don't want to pretend. I don't know if we can make it work, but I want..." He took a deep breath. "I want to be your boyfriend for real. Not pretend. If that's something you-"

Hans didn't even let him finish. He crashed his mouth against Chester's as he scooped him up in his arms. Chester responded immediately, kissing him back with desperate fervour, jumping up and wrapping his legs around Hans's waist, then grabbing a handful of Hans's hair. Their tongues sought each other out as Hans moaned, tumbling backwards until they crashed onto the bed.

Chester laughed and nuzzled their noses together as they wriggled on top of the mattress. "Is that a yes, then?"

"Huh?" Hans asked, forgetting what the question was.

Chester didn't seem to mind, though, as he giggled and kissed Hans's cheek sweetly. "Would you like to be my real-not-pretend boyfriend?"

"Oh," said Hans, sighing deeply in contentment and hugging Chester tightly. "Only if you'll be my real-not-pretend boyfriend, too?"

Chester took his time to kiss Hans's mouth thoroughly before answering. "I can't believe this is happening," he said with a slightly shaky laugh. "But hell fucking yes. I don't know how we'll make it work, but we will. Double-dare super-promise."

"Promise," Hans repeated. "And, you know, I think I've got an idea of how to make you believe this is happening." He grinned as he slipped his hand under Chester's T-shirt. "We have got *hours* until dinner."

Chester hummed and writhed against Hans's touch. "I think I like this plan a *lot*."

16

CHESTER

Seeing as they still didn't have any supplies, they had to make do with trading blow jobs again. But Chester had to confess he found it *no* hardship for them to strip down once more and kiss leisurely as their hands and mouths took care of their raging erections. Hans made him horny like he was a bloody teenager again. It was crazy.

Chester was extremely grateful for the physical distraction and not just because making out with Hans was a fucking delight. He was almost afraid to dwell on their conversation too long. Had they *really* just agreed to become boyfriends? Was this a bonkers, spur-of-the-moment declaration that they were going to have to retract in the cold light of day?

He sincerely hoped not.

He couldn't believe the words that had come out of Hans's mouth. But he didn't doubt their sincerity, or at least that Hans himself *believed* what he was saying was true. They'd both had feelings for the other when they'd been younger, and neither had realised what the other was going through. At least Chester had recognised his own attraction.

But he never would have dared hope that Hans would grow into those feelings, too.

Nana had been right.

But just because they wanted to be together didn't mean they *could* be. There were a lot of factors at play.

None of which Chester wanted to think about in that moment. His lips were wrapped around Hans's delicious cock as Hans moaned and carded his fingers through Chester's hair. Last night had been spectacular, but there was something to be said for the comfort and luxury of sex on an actual bed.

Chester was mad about Hans's body, and it made it all the sweeter knowing he truly had his heart as well. As they were in no rush, Chester took his time swallowing Hans down, pleasuring him for as long as he could, then slowing down when he sensed he was getting too excited.

"Tease," Hans whimpered the third time Chester popped off his cock to lick at his tip and then take his salty, heavy balls into his mouth. Chester just laughed, knowing the vibrations would only add to Hans's torment and pleasure as he wrapped his hand around Hans's shaft and began to gently stroke. That was the whole point. The longer he was wound up, the more explosive Hans's release was going to be.

As Chester kissed the inside of Hans's thigh, he stroked himself, making sure that Hans was watching him hungrily as his slippery erection pulsed through the hand he had closed around it. "Have you had enough to eat today?" Chester asked, trailing his mouth up along Hans's hip and his delicious hairy chest. "I've got some dessert for you, but only if you're not too full from lunch."

He wrapped his lips around Hans's nipple, sucking and nipping at it as it became a hard nub. Hans breathed heavily as Chester took care of him, running his hand up and down

Chester's spine. But then suddenly, Hans apparently broke and had enough. He grabbed Chester's hips and hauled him up his broad body.

Chester shrieked and laughed until he remembered they were supposed to be being quiet. They had no idea if Mr and Mrs Jager were back yet, and Greta *definitely* didn't want to hear their sexcapades, especially if she was feeling fragile and hungover. But in his defence, Hans had shimmied down the bed as he'd pulled Chester up it, and he devoured Chester's weeping length in one swift swallow.

Chester wondered how long they could keep tormenting each other in the most delicious way until they finally came. He glanced at the clock on the bedside table. They still had a couple of hours to find out. He braced himself on the bed and thrust his cock down Hans's throat, gently fucking his face and feeling like he'd won the lottery. Hans was so sweet and strong and hot. It was like they were a perfect match, their bodies slotting together like they'd been made to fit that way.

"Hans," he warned as his climax built. Hans just dug his fingers into the flesh of Chester's arse and sucked him off harder. Chester bucked, shooting his load, but Hans swallowed every last drop. "Fucking hell," Chester said shakily as he gasped for air. Once he stopped seeing stars, he pulled himself free, then crawled back down the bed to kiss Hans's plump, wet lips, tasting his own intimate flavour there. "Get comfy," he uttered to Hans. "Head on the pillows."

He was trembling and boneless from his orgasm, but there was no way he was going to leave Hans with blue balls. Hans grinned and did as he was told, so Chester hardly had to move much in order to get Hans's gorgeous cock back in his mouth. There was no teasing this time. Hans had been incredibly patient with Chester, and Chester intended to reward him with a magnificent finish now.

"Chester," Hans moaned, writhing beneath him. "Feels so good. Don't stop – close." He was breathless and flushed red and damp with perspiration.

Chester couldn't imagine him being any more beautiful. He popped off his cock for just a second, keeping up his ministrations with his hand, though. "Come down my throat, teddy bear," he told him hoarsely. "I want to taste your Christmas icing."

Hans snorted, but he was soon gasping again as Chester took him all the way down, giving him everything he had. Hans barely had time to cry out a warning before his bitter, salty cream hit the back of Chester's throat. He swallowed him down hungrily, wringing every last drop of his release from him. Even after it seemed he'd stopped, when he flopped back against the mattress, Chester continued to stroke him with his hand and lap at his tip. He loved the way Hans hummed and shivered, enjoying every second of it.

Eventually, Chester declared himself victorious in completely destroying his new boyfriend, and crawled up the bed to collapse next to him. Hans immediately enveloped him in a tight hug, peppering kisses against the side of his head and along his jaw.

"That was amazing," he murmured.

Chester pressed his lips to Hans's neck. "I told you next time we'd cuddle."

But Hans scoffed. "Actually, you promised that 'next time' you'd fuck my arse with me on my hands and knees. Don't think I've forgotten."

Chester laughed and hugged his lover happily. "Oh, don't worry, I haven't forgotten either. We just need to be a little more prepared next time."

"Double-dare super-promise," Hans said.

Chester gazed at Hans, drinking in that face he knew so well from before but was still getting used to its changes. "I feel like I'm in a dream," he said, stroking his fingers along his bristly cheek.

Hans turned his head to him and frowned. "I hope not," he mumbled. "I'll be really pissed off if I wake up alone with a wet spot."

Chester snorted and kissed his lover gently. "You're not alone, I promise."

For a moment, they just stared at each other, warm and cuddled close as their gazes searched each other's. "Thank you," Hans whispered. "For being here today."

"I'll be with you any time you like," Chester said, unable to stop the anxiety from bubbling up in him.

"I know," said Hans, but Chester wasn't sure he really did.

He bit his lip. "In case it wasn't obvious," he said tentatively, "this is me asking you to stay. Or asking to work out *some* way we can be in each other's lives. I know your family situation is tricky, but I want to try and make this work. Long term."

Hans nodded and pressed his lips to Chester's cheek, running his fingers lightly over Chester's drying hair. "Me, too. Absolutely. We'll work something out."

Chester wished there wasn't this uncertainty between them, but at least their intentions were clear and honourable. Chester was still struggling with the idea that it was just Miriam who was making Hans feel like he couldn't stay here in Gingerbread, but on the other hand, he did appreciate how hideously awful and manipulative she was.

Where there was a will, there was a way, and he had faith in his and Hans's ability to take care of the other's heart. It was what they'd done as teenagers, and now they were getting a second chance as adults to do it with real love.

"So," said Chester, propping himself up on his elbow and brushing back Hans's hair from his forehead. "This dinner you missed last night. Your dad and Miriam wanted you there so much they postponed it to do it tonight instead?"

Hans hummed and traced his fingertips along Chester's ribs. "Yeah. Considering how much she hates me, I would have thought Miriam would have just thrown a hissy fit and gone ahead with their plans last night regardless. I reckon my dad wants to talk to us about, well..."

"His illness?" Chester filled in gently. Hans nodded. "Do you really not know what it could be?"

"Nope," Hans said, dropping his head back on the pillow and looking up at the ceiling. "I mean, I've had plenty of guesses. But he just said that he's had some tests and the doctors have told him it's serious." He sighed. "I have a feeling tonight he's going to elaborate on that, and maybe...I dunno, something to do with his will, maybe? Or the house and the estate? All this was mum's, after all. Passed down through her family for generations. But I bet you anything that Miriam wants every single penny. It could get ugly."

Chester picked up his lover's hand and kissed his knuckles. "Well, it's a good job I'm here then, isn't it?"

Hans bit his lip and gave him a searching look. "Only if you really want-"

"I'll *be* there," said Chester. Then he flashed Hans a knowing grin. "This time as your *actual* boyfriend. That's basically Miriam Kryptonite, I promise. She can't hurt you whilst I'm around. Just like Ethel couldn't hurt you when we went into the Candy Cauldron as kids."

Hans frowned. "I hate that you still have to battle her every day," he said tenderly, brushing his fingers over Chester's hair and down his jaw. "I know it was our special place as kids, but is it really worth it when she's so awful to you?"

Chester sighed. He'd had this discussion with his nana so

many times. He knew his argument was thin, but he wasn't backing down.

"I'm not kidding when I say that place would fall apart without me. The shop would go under, and half a dozen people would lose their jobs. Which isn't loads, I know," he admitted, "but this is a small town. There aren't a lot of options for employment close by. Like Heather – she's a single mum without a car, and that job keeps food on the table. She'd be screwed if the shop folded. Besides"- he poked Hans's chest fondly -"it's the jewel of the village. Kids come from miles around, and it just makes them so happy. It's stood for generations in one form or another, and I'd hate if I was the reason it went under."

Hans frowned and scooped up the hand Chester had jabbed him with to kiss the finger. "Not to disrespect you, gorgeous, but Ethel ran the place when we were kids. It survived before you arrived."

Chester sighed. "That's because I took over from the last assistant manager. And yeah, someone could replace me if I left, but the last person was there for twenty years. I don't know who else would put up with Ethel if I threw in the towel. Not to mention that she's getting older and can't do as much as before. A lot of the physical work is down to me." He screwed up his face. "Besides, when she's not there, I really do *love* my job. People don't need sweets. It's purely for pleasure, and I love making that happen for them. Spreading joy into the world, you know?"

Hans gave him a look filled with fondness. "I do know. And you were always amazing at spreading cheer and goodwill. I just want you to be happy, too."

Chester shook himself and smiled. Hans didn't need Chester's problems on top of his own. But it was important to him that Hans knew why he couldn't just up and leave Gingerbread if Hans went back to London. As well as the fact that Chester didn't want to leave his nana or his community here.

But today was about Hans's family, and they could only tackle one fire at a time.

"Anyway," Chester continued, "there's a strong chance the old bag will drop dead any day now, fingers crossed!"

They laughed like they were naughty schoolboys again. "Chester," Hans scolded, tickling his ribs. "Even you wouldn't wish an old lady dead. Besides, we've been saying that since we were kids, and the battle-axe is still going strong."

Chester snorted. "Okay, yeah," he conceded. "She's definitely using dark magic to keep herself alive and kicking. I'm sure her office is filled with voodoo dolls and pentagrams. But I wouldn't be sorry if, you know, she accidentally fell into the industrial oven we have out back or something."

Hans tilted his head. "There's an oven on the shop premises?" he asked, interested.

Chester shrugged. "Yeah, we never use it, though. That would cost *money*."

"Oh, no! Not *money!*" Hans pretended to be shocked. "Will no one think of the starving orphans who should get *all* of our money?"

They giggled and snorted, then tickling became kissing again, and it wasn't long before Chester was trying to coax another orgasm out of his new boyfriend. Before they could get too far, though, Hans sighed and leaned back to study Chester's face, running his fingertips along his jaw. "I love you, dickhead," he said fondly, using the very nickname that Nana had remembered from their teenage years.

"Love you too, teddy bear," Chester told him back. He'd honestly forgotten how much they used to say they loved each other.

Chester wondered if things would have turned out

differently if he'd told Hans how he'd felt back when they were eighteen. But Hans had mentioned several times that he hadn't been ready to come out until he was in his mid-twenties, and Chester decided that despite all his heartache, he wouldn't change things. He might have scared Hans away completely when they'd been younger. This way he got to be with his best friend when he was comfortable with his sexuality.

No matter all the other complications, Chester was certain of Hans's feelings towards him now, and was extremely grateful that they didn't have to contend with any gay panic. They were happy in their own skins, and if they could just sort the rest of their issues out, they really could be incredible together.

The use of 'teddy bear' really did make Hans laugh. "Please don't call me that at dinner," he begged. "Greta will never, *ever* let me hear the end of it."

Chester hummed. "I don't know. It depends. What are you willing to do to help me keep my mouth shut?"

Hans growled and rolled them so Chester was on his back. They'd only just come, but he could feel a fire stirring inside him regardless as Hans ground his heavy body over Chester's, their soft, sensitive cocks rubbing against each other between their bellies.

"I could keep your mouth *full* for a bit longer up here in the bedroom," Hans suggested playfully.

Chester raised his eyebrow. "Already?" he said doubtfully.

Hans gasped, looking scandalised. "I meant with all the chocolate and sweets Greta bought me yesterday! What on earth were you suggesting, Mr Wild?"

Chester captured Hans's lip between his teeth, letting it drag through. "You're free to do anything you like with my mouth, Mr Jager," he teased back.

Chester couldn't change what Miriam might have in store

for them or what fuckery might be going on with Hans's father's will. But he could be there for his boyfriend for the next couple of hours to love him and distract him from things beyond his control. Whatever happened, Chester would be by his side for as long as he could.

Just like he always used to be.

17

HANS

"Oh, you're here," said Miriam as Hans and Chester walked into the kitchen later that evening. She spun around, martini glass in hand, as she assessed them. Her eyes flicked up and down them like she was inspecting for dirt. Then in a flash, her big crimson smile was back, even if it didn't reach her smoky eyes. "Both of you. Isn't that…nice?"

Hans narrowed his eyes and placed a hand on the small of Chester's back as he glanced at the clock on the wall. They'd managed to avoid seeing anyone else all afternoon, but Greta had texted him with what time to be downstairs, warning him not to be late. So here they were, five o'clock, on the dot.

He noticed that she wasn't there yet.

"Yes," he said, rousing his Christmas cheer and smiling at Chester before looking at his step-mother again. "Right on time. We were promised drinks and nibbles, and with the kitchen smelling so divine, we hurried on down."

Yes, he was buttering her up in the vain hope that she might not be a total cow towards Chester, but he was also telling the truth. The air was filled with the scents of roasting meat and potatoes, sweet and cheesy sauces, and the tang of salty vegetables. Miriam might have been an awful gold-digger, but credit where credit was due. Hans had assumed that she might have hired a cook or even have live-in staff since he'd moved out. But Miriam had always known her way around the kitchen, and apparently still did.

Even if said kitchen was nothing how it used to be.

Miriam's refurbishments had begun the second she and Hans's dad had come back from their honeymoon. The space was all gleaming chrome and marble now – nothing like the warm wooden finishes Hans recalled from his childhood. The delicious smells of their upcoming dinner went some way to help him accept the new décor, but like everything in this house, it was difficult to ignore the coldness of the room regardless of the heat coming from the appliances.

Of course, Miriam hadn't broken a sweat despite the glowing oven and bubbling pans. In fact, she still looked like a Stepford wife, with a full-on fifties A-line dress, including voluminous petticoats, as well as curled hair and high heels. The shade of red on her apron perfectly matched the roses on her dress and the sparkly teardrop earrings she had on. And of course, her blood-red lips.

She took a sip of her martini and looked Hans and Chester up and down again as she stirred a simmering pot of gravy. They were thoroughly showered after their afternoon of making out like horny teenagers, but they were both just in T-shirts, their sock-clad feet poking out from the legs of their jeans. Hans had planned on wearing a button-down over his T-shirt, but he'd been too hot after all the sex. Now he was wondering if he should have.

He was just about to panic that they'd missed some sort of dress code announcement when Greta came strolling in to join them in the kitchen. She appeared bright-eyed and bushy-tailed, having apparently slept off her hangover. But more importantly, she was not wearing either a ball gown or tuxedo.

In fact, along with her black leggings, she was wearing a Christmas jumper that he'd never seen before, which on her Hans saw as nothing less than the sign of the oncoming apocalypse. It appeared that the prospect of another dinner with Miriam had made her come over all frivolous. It read 'Dear Santa…define good…' and had literal bells on it.

"What the bloody hell is that?" he asked before he could think of something more tactful to say.

Greta grinned and plucked a *vol-au-vent* from its tray, popping it whole into her mouth. "I'm just getting into the spirit of things, dear brother," she said as she swallowed. Then she leaned in closer to Hans and Chester. "I have a feeling tonight is going to be *fun.*"

Before Hans had a chance to ask her what she meant, they were accosted by a chocolate-coloured blur on four legs, barking the house down.

"Dodger!" cried Chester, immediately dropping to his knees to fuss over the happy puppy. "Hello, handsome boy. Yes, you are!"

Greta gave Hans a shrewd look, grinning wickedly. "Looks like you boys had a…cosy afternoon."

Hans realised with a jolt that from this angle Chester's love bite was visible, and he felt himself blush immediately. "I, um…"

He wasn't embarrassed exactly. But Greta clearly wanted details of how they'd gone from being fake boyfriends to real ones, and Hans didn't want to discuss that in front of Miriam.

Speaking of which, the she-devil spun on her heels, making her dress billow out. "No dogs in the kitchen!" she shrieked, waving a spatula around. Then she plastered a smile on her crimson lips and fluttered her fake eyelashes. "I mean, I need space to work my Christmas magic. Why don't you children find your father in the living room?"

Hans frowned, not impressed by the use of the word 'children'. They hadn't been kids for a long time, and she was no kind of mother to them in any case.

"Sorry," he apologised anyway for the sake of peacekeeping. "You said for us to come down for drinks and nibbles at five, and it's-"

"Yes, yes, I know what I said," Miriam snapped, the smile still frozen on her face as she bustled about. "Take the trays with you, and the bar is all set up in the living room for tipples. None for your father, though!" She wielded the spatula like a sword once again. "Doctors' orders. Or so I assume. Your father is being *very* cagey about all this." She laughed, slightly hysterically, and shook her head like she couldn't *believe* she was being kept out of the loop. "But best to be safe than sorry, however, I think."

Hans narrowed his eyes, very surprised that Miriam hadn't interrogated his dad's doctors herself. His anticipation of what was going to go down this evening was growing. That was very strange if even she didn't know what his prognosis was. If Johan was that ill, why hadn't he discussed it with his wife? There was definitely something fishy afoot.

And he didn't just mean the tray of salmon *vol-au-vents* that Greta grabbed from the kitchen island to accompany them to the living room.

Hans's concerns about their family drama were overruled by his stomach. After all the sex he and Chester had indulged in over the past twenty-four hours, he didn't hesitate to follow Greta's lead and snag a plate of mini quiches whilst Chester opted for a bowl of honey-glazed cocktail sausages.

As they made a hasty exit from the kitchen, Chester leaned into Hans and kissed him on the jaw. "That could have been worse," he murmured.

Hans huffed, but he smiled down at Chester. "I imagine she's just warming up. But yeah, I'd rather have some food and booze in me before the fireworks start."

They followed Greta down the hall, past some truly cringey wedding photos of Hans's dad and Miriam. In every picture, Hans's dad looked to be in a mild amount of discomfort whilst Miriam poured herself all over him. There were no photos of Hans and Greta on display from the day, probably because they'd spent the entire time scowling before they'd gotten drunk on alcopops that the sympathetic bartender had snuck them.

Considering how resistant Hans's dad looked in the photos, not to mention his secret bunker to escape his second wife, it was a mystery why Johan had ever married Miriam. A question he hadn't been able to answer for thirteen years.

Also, Hans had to wonder where his mum's wedding photos were. The house had been full of them growing up. But after seeing the bunker, he was at least hopeful that his dad had rescued them and they were in a box in the attic or something.

Speaking of his dad, the three of them did indeed find him in the living room with a very excitable Jammie Dodger leading the way. The fluffy puppy was beside himself as they entered, barking and scrambling over the hardwood floors to jump up at Hans's dad where he was sitting, then coming back to run around their legs like he'd thought the three of them had been lost forever instead of merely being upstairs.

"Now, shush, come on, Dodger," Hans's dad gently chided, but his warm laughter undermined the command somewhat.

Dodger ran back and forth between the threesome and Hans's dad as if ensuring that they couldn't *possibly* miss each other. When he was satisfied that everyone was where they should be, he calmed down and stopped barking, settling down by his dad's slipper-clad feet. Judging by Johan's cardigan and slacks, it was only Miriam who had decided to dress up for the evening, probably to try and intimidate them or something.

She could try all she liked, but all Hans cared about was that he and Chester felt comfortable, which they did. Greta was always going to do her own thing, and his dad...

Well, Hans didn't know his dad at all anymore, but he looked happy enough as he fussed over Dodger from his chair.

With a jolt, Hans realised his dad was sitting in *his* chair. The one he'd always had when he and Greta had been growing up. They'd always known not to sit in Dad's special chair unless it was to crawl into his lap and be read to.

Hans felt a lump rise in his throat as they placed the food they'd carried in onto the black, square coffee table. He looked around the room that was otherwise all grey, chrome, and black. Even the eight-foot-tall Christmas tree was decorated so precisely and symmetrically Hans could picture Miriam placing each silver bauble or bow on with a ruler and spirit level.

But his dad's chair was a battered old red-and-cream thing with plump arms and a high back, the fabric worn away in patches. It was his favourite place to read. Indeed, he was putting a bookmark in another thriller book as he laughed at Dodger running around the room again.

Whatever battle Miriam had won throughout the rest of the house, she'd lost it with that chair.

Pride welled up in Hans. He didn't know the full story, but that chair showed that some part of the dad he knew was still in there.

"Well," said Johan, rising to his feet to shake their hands. "You boys are looking remarkably well, considering your adventure last night. I hope your car's okay, Chester?"

For some reason, nerves fluttered in Hans's belly. He may have some good feelings towards his dad now, but he still kind of felt like a stranger after all these years apart. Were they supposed to talk about the bunker? It was clearly his secret hideaway from Miriam.

"Yes, thank you," said Chester, coming to Hans's rescue, shaking Johan's hand with gusto. "It just needed a jump-start in the end after the fog got into the engine."

"Yeah, but…" said Greta, already uncorking a bottle of red wine she'd got from the fancy display cabinet. Clearly, hair of the dog was the way to go as far as she was concerned. "Where did you *sleep?* What's this business with the shelter? Surely it wasn't mum's old Anderson shelter?" She arched an eyebrow at their father. "Dad was all very hush-hush about it last night. Told me not to mention a thing in front of Miriam. In fact – *she* thinks you got a lift back to Chester's place."

Ah-ha! So it *was* a secret. Right, Hans could work with that.

"Dad probably didn't want her to worry," he said placatingly with a shrug, accepting the glass of wine as she offered it. He and Chester sat down on the couch as Hans's dad retook his own seat. Dodger settled immediately by his feet. "Dad's kept it pretty decent. We were fine."

He met his dad's eye, and he could have sworn he winked, but Greta wasn't done. She huffed as she passed Chester his glass of red, and Hans looked nervously down at the pale grey sofa they were perched on. If they spilled anything, Miriam would definitely kill them. But…he wasn't sure how much he cared anymore.

"So you huddled in a war bunker all night? That's not very romantic." Greta waggled her eyebrows as she took a seat on the other end of the large L-shaped couch, and Hans sighed. Nothing got by her. She could clearly tell *something* had shifted between Hans and Chester for real, especially if she'd clocked that love bite of Chester's. But Hans kind of wanted their time together in the shelter to stay private, for now. Not to mention not wanting to drop his dad in it.

It was a strange line he was walking, protecting his dad's secret when they'd never even discussed it.

Hans wanted to tell Greta all about the corkboard where every single one of their cards had been preserved. He wanted to assure her about the photos that had vanished from this house but had found their new home there. He wanted to take her there and show her all of Mum's precious snow globes, all standing proudly as a monument to her travels and adventures.

But tonight was a dance, and Hans had to be patient. He didn't know what his dad was up to, and it was probably best if Hans let him take the lead.

"We were fine," Hans assured his sister. Then he looked at his dad. "I'm just sorry we spoiled dinner."

"Oh," said his dad jovially, waving his hand. "It's fine. Miriam loves entertaining and cooking, so it was no struggle to host a second night. And it meant I got time to spend with Greta, didn't it?"

She looked slightly confused as she turned to Hans. "We played board games, and Dad showed me the photos he took from his trip to India. A trip he took last year *alone.* It was… fun." Her confused expression seemed to deepen, like bonding time with her dad had been the last thing she'd been expecting.

"Yes, unfortunately, Miriam came down with a headache last night," said Dad in concern, his brow furrowing. "But she seems to have rallied for tonight, lucky us!"

The other three hummed as they sipped their wine. Hans believed Miriam had come down with a headache as much as he still believed in Father Christmas.

He jumped a little in surprise as Chester's hand slipped over his knee. He wasn't used to having a boyfriend, and he'd certainly never introduced one to his dad. But he had to admit that the touch was immediately welcomed, and he relaxed.

"Sounds like you two had a lovely evening," said Chester warmly to Hans's dad.

"As did you two," said Greta slyly to Hans, still fishing for gossip.

"So, uh," said Hans, ignoring her and casting around for another conversation topic. He latched onto the first thing that came to mind. "I saw the stable from my bedroom window. It still looks like it's in action?"

He hadn't been able to get a close look, so what he was really asking was whether or not Peanut Butter was still there. But he wasn't sure if that would be a tricky subject with his dad.

On the contrary, Johan beamed, sitting up in his seat and stroking Dodger's head when he got up in excitement.

"Oh, yes," said Hans's dad eagerly. "Of course, I still know very little about horses, but we have a lovely girl from the village who comes in and takes care of Peanut Butter almost every day. I let her sort of adopt him when she was a teenager so she could have her own horse without all the great expense." He smiled down at Dodger, and Hans wondered if his eyes got a little misty. "We go down and talk to Nutty, don't we, boy? He's a very good listener."

"I bet he is," said Chester warmly.

Hans cleared his throat as he realised he had a lump in it. He'd been bracing himself to hear that the horse had been sold or something even worse. But to know he was still here was almost like a bit of his mum was still here, too. His dad really did have more of a backbone than Hans had given him credit for.

"I might go and say hello in the morning in that case," he said.

His dad nodded earnestly. "Please do. And Chester is more than welcome as well if he's staying the night."

Chester looked down at his wine in alarm. "Oh, whoops. I didn't think-" he began, but Johan waved him off.

"Don't give it a second thought. We're delighted to have you and wouldn't dream of sending you back out into the dark after what happened to your car last night."

Hans beamed and nudged Chester's knee with his own. "Thank you for including Chester in the invitation tonight," Hans said softly, tearing his eyes away from his gorgeous man to smile at his dad.

Johan scoffed and shook his head at Hans. "Nonsense, of course. We're thrilled to have him over. I'm only sorry we didn't welcome you when you were lads, Chester." Hans's dad frowned. "I'm not sure why that was now…"

"Well, isn't this cosy?" Miriam announced as she came swanning into the room, saluting her fresh martini glass at them all. Her smile was sharp like a shark's, showing all her teeth as she surveyed the room. "What are we all talking about…" Her question trailed off as her eyes narrowed dangerously, and it was only then that Hans realised his dad also had a glass of red wine in hand.

Greta looked guiltily away, suddenly very interested in a bland bit of art on the wall, that just seemed to depict a dreary, rain-soaked street.

"Johan Jager!" Miriam scolded, her gaze turning on the twins. "You two should have known better."

"Why?" said Hans loudly and clearly, surprising everyone, most of all himself. "Why should we know better? We don't know anything at all about Dad's illness, his symptoms, his medication, nothing. If he wants a glass of wine, why shouldn't we trust that he knows what he's doing and give it to him?"

Miriam looked like she was going to combust, but Hans's dad chuckled, diffusing the situation. "Now, now. There's no need for any of that. I'm fine, Miriam. How's the dinner coming along? It smells wonderful."

She opened and closed her mouth a couple of times but seemed reluctant to fight with him in front of Hans, Greta, and Chester. Or maybe she had another reason for plastering that big, fake smile back on? Hans really didn't know.

Instead of arguing further, she took a dainty sip of martini, swishing her voluminous skirts as she did.

"Yes, wonderful, my darling," she said, batting her eyelashes. "In fact, I'm about to dish up, so perhaps we'd all like to make our way into the dining room, hmm?"

By the twitch of her jaw, it looked as if the prospect of being in the same room as Hans and Greta for the next few hours pained her. But she managed to keep up her shiny facade for as long as it took everyone to agree and rise to their feet.

"Here, let *me* help you, Johan," she said as she tottered over to Hans's dad so fast that she almost skittered off her high heels.

The olive swung on its cocktail stick inside the martini glass. Poor Dodger ran for cover, cowering behind some cold black sculpture that looked like a melting man reaching out for help. Chester just leaned back in time so as to not get sprinkled with Miriam's escaping drink. Luckily the liquid was clear, and therefore not as much of a danger to the sofa as their red wine.

Chester slipped his hand into Hans's as they stepped back to let Miriam escort Johan from the room. It was as if she was terrified that if his children got too close to him, he'd disavow her on the spot.

Who was Hans to say that wasn't the case?

Greta grabbed the bottle of red and sauntered after Dad and Miriam, and Hans was happy to walk with Chester at the back of their small entourage, with Dodger scampering between all five of them.

"Are you ready for this?" Chester asked quietly.

Hans pressed his lips gently to Chester's. "We'll see. I'm so glad you're here."

Chester bumped into his side and kissed his jaw. "I wouldn't be anywhere else."

Hans was very doubtful of that. But there was only one way to find out.

They headed to the dining room.

HANS

You could cut the atmosphere with a knife.

Oh, the dinner was perfect, all laid out in Wedgwood china dishes for people to help themselves. The table cloth was so white it was like freshly fallen snow, and the crystal chandelier overhead bathed everything in sparkling light. The table was enormous, lit by real candelabras with dripping wax candles between the abundance of food, and Hans felt like he was in one of those fancy period dramas on the TV at the lavishness of everything. All they needed was footmen to serve them.

But no one was saying a word. Luckily, Miriam had put on a Christmas album, so there was a bloke crooning quietly in the background to accompany the scrape and clink of cutlery on crockery, which meant it wasn't completely awkward. But Hans felt like there was a bomb waiting to go off. Even Dodger was lurking in the doorway, unsure if he wanted to come inside the dining room.

At least Hans had Chester's warm, sturdy presence beside him. Chester was able to reassure him without speaking that he was there for Hans by touching his thigh or bumping their shoulders together. No matter what was going to happen, Chester would look after Hans, like he always did.

Then there was Greta sitting opposite. She and Hans had been able to communicate nonverbally since birth, so when she arched an eyebrow and picked up her drink to sip it, Hans knew she was saluting him, waiting for the fireworks to begin.

He was glad someone was having fun. He was so apprehensive he was struggling to eat, despite the food tasting as good as it had smelled in the kitchen. Hans pushed some peas through his thick gravy, then glanced around at the fancy garlands hung around the room. He felt like he was in a department store display, with Miriam watching their every move from the head of the table, as if she was looking through the shop's glass window.

Hans's dad was sat beside Greta, and not at the head of the table. Hans wasn't even surprised that Miriam had taken that spot from him. Johan threw Greta and Hans little smiles as they ate, but made no attempt at conversation. Greta stood up to retrieve a second bottle of wine to open from the sideboard. Apparently, there were stashes of booze everywhere in this house.

Not to be left out, Miriam picked up her cocktail shaker and shook it violently, making the rest of them jump. She smiled closed-lipped at Johan, then saluted him with her topped-up glass.

Greta filled up the red wine glasses almost to the brim.

Hans felt like there was a storm brewing in the air.

It was only Chester's hand on his knee that stopped him from fidgeting and kept him calm. In fact, Chester seemed to be eating his entire dinner one-handedly. Hans caught his eye and felt a surge of courage run through him. Johan had *invited* them here. There was nothing to be nervous about.

The only thing that mattered was Chester's heart, and

come hell or high water, Hans had that. But life would be a lot easier if he could sort out this mess with his family.

He cleared his throat and took a sip of wine.

"So," he began. Someone had to say something, and it seemed it was going to have to be him. "Shall we address the elephant in the room?"

"Which one?" Greta muttered into her wine glass.

Miriam beamed at the two of them, her martini glass aloft. She might have been smiling, but her eyes were like daggers. "Now, now, children. There's no need to be uncouth."

Hans frowned at her. "We haven't been children for a long time."

"And we're not *your* children," Greta grumbled.

The brewing argument was interrupted by Hans and Greta's dad sighing. He smiled warmly at them, and Chester's comforting hand on Hans's thigh squeezed tighter. "You're right, son," said Johan. "We do need to talk. Thank you for coming this weekend, and thank you, Miriam, for graciously hosting. I wanted to speak to you all at once. It makes me very sad that the family drifted apart in the wake of your mother's death, but I sincerely hope that maybe that could change now."

"Drifted apart?" Greta spat, putting her wine glass down with such force she narrowly missed sloshing its contents over the white tablecloth. Miriam audibly gasped at the near miss. "That's an interesting way to put it."

Hans waved her down. "I know there's a lot of history between us," he said urgently. "But before we start accusing one another of past sins, I want to know what we're dealing with here. Please. Can we all just stay civil long enough to talk about Dad's illness?"

"You're quite right, dear," said Miriam, positively overspilling with contriteness. That and the 'dear' rankled

Hans, but he pressed his mouth together and let her speak. "We're all very anxious to hear what's going on with your diagnosis. I know you wanted us all together to explain, but I've been *so* very worried. We need to make arrangements, after all."

Greta blinked. "Arrangements?"

"For Dad's care, you mean?" asked Hans.

Miriam blinked slowly, as if processing what he'd said. "Yes, his care. Absolutely." She reached over and squeezed Johan's hand, which took quite a lean at this ridiculous table.

Hans huffed and caught Chester's eye, and he raised a brow. He'd bet anything the 'arrangements' she'd been referring to meant the will and their family estate.

Gold-digger.

Hans's own feelings were so far from thinking about money. "Dad, I was so worried when I heard you were sick. What's going on?" he asked, a lump rising in his throat as he looked at Johan. He still didn't *appear* ill. He hadn't all weekend. But then, some illnesses were invisible, and Hans shouldn't make assumptions based on appearances.

Johan sighed and toyed with his fork. "I was told to get my affairs in order. I'm not sure what time scale we're looking at, but Miriam is right. I need to talk to you two about your inheritance and explain how my will is set up."

"I didn't – that's not what I said at all, darling," Miriam spluttered, halfway through carving the bloody lump of beef on her plate. Her lipstick must have been made of concrete because her fake smile was just as shiny and crimson as ever, even after all the food and drink.

Johan gave her a patient smile. In that moment, he looked so tired. "It is an important consideration." He turned back to look at Hans. "I know we've been estranged for so long, and that breaks my heart. But I wanted to make sure that you two knew you were going to be taken care of."

Miriam's fork screeched on her plate. "Oh, really?" she said pleasantly enough, but Hans was suddenly wondering just *how* sharp the knives were.

He glanced at Greta, grateful for Chester's solid presence beside him. This was a hell of an awkward conversation to be party to, but Chester was there for Hans like he had been all throughout Hans's teenage years. If Hans hadn't scared him off by now, he hoped he never would.

"Why now?" Greta asked, and Hans had to agree. "Why reach out to reconnect now? I know you're ill, but I don't really see how that's changed anything. The past is still what it always was, what it will always be."

"You were the one who wanted us gone all those years ago," Hans added. "You didn't want to support us then after what we did. Greta's right. Why now?" The words burned in his throat as he repeated his sister's question. He wasn't sure that he wanted answers or not, but they'd started, so they had to finish.

Or so he thought.

"Oh, let's not hash over bad feelings from the past," said Miriam with a high-pitched laugh. She gulped the last of her martini down and grabbed her silver drink canister, shaking it vigorously. The loud clattering of ice made Hans wince, and killed the conversation for a few seconds. "The important thing is that everyone is treated *fairly* now." She poured her fresh cocktail with a flourish, like she'd won the argument.

Hans was only just getting started, and he knew that Greta was as well.

But it was their father who spoke. "What do you mean, 'I didn't want to support you then'?" He looked between them, his eyes glassy. "What on Earth could you have ever done that I wouldn't want to support you? You mean when your mother died? I…you pulled away from me. I was trying to give you space."

"Yeah, right," said Greta, taking a glug of wine. "We knew you blamed us for her death, just like everyone else."

"We were just trying to respect your wishes," said Hans quietly, trying to rein his emotions in. He was afraid he might begin to cry, and then he'd never stop. "We know seeing us was painful for you, but…we needed you, Dad. We were grieving, too."

Hans expected his dad to look sad or contrite. But instead, he looked thoroughly confused. "Why would I…?" he started to ask, his voice faint. *"Blame* you? Why on Earth would I *blame* you? Her horse bucked. It was just an accident!"

"But we'd just had that argument," Hans said, his throat thickening and his eyes burning despite his best efforts. "The last thing Greta and I said to her was that she was mean, that we hated her. If we hadn't had that fight with her, she would have been more careful and kept control of her horse. It was our fault she died, and everybody knows it, so there's no point in trying to sugar-coat it now."

He sniffed and lost his battle with the tears that spilled down his face. He'd known that truth for so long, but speaking it out loud again after all these years shattered his heart. He'd tried to numb the pain, but in that moment, it was as fresh as the day she died. He would never, *ever* forgive himself for what he'd done, and speaking the words aloud helped him to own that responsibility, at least.

Chester was looking at him in confusion. Hans hated that more than anything. But it was time they talked about this openly, especially if they were going to be together.

Greta bit her lip and looked at Hans with tears in her eyes, too. "I'm so sorry, Dad," she whispered.

Hans clung to Chester's hand, trying not to let the room

spin. He'd avoided speaking about his guilt out loud for the past fifteen years. Not even to Chester. "We don't blame you for blaming us," he said thickly. "But to cut us out-"

"That's a little dramatic, don't you think?" said Miriam with a chuckle and another big glug of martini. "You wanted to spread your wings and move out. Didn't they, Johan?"

But Hans's dad wasn't looking at her or apparently even listening. "There was no argument. What are you talking about? Hans, Greta – your mother loved you more than anything else in life. You know that, don't you? Please, tell me you know that."

Hans openly sobbed. No, he wasn't sure about that at all.

"Oh, baby," Chester murmured, moving his chair noisily over the wooden floor to wrap his arm around Hans.

"Watch the varnish!" Miriam shrieked.

Greta scoffed. "Nobody cares about your fucking floors right now, Miriam," she snapped.

Miriam slammed down her glass, getting her drink on her plate, the alcohol mixing with the gravy. "This is *my* house, and you will respect me!" she cried as she stood up.

Hans stared at her mulishly. "Actually, it was our mum's house, and Dad might not remember, but you were *always* reminding us about the fight we had over our bikes just before she died. If she'd never died, you wouldn't be here, so maybe have some respect for *her*."

Johan looked over at Miriam in shock. "The bikes?" he said faintly. "How did you even know about that?"

Miriam waved a hand dismissively, still standing and towering over them all in her high heels. "The children mentioned it. You mentioned it. Everyone knew about it," she added with a tinkling laugh. But then her expression became incredibly grave. "Look, I know it was a tragedy. No one is disputing that."

"But everyone knew it was our fault she died, right?" said

Greta, her jaw set and her arms crossed as she looked to be fighting back tears. "Why would we stay here when everyone hated us. You'd already packed us off to boarding school. By the time we turned eighteen, we knew we weren't wanted. We were the little murderers of Gingerbread."

Hans was familiar with all of this. It was etched into his and Greta's memories like stone.

So why did his dad look so shell-shocked?

"*That's* why you left?" he rasped, his face even ruddier than usual and his eyes brimming with tears behind his glasses. "I thought you wanted to get away from the grief – that you *wanted* to go to that fancy school and then off to London, to follow your dreams. I tried to pay for your university, but you didn't want that, so I let you go, even when it broke my heart!"

"What?" said Hans, unable to believe what he was hearing. "That's not-"

"Nobody thought that you were responsible for your mum's death." Chester was staring at Hans in horror. "That's what you thought? That's why you left?"

"We couldn't go into the village without people staring at us," said Greta stubbornly. "It was obvious."

Chester spluttered, looking between the twins. "They were probably looking because they felt sorry for you, because everyone *loved* your mum, and couldn't believe your new step-mother had been so cruel as to ship you off to boarding school the second she married your dad! And when they heard you were leaving, that made a lot of people think you were abandoning the town as well as your dad. But if they'd known what you'd had to deal with, they would have understood, like I did!"

His cheeks were tinged red, and he was trembling as he tore his gaze away from Hans and glared at Miriam.

Hans couldn't blame him. He felt like his whole world was crashing down as he too looked at Miriam.

In fact, the whole table was now staring at her with varying degrees of incredulity.

Miriam just let out a peal of laughter and drank what was left of her martini. "I don't know what you're talking about, darlings. You practically begged us to go to that fancy school. I thought you wanted to go to a good university. It surprised us both that you didn't pursue your further education, didn't it, dear?" She fixed her gaze on Johan, but Hans's dad's mouth was in a thin line, his jowls quivering.

"My memory isn't what it used to be," he said, his voice dangerously low in a tone Hans had never heard before. "But I'm pretty sure that *you* convinced me that school would be the best thing for my children. You told me they were too shy to ask because the fees were so high. *You* told me they didn't want to attend university, that they wanted to make their own way to London. That it was a matter of pride. And," he said, turning back to the twins, "just for the record, there was no big fight over your bikes. I think you're confused with a different day when you fought about being allowed out on your own, when you were younger. That I remember."

He shook his head and took a deep breath.

"But the day of her accident, you asked for new ones, and your mother said that we'd all discuss it when she returned, because you hadn't had the old ones that long. That was it. I don't know where you got the idea that everybody blamed you, but I can assure you, that's nonsense."

Hans felt like he couldn't breathe. "No, t-that's not," he stammered. "It was a fight. I remember...I think?" He looked at Greta. Was he remembering things correctly? Or...was he just remembering what he'd been *told?* What he *thought* people thought? "Right? Everybody blamed us."

"*Nobody* blamed you," Chester growled. For someone so

small, it was amazing the anger he was radiating. He gripped Hans's hand in his own, his face blotchy with emotion. "Even if you'd had a fight with your mum, you still didn't make the horse buck. But I've never once heard anyone in the whole village say anything like that. They were miffed you left because it felt like you were too good for the village all of a sudden. But I knew that wasn't true, and now no one thinks that either." He glanced over at Greta. "I don't know how you got it into your head that the town hated you both, but I promise you that was never the case!"

He looked back to Hans, and they stared at each other as Hans blinked free another couple of tears. "Do you swear?" he uttered.

Chester grabbed either side of his face, trembling with sincerity. "I wish you'd told me this years ago," he said, his voice cracking. "I could have saved you so much heartache."

Greta's eyes narrowed at Miriam. "I'm starting to get an inkling as to where all these crazy ideas came from."

Miriam rolled her eyes and laughed again. Her constant tittering was becoming incredibly annoying. "Now, look. Memory is fallible – unreliable! I think you'll find-"

"Why didn't you tell us any different?" Hans cut her off, asking his question to his father in little more than a whisper. "We *needed* you. But you closed yourself off. You let *her* swoop in and – I don't even know! Brainwash you or something!"

Miriam looked ready to snap again, but Johan held up his hand. "Let me speak, Miriam," he said firmly. "Yes, I owe you both an explanation and an apology. I did a lot of soul-searching during my time in India last year, as Greta knows. But...I owe you the shameful truth. There have been too many lies, too much misunderstanding. More than I ever realised, so let me say this now."

He swallowed, looking tearful. Hans reached over and

rubbed his hand over his dad's. "It's okay," he said, nodding. "I think we're all ready to talk, to hear the truth. Even if it's painful."

"Johan, I don't think-" Miriam began, but Hans's dad spoke over her.

"Miriam and I knew each other several months before your mother died," he said loudly, closing his eyes. "From the town council. We…flirted. It felt harmless to me at the time. But then your mother was gone in an instant, and the guilt that overwhelmed me for straying from her, even for a moment, was crippling."

Tears ran down his face, and he blinked his eyes open, not moving to wipe the wetness away.

"When Miriam was still interested in me…when she came to comfort me, I thought…I thought if we had a relationship, that it might make the flirting *mean* something. I was so lost and empty, I didn't know how to reach out to you kids, and she seemed to do such a marvellous job of taking care of everything, so I let her." He hung his head and shook it. "I was such a fool. Such a *blind* fool."

Hans didn't know what to say. He'd felt as if the whole world was falling down, but now it was like the ground had opened up beneath him. "You felt guilty…for *flirting?* That's why you *married* her?"

"And because he loves me," Miriam shrieked, her eyes wild. "Right, darling?"

Greta was just staring at their dad. "You know flirting isn't cheating, right?" she asked, completely dumbfounded. "You didn't have to *shackle* yourself to her out of guilt. Mum would never have wanted that."

"Watch your tone, young lady," Miriam snapped at her. "Your mother wasn't the saint you all made her out to be, for heaven's sake."

"Don't speak about my mum that way," Hans barked,

trembling with rage. "She was *ten* times the woman you'll ever be, you lying, manipulative-"

Miriam burst into tears, shocking Hans into silence.

"You all act like she was this saint!" Miriam wailed as her mascara ran down her face. "That she could never do anything wrong! I'm sorry you thought her death was your fault, children. I don't know how that happened. But the truth was she wasn't perfect! She should never have been riding an inexperienced horse that close to the road where it could be so easily spooked by a *car engine!* She wasn't flawless! But I've still been living in her perfect shadow for fifteen years, and I've had *enough!* Maybe I remembered some things wrong or acted in what I thought was your best interests, but does that really make me a bad person?"

She hiccuped and gulped down another slug of martini from her once more filled glass. Then she turned to face Hans's dad.

"I'm *sorry* I'm not Anna, but I tried, Johan. I really did. I flirted because I loved you from the moment I met you, and then I was so sad for you, I wanted to try and make you happy. But am I really a terrible person for being thrilled when you reciprocated my feelings? *This!* This was why I didn't want to rehash the past! It's messy and complicated, and all I want to do is focus on you and your well-being." She took a dramatic, shaky breath and held her hand to her chest as she looked towards the ceiling. "For however long we have left with you on this Earth."

Hans's resolve wavered, and empathy started to creep in. Maybe they had been too harsh on her. Maybe it was all a big misunderstanding? She was right. They were squabbling when all that really mattered was his dad's health. Maybe-

"What car engine?"

Everyone turned to look at Greta. Miriam sniffed and frowned at her. "W-what?" she asked breathlessly.

Greta flicked her eyes at Hans and then their dad. *"What car engine?* You said that's what spooked Peanut Butter, but we never knew what caused him to buck. He might have been young, but Mum said he was always a steady horse, and she was an exceptional rider."

Miriam opened and closed her mouth as she looked around the table. All the colour had drained from her face, making her red lipstick look ghoulish. "I – everyone knows it was a car," she said with a nervous laugh. "She was found by the side of the road. What else would it have been?"

Hans saw Chester frown from the corner of his eye. "I never knew where she was found," he said, looking to Hans and then Johan for confirmation. "Neither did my nana or anyone I spoke to about it. It's always been assumed she was found deep *in* the forest."

Hans swallowed, dread and clarity washing through him at the same time. He wasn't sure if he was crazy, but he glanced at Chester and found his strength.

"Dad found her not far from the bend where your car gave out," he said, his voice sounding to him like someone else was speaking using his body. "We didn't tell anyone because we didn't want people laying flowers there. We didn't want people to think of her out there, cold and alone, not when she'd been so full of life. She would have wanted the lovely plot where we laid her to rest."

Miriam looked between them all, the guilt clear on her face. "I – I must have heard a rumour or something, I don't know. *See!* This is what I mean! I can't even speak about her death without becoming the bad guy!"

Something was slotting into place for Hans, though, and he glanced at the wall in the direction of the driveway. "Peanut Butter wouldn't have been spooked by a regular car. He was used to those. But you've always had the loudest throttle rev I've ever heard, Miriam."

It didn't matter that she'd changed cars since then. All of her cars had the kind of engines that would scare the crap out of anyone.

Miriam was definitely panicked now, and the tears came back with a howl. *"It was an accident!"* she sobbed. "When I saw that bloody horse throw her off, I fled the scene! I didn't know what else to do, and I certainly didn't know that she was *dead!* Johan, you have to believe me. I loved you so much, and it was bad enough living in her shadow without you blaming me too. It was just an *accident!"*

"I can't believe what I'm hearing," said Johan in disbelief. He dragged his hand over his mouth and shook his head. "So you let two barely-teens believe that *they'd* caused their mother's death instead? You…you took my beautiful Anna away from me? From us?"

Tears were running down Hans's face now, but with Chester's arm firmly around him, he held on to his strength. He reached out for his dad's hand again and glared at Miriam, not letting her get away with this. "All along, it was you? You took her away? And why were you driving down that road anyway? It only leads to our house."

Miriam was still crying ugly tears, smearing her make-up over her face as she sobbed. "I *told* you! I *loved* your father! It wasn't a crime. We never acted on it! Sometimes I would drive by the house to see if I could catch a glimpse of him, to ease my broken heart!"

"You fucking stalker," Greta said incredulously, whistling and downing half her wine in one gulp. "I knew you were a crazy bitch, but-"

"I'm not crazy! I was *there* for your father when you two ran away!" She thumped her chest like a gorilla, jumping back to her feet. *"I* was there for him! And you're not going to come crawling back now and take everything from me! This is *my* life! I worked hard for it! You little ungrateful shits don't deserve a *penny!* I'll make sure you're cut from his will *if it's the last thing I do!*"

There was a horrible silence that lingered for about three seconds.

Then Johan Jager cleared his throat. "Well. It's a good job I'm not actually sick, then."

For another few seconds, nobody moved. Then one by one, every head turned to stare at Hans's dad, mouths open and eyes wide.

"I – you – *excuse* me?" Miriam spluttered.

Johan shrugged and took a sip of his own wine like he hadn't just dropped a massive bombshell. "Greta, Hans, I'm terribly sorry. From the bottom of my heart. I didn't want to mislead you. But one, I didn't know how else to get you home when I thought you'd abandoned me, and two, I thought bringing my will into question might show Miriam's true colours." He sighed with great sadness. "I've suspected for quite some time now that she didn't have my best interests at heart."

Miriam had gone from china white to puce. "No – but – I drove you to all those hospital appointments!"

Johan shrugged, and his mouth twitched in half a smile. "I was getting my prostate examined. A man my age can't be too careful, you know." He chuckled sadly. "Then there were blood tests, an ECG on my heart. Just routine check-ups I thought I should catch up on if I was going to speak to my lawyer and alter my will." He smiled and shook his head, looking between the twins. "Which I will be doing first thing Monday morning, as well as filing for divorce."

Miriam's scream was like a volcano blowing its top, and poor Dodger ran for cover somewhere down the hallway. "You can't *do* that!" she bellowed, slamming her fists on the table and making its contents rattle. Then she rounded on Greta and Hans and therefore Chester too, which Hans didn't like. "This is all *your* fault! You've always ruined everything! We were so happy without you awful brats!"

Johan sighed. "I suggest you go start to pack, Miriam. I'll expect you to leave *my* and my *children's* home tomorrow. I'll put you up in a local hotel until you can find your feet."

Greta leaned forwards, her eyes sparkling with righteous anger as she glared at their soon-to-be-former step-mother. "You do know that there is no statute of limitations in the UK, right? After that little confession of yours, I'd say you've opened yourself up to prosecution for leaving the scene and failure to report an accident, involuntary manslaughter, and maybe even hit-and-run." She winked at Miriam. "So if I were you, I'd disappear far, far away."

Miriam looked like she was going to cry and beg or maybe scream some more. But in the end, she just snatched up her cocktail shaker and martini glass, then stomped from the room with her high heels *clack-clack-clacking* on the wooden floor until she disappeared upstairs.

"How did you know all that?" Hans asked in disbelief.

Greta puffed out her cheeks and picked up her wine glass to take a big gulp. "I watch a *lot* of cop shows."

"I can't believe that all really just happened," said Chester, rubbing the back of his neck.

Johan shook his head again and sighed deeply. "I've been such a fool. I've done so much harm to you both. I don't know if you'll ever be able to forgive me."

Hans and Greta reached out to him at the same time, squeezing a hand each. "We were all fooled by her," said Hans firmly. "I saw your corkboard in the bunker. I know how much you've missed us, and we missed you too. Maybe that's enough of a place to start a new chapter in our lives?"

"What board?" asked Greta.

Chester rubbed Hans's back and smiled at the twins.

"Your dad's kept every single card you two ever sent him, from the looks of it."

"I even rescued a couple from the bin once or twice," Johan admitted thickly, confirming what Hans and Chester had suspected about the ripped ones.

Greta bumped shoulders with their dad. "I'm so glad we never stopped sending ours to you in that case, even when all hope seemed lost."

Hans shook his head. "I know it doesn't really change much…Mum's death was still an accident. But I can't believe it was *Miriam* who spooked her horse. All this time we stayed away from home because we thought everyone blamed us, but…it was her all along." He swallowed, not wanting to cry any more, but his relief was pretty overwhelming. "Mum didn't hate us," he said, looking at his sister, who gave him an uncharacteristically wobbly smile. "Are you sure we didn't fight before her accident?" he asked their dad.

Johan scowled. "No, I'm certain you're getting two arguments muddled. I'm not surprised after the trauma of her sudden death, especially if someone was whispering poison in your ears." He shook his head angrily. "But no, I assure you, you kids were slightly grumpy at most about the bikes. Your mother and I laughed about it before she went to the stable."

He placed his hand over Greta's, then beamed at her and Hans.

"She left this world loving you more than anything, and now I'm going to spend the rest of my life making up for all the ways I neglected you since she departed. Starting by transferring you the funds you should have had for your higher education. I want you to have every opportunity available to you from now on. And I'm very much hoping I can be in your lives to help you with anything you need for many years to come."

Hans swallowed his emotions and smiled. Above all else, he was *happy*. "I'm looking forward to it."

"Me too," Greta agreed.

Chester got Hans's attention back by taking his hand between both of his, then bringing it to his chest as he looked Hans in the eye. "I'm so sorry. You kept saying you weren't welcome here, but I never understood what you really meant. I promise you, from the bottom of my heart, no one ever blamed you or wanted you to leave town."

"In fact," said Hans's dad, and Hans looked over to see him looking earnestly at him. "I'll go so far to say you were greatly missed, and I hope now that we'll see you much more regularly."

Happiness threatened to overcome Hans. He was still sad over the fresh news about his mum, but he'd been grieving her a long time. Now felt like the time for moving forwards. After a lifetime of uncertainty and feeling like he'd never belonged anywhere, everything suddenly seemed so clear to him.

"How about…all the time?" he asked.

It was his dad he was replying to, but it was Chester he was looking at. Chester's blue eyes went as wide as saucers. "What do you mean?" he asked.

"I mean," said Hans, licking his lips, nerves and excitement fluttering in his belly. "I think it's high time I moved back to Gingerbread. It's where my heart's always been, after all."

Chester bit his lip, his eyes shining with tears. "Are you serious?" he whispered.

Greta scoffed, topping up all their glasses with more wine. "Of course he is. You two are so in love it might make me sick if it wasn't so awesome." She winked at them and raised her glass. "A toast! Here's to coming home, happy endings, and just desserts. Well done, Dad, for finally seeing the light."

Their father sighed, but a ghost of a smile played on his lips as he joined the other three in lifting his glass to clink them together. Dodger even crept back to the door and finally trotted in when he saw there was no more fighting, wagging his tail.

"To a fresh start," Johan toasted. "Your mum would be so proud."

"To finally seeing the bloody obvious," said Hans, kissing Chester on the lips. "I'm sorry it took so long."

Chester beamed at him, happy tears falling down his cheeks. "You were worth the wait."

19

CHESTER

CHESTER COULDN'T SAY HE WAS A FAN OF REALITY TELEVISION, but for a minute there, he'd felt like he might finally understand what it was like to live through one of those big drama scenes. He was amazed nobody had got a drink thrown in their face.

But once the dust had settled and Miriam had stormed *very* loudly out the front door, presumably to head off to a hotel early, they'd all been able to relax. Sure, Chester had felt a little guilty over eating the food she'd prepared, but then Greta had informed him that it counted as she-devil tax and he should enjoy himself.

It was a lot easier the more the wine flowed.

There was so much that had happened in such a short space of time, Chester couldn't quite wrap his head around it. Mr Jager wasn't sick. Miriam had inadvertently caused Hans's mum's accident. Worse, she'd convinced the young twins that their mum's death had somehow been their fault and that everyone in town blamed them. No wonder they'd left and never looked back until now.

It was tempting for Chester to feel bitter or resentful about that. Like if he'd known what Hans had thought, he could have somehow changed things and made him stay. But deep down, Chester had already resolved himself for not drifting into 'what ifs'. The only thing that mattered now was that the many truths had come to light. It wouldn't do them much good to dwell on the past. Chester wanted to heal that, of course, but he was also far more interested in looking to the future.

Where Hans was maybe going to move back to Gingerbread.

Could that really happen? Chester's heart was already very hopeful, and with the help of the wine, his mind was already running away with the possibilities. Still, after so many years of disappointment, there was still a niggling doubt lingering inside him.

Despite that, he felt like he was walking on a cloud when they left the dining room table, and not just because of all the wine. Hans had been living his life based on so much misinformation, and not only about his family. He'd had no idea about Chester's feelings for him, and now that he did, he'd been so sure of their relationship that he'd pledged to move back home on the spot.

Chester didn't want to get his hopes up too much, but that was a bloody good sign that things might finally be going his way. After all these years of pining and trying to make it work with other guys, it felt like a Christmas miracle had brought back to him the one that got away.

He never intended to let him go again.

Chester slipped his hand into Hans's as they left the living room. The night was far from over, and he was looking forward to some more playtime with his smoking hot new boyfriend.

"Are you sure you don't want to join us for some card

games?" Mr Jager asked as their small group came to a halt in the hallway by the living room. Dodger looked up at them expectantly, wagging his tail, and Chester almost relented. But Greta groaned and patted her dad on the back.

"Let them be, Dad," she said fondly, winking at her brother. "We'll have plenty of fun, just the two of us. The boys need some alone time."

Hans was burning red as he glared at his sister. "Thanks," he muttered, and she cackled gleefully.

Chester was grateful, though, and he hugged Hans close as he beamed at Greta. He needed to reassure himself that this was all real and not going to vanish in the morning like melted snow.

"It's been an eventful evening. But I'd love a games night another time?" he suggested hopefully, testing the waters about Hans's pledge to move back here. However, Chester's worries were eased slightly as Hans perked up.

"Oh, yeah," he said, nodding at his dad and sister. "That sounds fun. Rain check?"

Greta snorted. "Don't you mean fog check?"

Mr Jager tutted but smiled at her, then pulled Hans in for a hug. "I'm so glad you're both home," he said with a sigh. "It's been too long. Let's make sure we make the most of our time to come."

"Absolutely," Hans agreed.

Chester was about to lead his boyfriend towards the staircase when Greta reached out and tapped him on the shoulder. "Oh, Chester?" she said as he turned back around. "I think you should check the registered charity number on Ethel's tin."

He blinked, shaking the wine from his brain as he tried to process her words that didn't feel like they were related to anything anyone else had said all evening. "Uh...what?"

She grinned at him and sipped some wine from the glass

she was still holding. "Just a hunch I had whilst working through my hangover. Check it's a real charity. If it's not… you might want to have a little chat with the police."

"Uh…I…" Chester stuttered, but she waved him off.

"Not *now*, of course. Later. Okay, have fun!" She steered Mr Jager away into the living room, winking over her shoulder. Dodger seemed torn between who to stay with, but ultimately, he barked once, then scampered after his dad.

"What was that about?" asked Hans.

Chester shook his head. "I'm not sure, but"- he laughed then waggled his eyebrows at Hans -"let's worry about it tomorrow. Right now, I have other plans."

Hans licked his lips and looked down at Chester. "Oh, really?"

"Uh-huh," Chester said, slipping his hand over Hans's hip and pulling him close. "I think we've got a lot to celebrate, don't you?"

Hans ran his hand down Chester's arm, his eyes heavy with lust.

Chester *loved* that look on him.

"Naked celebrations?" Hans asked hopefully, making Chester burst out laughing. He stood on his tiptoes and pressed a kiss to Hans's lips, tasting the red wine that lingered there.

"Of course. Only the best for my *boyfriend*."

Hans brushed the backs of his fingers along Chester's cheek and jaw. "Come on," he murmured and began leading him up the two flights of stairs back to his bedroom.

Chester wondered what the house had looked like before Miriam turned it into a cold, sterile magazine display rather than a home. He was even more glad that he'd seen the bunker first, as he felt he'd got a much better impression of the family than he would have if he'd just seen this place on its own. Maybe now Miriam was gone, Johan would change it?

And maybe Hans would be around to help him?

Chester looked up at him as they walked along the top floor hallway, nervous excitement fluttering in his belly. Was this the start of the next chapter in their lives?

Hans didn't seem worried. He looked like he was singularly focused on hurrying them down the hall and getting them behind the closed door of his bedroom again. Chester didn't exactly disagree with this sentiment, but when the door clicked shut and Hans went to tug him towards the bed, Chester paused.

Hans turned back to look at him, his face falling. "Everything okay?" he asked tentatively.

Chester smiled at him, rubbing the back of the hand he was holding with his thumb. "I know a lot's happened," he said, fighting the lump in his throat. "So I don't want you to feel like you have to promise anything."

Hans frowned at him, stepping closer and taking Chester's other hand as well. "Like what?"

Chester looked into his deep, brown eyes. "Like about moving back here. That's a big commitment, and-"

He was cut off with a *whoomph* as Hans's mouth slammed into his, their lips crashing together as he grabbed either side of Chester's face, snogging him like the world was about to end.

"Chester Wild!" he cried when they surfaced for air a few moments later. His gaze burned as he stared into Chester's eyes. "I am going to move here to be with you, because I love you, and I want to see you every day. I understand if that's a bit fast and you might need some time. I'm sure I can live here for a bit if necessary. But honestly, I want to wake up beside you every day, too. I am in this one *hundred* percent, so long as you are too." He raised his eyebrows, asking the question.

Did Chester feel the same?

A relieved laugh bubbled up from inside Chester, escaping his throat as his eyes pricked with tears. "Okay, then," he said happily, placing his hands over Hans's. "In that case, I'll stop checking you're really sure about this…about me…and start enjoying it."

Hans's look was serious as he pressed their foreheads together. "I get the feeling you're scared to trust me because I let you wait so long. I'll never not be sorry about that, but the only way I can see to make it right is to jump in with both feet right now, Chester. We've wasted too much time already. I don't want to hang around any longer than we already have. Life's too short. I know my mum would want me to be happy, and I know she'd smack me over the head for not realising how happy you make me sooner. I'd like to put an end to that, starting tonight. I'm *yours*, heart, body, and soul."

Chester sniffed and threw his arms around Hans's back, hugging him close. "My teddy bear," he mumbled into Hans's chest.

Hans kissed the top of Chester's hair and then nuzzled his nose into it. "Your teddy bear," he agreed. "One who is very, *very* hard for you right now."

Chester barked out a laugh, his melancholy mood well and truly dispersed. He grinned slyly as he slid his hand between Hans's legs, feeling the magnificent bulge there. "And what would you like me to do about that, teddy bear?" he asked.

Hans groaned and captured Chester's lower lip between his teeth, giving him a little bite. "I think it's about time you made good on that promise of fucking me on my hands and knees."

Chester growled in frustration. He would actually be

confident having sex with Hans without condoms if they both agreed there was nothing to worry about. But Chester wasn't topping Hans for the first time without lube, no matter how tempted he was to try and wing it with spit and a prayer. He wanted their first time to be absolutely magical.

"We don't have the supplies," he grumbled, not ashamed of the fact he was pouting. His disappointment was strong.

But Hans grinned, pinching Chester's chin gently between finger and thumb, then turning his head so he was looking at the bed. "I think Father Christmas came early and left something to help *us* come early," he said in delight.

Chester hadn't looked at the bed when Hans had dragged him back into the bedroom. He'd been too preoccupied with his worries. But apparently, Hans had been on the ball. There was only a bedside lamp on, so it wasn't clear at a glance. Now he was focusing on it, though, he could see there was something on the bed.

It looked like a box of condoms and a bottle of lube. There was a shiny wrapping bow on the box.

He giggled, not believing what he was seeing as he moved to the bed. On closer inspection, there was also a gift tag.

"For you, dear brother, so you can be nicely naughty," he read aloud.

Hans hugged him from behind. "As much as I absolutely do *not* want to think about my sister getting me sexy supplies, I think I can maybe forgive her outrageousness on this occasion."

Chester dropped the gift tag back on the bed and spun to wrap his arms around his boyfriend's neck. "I think I can forgive her, too," he said, feeling sinful as he kissed Hans with gusto, his tongue exploring his lover's mouth as he pulled them down on top of the bed in a tangle. "Now we know why she was late down to dinner, at least."

Hans laughed and groaned, covering Chester's mouth

with his hand as they rolled over the mattress onto their sides. "No more discussing my twin or any other family members whilst we're in this bed, starting this instant," he said with a chuckle. "It's just you and me and our fun little present that *magic elves* brought us to have some fun with."

Chester snorted, licking Hans's palm, then biting at his fingers when he tried to pull his hand back. "Okay, teddy bear," he said. "This is Santa's workshop, and this naughty elf is going to have his way with you *all* night."

Hans hummed and kissed Chester's neck next to the love bite that was already there. "I wish we had another candy cane," he said, sending electricity straight to Chester's balls.

He squirmed against Hans and nipped at his earlobe. "Well," he uttered wantonly. "I spy your Candy Cauldron bag over there. Want to see what we've got?"

Hans blinked at him, then raised himself up to look over by the wardrobe where someone (presumably another magic elf) had left the bulging bag of sweets and chocolate that Hans and his sister had bought at the shop yesterday. "Oh," said Hans, his cheeks flushing in the lamplight.

Chester winked at him before scampering off the bed and dashing over to rummage through the bag. *Jackpot.* He snatched up several items, the cellophane bags crinkling in his hand as he dashed back to the bed.

Hans had set himself up with the pillows propped behind his back, watching Chester as he returned. Good. That was exactly where Chester wanted him.

Time for some more teasing.

Chester dropped his goodies beside them as he crawled into Hans's lap, straddling his legs. Hans grinned and hummed as Chester kissed him, then raised his arms obediently as Chester pulled his T-shirt off. "That's better," Chester murmured as he ran his hands over Hans's broad, hairy chest, tweaking his nipples and kissing his mouth filthily.

Hans groaned and twitched deliciously, gripping Chester's hips. Their crotches ground against one another, promising good things to come. But Chester wasn't quite ready for that yet. He wanted his man completely desperate by the time he finally started fucking him.

"Are you my good bear?" he asked between kisses.

Hans nodded, grabbing Chester's arse through his jeans. "So good," Hans said, nuzzling their noses together. His beard tickled Chester's cheek. He was going to have to deal with a bit of beard burn before his skin got used to it, but he didn't mind. He'd put up with a great deal to be with Hans Jager.

Chester leaned back, whipping his own T-shirt off and then picking up one of the bags he'd selected. This one was filled with Champagne truffles. He pulled open the top of the bag and retrieved one of the chocolate balls, placing it between his lips. Then he pressed his mouth back to Hans, cracking the chocolate casing with his teeth as he did. The liquidy-goo spilled out between them, and Chester's cock ached as he lapped up the Champagne-laced ganache from Hans's lips and tongue.

Chester fed his love a couple more tasty treats this way, all the while rutting himself shamelessly against Hans's cock. By the fourth truffle, Chester slipped his hand between them, taking mercy on Hans as he unzipped his jeans and fishing his hand through Hans's underwear, wrapping his hand around his rock-hard, weeping member.

"Is this lollipop for me, handsome?" he asked.

Hans kissed him hungrily, licking chocolate from Chester's own lips as he bucked in his hand. "Yes, baby, all for you."

Chester dragged his hand over his mouth to wipe off any

excess chocolate, then yanked at Hans's jeans, tugging them down his legs with Hans's help.

It was time they got naked.

Once they no longer had any clothes in their way, Chester wasted no time in straddling Hans again. But this time, he broke apart a couple of the truffles in his hand, then proceeded to smear the yummy sweetness over his own nipples, then used the rest to lubricate both their cocks as he rubbed them together. Slipping his clean hand behind Hans's head, he guided his lover's mouth to suck at Chester's nipples. His toes curled as the little buds hardened under Hans's lips, tongue, and teeth.

They were going to make a mess of the bed. Chester didn't care. He'd take the sheets home himself and wash them. They were having way too much fun to stop now.

One way to try and save the bedspread was to eat as much of the chocolate as possible. Which was why when Hans had licked Chester's nipples until they were shiny and clean, Chester pushed him down to lie flat on the bed, then spun around so they could 69.

Chester could have probably come like that, but he'd promised Hans a very specific kind of fucking, and Chester wasn't about to break that promise on their first night as boyfriends.

Hans groaned as Chester changed positions again, sliding his cock from Hans's mouth and popping off Hans's own delicious length, then turning back around. "Chester," Hans complained, but he was grinning, so Chester knew he wasn't really grumbling.

Which was why Chester slapped his thigh, hard enough to sting and hopefully leave a hand print, and both their cocks jumped. Hans's eyes went wide as he looked at Chester with a sort of awe, his mouth falling into a little 'O' shape.

"Naughty bear," Chester said. "Onto your tummy now. Let your elf take care of you."

Hans didn't move for a second, so Chester took the opportunity to grab a couple of gummy bears from one of the other sweet bags and stick them onto Hans's nipples. Hans dropped his head to look, then leaned back as he roared with laughter.

"Shh," Chester scolded him half-heartedly, dipping down to lick the gummies into his mouth. He plucked a couple more bears out of the bag and fed them to his own man-sized bear, loving how Hans licked his fingers. "Be quiet, teddy bear."

Hans waggled his eyebrows. "If I don't, will you spank me again?" he asked hopefully.

Chester's heart sang. He wasn't sure if Hans would want more of that kind of play, and he was thrilled to hear he did. "How about I spank you again if you're nice and quiet for me?" he asked.

Hans's breath hitched. "Yes, please," he rasped.

"There's my good big boy," Chester purred, giving Hans's nipple another pinch. "Now do as you're told, and flip over. I want your arse."

Hans caught his mouth for a quick kiss before doing exactly that, wriggling his bum and making Chester laugh almost as loud as Hans had. "Shh," Hans mimicked him, winking over his shoulder as Chester leaned down and bit his plump, round cheek.

"Let's be quiet little Christmas mice," Chester agreed, fetching a white chocolate mouse from the last bag. He showed it to Hans, whose eyes grew wide. "Now you just get comfy and let me take care of you."

Hans licked his lips, then nodded before dropping his head down on the pillow. A thrill rushed through Chester. He loved that Hans trusted him like that.

The mouse was kind of a bullet shape, but Chester still squirted a fair bit of lube over its head, delighted to discover the 'elves' had got them peppermint flavour, perfect for Christmas. Positioning himself between Hans's spread-out legs, he placed the other end of the mouse between his teeth, pulled Hans's fleshy globes apart with his hands, then moved down so he could push the chocolate treat inside his most intimate area with his teeth.

"F-fuck!" Hans cried into the pillow, his whole body quivering as he laughed and squirmed in delight.

Chester hummed, digging his fingers into Hans's backside as he began to suck on the chocolate, licking around Hans's hole and up the base of his sack. As full as he was from dinner, he intended to make a meal out of this, and Hans certainly wasn't complaining.

"Chester," he moaned, gripping at the bedsheets as he writhed, humping his still hard cock against the duvet. Chester slapped his bum, making it jiggle deliciously and earning another gorgeous moan from Hans.

"Do you like this, naughty bear?" Chester asked, sucking at the melting chocolate mouse again. The white goo was spreading around Hans's entrance, and Chester could hardly wait until that would be his cum. He hoped it would be sometime very soon.

"I love it, baby," Hans panted, his skin damp as his back rose and fell with his heavy breathing. "Stretch me out. I want you to fuck me."

Chester rubbed a soothing hand over the flesh he'd spanked on Hans's leg and arse, kissing the curve of his fuzzy cheek. "I will, I promise," he whispered. "You just lie there and let your elf do all the work."

The mouse disappeared quicker than Chester would have liked, but his dick was getting impatient, so he resisted the urge to insert another one. Instead, he trusted the chocolate and his tongue had started stretching Hans out, so he lubed up two fingers and pushed them in without warning. Hans jerked and moaned, raising his arse to accept the intrusion.

"Yes, baby, like that," Hans begged.

Chester grinned, pumping his digits in further, searching for Hans's prostate as he wanked himself off. He wanted to make sure he was as hard as possible for his lover. "Am I your Santa Baby?" he asked.

Hans chuckled and groaned. "I thought you were my elf?"

Chester tutted, crooking his fingers and stroking Hans's prostate, making him cry out. "I can be both if I want," he grumbled.

Hans laughed and nodded, his forehead beaded with sweat as he looked over his shoulder at Chester. "You can be whatever you want, just, *please*, Chester. I need you inside me! I'm ready."

Chester kissed his beautiful bum and withdrew his fingers. If Hans said he was good to go, Chester believed him. His cock wasn't as small as his slender stature might suggest, but Chester would ease in slowly so as not to hurt his lovely teddy bear.

Much.

He slapped the other arse cheek before reaching for the condom box. "Up you get, then," he said playfully. "You know how I want you, you delicious treat, you."

Hans was on his hands and knees in a flash, wiggling his bum eagerly for Chester's attention. Chester giggled and hurried to rip the condom open, not wanting to leave his boyfriend hanging long.

But then he paused as he burst out laughing.

"What?" Hans demanded.

Chester showed him the open wrapper. It had a checklist of nice, naughty, or *very* naughty. But that wasn't what had made him cackle. The condom itself was red and white striped, and Chester hurriedly rolled it down his cock. "There you go!" he announced proudly. "Now I really *am* going to give you my candy cane!"

Hans snorted with mirth, but Chester soon had him moaning again. He kissed and nuzzled the cheek he'd just slapped, then positioned himself behind Hans once again. Hans's legs were so wide as he eagerly presented his hole to Chester, Chester didn't need to pull his cheeks apart much at all. He just used one hand as he pressed his tip through the tight ring of muscle, gripping Hans's hip with the other hand to aid in steadying him.

"That's it, gorgeous," Chester grunted as he inched further into Hans's tight, perfect hotness. Even through the condom, Chester was in heaven as Hans's arse swallowed his cock hungrily. "Take it all. Let me feed you my candy cane."

"I love it," Hans gasped, pushing back and taking Chester up to the root. "You're perfect, Chester. Pull my hair."

Lust rolled through Chester as he let go of Hans's backside to do as he asked, gripping his thick, damp hair firmly. He kept his hold on his hip and began to ride him. He watched his cock sliding in and out of that beautiful round arse, loving the heavy *slap-slap-slap* of their thighs hitting together. From this angle, he could just see Hans's Adam's apple bobbing in his elongated neck.

He was the most edible thing Chester had ever seen.

"You're fucking *stunning*," he gasped as he ramped up his thrusts. "I'm going to come inside you. You're my big, hunky teddy bear. I'm going to fuck you until you fall apart, Hans."

"Yes, fuck, *please*, Chester," Hans sobbed, bucking backwards to meet Chester thrust for thrust. "I'm yours. *I always have been.*"

Those words broke something beautiful in Chester. He cried out, emotion overwhelming him as he thoroughly claimed his man. The bed was probably creaking and banging against the wall, but at this point, he didn't care. He pummelled deeper and deeper, feeling his climax suddenly build. Whilst he still had some wits about him, he let go of Hans's hair so he could reach under them and wrap his hand around his hot, bobbing cock.

"Come for me, gorgeous," Chester begged. He was close, but he didn't want to climax before he knew his man was sated. "I want to see you spill everywhere. I've been waiting so long."

Hans grunted and trembled as he rutted frantically. "I love you, Chester," he managed to gasp, just as he started creaming over Chester's hand. "Fuck, yes! Don't stop!"

Chester bit his lip as he pushed for the big finale, hammering into Hans as he shook and rode out his orgasm. Losing himself in Hans's pleasure, Chester was soon falling over the edge himself, filling the condom as he pulsed his load deep inside Hans, the way he'd fantasised about for years.

Except this had been so much better than any daydream he'd ever had. As the two of them collapsed on top of the mattress, Chester still buried inside Hans, they gasped and trembled together, the air thick with their musk and the sweetness of the chocolate and peppermint. Chester fumbled until his hand landed on top of Hans's, and he interlaced their fingers as he kissed Hans's shoulder blade.

"That was incredible," he said breathlessly, sleep already threatening to envelop him after such an energetic end to a long day. But he had to make sure this finished the right way, and that meant being certain that everything was perfect for Hans. "I hope you enjoyed our little midnight snack?"

He hated that anxiety crept into his voice, but after so many years, he needed to know that Hans had loved it too. But he needn't have worried. Hans grinned lazily over his shoulder, looking drunk on his orgasm as he leaned up and claimed Chester's mouth for a sweet kiss.

"That was mind-blowing," he said, shaking his head. "Please tell me that we're going to be doing that all the time."

Chester nuzzled their cheeks together, relief filling him up like water replenishing a long dry well. "Double-dare super-promise," he said.

EPILOGUE

HANS – ONE YEAR LATER

"THANK YOU. COME AGAIN!" CHESTER CRIED CHEERFULLY AS the waving customer left the bustling shop. Hans watched his boyfriend warmly, marvelling at all they'd accomplished in just a year.

The grand re-opening of Gingerbread's old-fashioned sweet shop was going incredibly well. It probably had something to do with the new owners.

Hans pulled Chester to him where they were standing on the shop floor. He kissed his temple with fierce pride and enough love to make his heart want to burst from his chest. "I think it's going pretty good. Don't you agree, Santa Baby?"

Chester covered his mouth and laughed incredulously, wide eyes roaming the packed space of the shop that used to be called Candy Cauldron. "This is unbelievable. I never truly believed this would work, but we've done more business today already than our entire first week of December last year!"

Hans hummed and kissed his boyfriend again. "I had every faith," he said. "We did it."

It turned out that charity fraud was a very real crime, punishable by several years in jail.

Evil Ethel had found that out the hard way.

As it transpired, Greta had been deeply suspicious of Ethel's charitable donations when she otherwise hated children with the passion of a Dickensian villain. So Greta had taken a quick photo of the registered number whilst Hans had been distracted by Chester, and tried looking the charity up online.

Nothing.

All those years she'd been taking the village's generous donations, not to mention her staff's festive bonuses that she'd bullied them into giving, and been building a retirement fund. When Chester had reported her to the police last Christmas, she'd apparently only been months away from running off to the Cayman Islands where she might never have been caught.

But it seemed that after all these years, justice was finally being served. Ethel had been found out and forced to repay as much as she could from her savings, so that had meant some really *big* bonuses for the Candy Cauldron staff. As for the charity tin, the town council had held a meeting – chaired by Hans's dad – and the unanimous decision had been made to send that lump sum to the children's hospital in Gloucester, where it would finally be put to good use for real.

But Ethel hadn't just been required to pay back the people she'd duped. She'd had hefty legal fees and fines to pay as well, so had been forced to liquidate her business to cover the costs.

That had left the Candy Cauldron up for sale. The solution had seemed pretty obvious in the end.

Chester and Hans had taken over the business themselves, expanding the sweet shop to include a bakery by bringing the industrial oven back to life. They hadn't just had Chester's mega-bonus with which to buy and invest in the company. Hans had been able to take a substantial amount from the savings his dad had put aside for his university fees once upon a time, and invested in his dream of opening his own business, along with night classes to make sure the books never got cooked again.

Now here they were, partners in life as well as work, and Hans couldn't be any happier if he tried. He'd stepped into this shop a year ago and felt like a stranger, returning to a home that didn't want him. Now he'd spent the whole day greeting friends and acquaintances by name, all of whom wished him and Chester the very best of luck with their new venture.

Which of course had a new name to go with it.

"Thank you for visiting Sweet Tooth," Chester said as he handed out free samples of their signature vegan chocolate mice and candy canes, all wrapped in biodegradable cellophane. "We'll be open until Christmas Eve! Make sure you come back for our gingerbread people decorating day!"

"Oh, just *look* at you two," said Miss Nancy from the haberdashery as she bustled up to Hans and Chester, her basket full of goodies. "This is all so wonderful! I'm just pleased as punch for the both of you."

Chester handed his tray to one of the other members of staff and hugged Hans to him as he beamed at Nancy. "Thank you so much. We're thrilled," he gushed. "And thanks again for the new curtains. They're absolutely perfect in our living room."

Hans had made good on his promise and moved back to the village as soon as he'd been able to hand his notice in at his old London job and house. He'd had zero second thoughts or cold feet. This was where he belonged. For the first few months, he'd lived with Chester in his small flat. But then when things had settled down and their finances had improved, they'd started renting a real house with a garden big enough for their very own puppy, Elton.

"Is your dad here?" Nancy asked Hans as she looked around the packed shop. "I've got a couple of committee things I wanted to run by him."

Hans chuckled. Miss Nancy hadn't been joking when she'd said that she'd wanted to start up a local Pride. During the course of the year, she'd worked with the council to set up a committee with several of the other nearby villages, and everything was falling into place for the area's first parade next summer.

For a young man who'd been too afraid to come out of the closet until his mid-twenties, Hans was so overjoyed to think of the difference that was going to make to the local LGBT community. So much so, he and Chester were already planning on marching on behalf of Sweet Tooth and Gingerbread.

"Not yet. He and Greta will be coming by soon, though," Hans told Nancy. "I'm sure my dad will be thrilled to see you, Nancy."

Nancy, who was herself a widow, blushed. "Well, uh, I'll look forward to seeing him soon, then," she said. Someone else called her name, and she disappeared to go gossip with whoever it was, which meant she didn't see Hans and Chester share a knowing look.

"Do you think they'll finally get their act together by Valentine's?" Chester asked.

Hans snorted. "Miss Nancy is ten times the woman Miriam was. If she and my dad aren't dating by New Year's, I'll eat my hat."

Chester purred wickedly and leaned closer to Hans. "Your hat? Don't tell me you've gone off eating candy canes? I was saving a special one just for you later."

Hans felt heat rise onto his cheeks. He glanced around the shop, torn between worrying that anyone had overheard and squirming in delight at the little bit of public play. "I have been a *very* good teddy bear," he murmured back.

Chester discretely pinched his arse, making him jump. "You're certainly on Father Christmas's nice list," he said. "I think we can find something yummy for us both to feast on tonight."

Before they could get too lost in their game and Chester dragged Hans out back for a quickie, a gaggle of American backpackers popped up saying they'd read a blog post about the sweet shop's reopening. They asked Chester for the best British treats to bring back home, and so Chester was off, buzzing with happiness as he showed the tourists to his favourite goodies.

Hans watched him work for a moment, overflowing with adoration for the love of his life. A year ago, Hans was unhappy and lonely, just drifting through life with no idea of what he wanted. Now he was home, living with his favourite person in the whole world. He had his family back as well as his community. He was a business owner. He got to spend his days making cakes and pastries to bring people joy, and his nights in his and Chester's bed. It was perfect.

Well, almost perfect.

Before nerves could flutter in his belly, a couple of small children collided against his legs. He should have known who they were before he even looked down.

"Gemma! Jeremy!" he cried in delight, not bothered at being smashed into by the typically exuberant siblings. "Merry Christmas."

"Merry Christmas, Mr Jager," said Gemma excitedly. "We're so happy the sweet shop is back open! You're a *much* better boss than the mean old witch lady."

"Gemma," her mum scolded as she pushed through the

throng and found her runaway children. "That's not a very nice thing to say, is it?"

Gemma frowned at her mum. "But it's *true,*" she insisted. "Mr Jager and Mr Wild are much better at selling sweets and chocolate. I can already tell. They have *cake* as well now!"

"Cake and lock-lock," Jeremy agreed happily. His hands and mouth were sticky and red, and Hans wondered if he'd helped himself to a free sample or just opened one of the jars on the lower shelf.

Well, he couldn't say he was cross. Those kids had been through quite a year, and he was glad he and Chester could give them a cheeky free treat again.

"How are things with you, Lena?" he asked their mum.

To his surprise, she replied to his question with a beaming smile for once. "Great, thanks," she said proudly, then glanced down at the children. But they were already more interested in some rainbow lollies they'd found. "The *You-Know-What* papers have been submitted. It's all going to be finalised in the new year. It's been an adjustment for the little ones, but we're already so much better now *Mr Scrooge* has gone."

Hans rubbed her arm with genuine happiness on her behalf. "Good for you," he said. It was about time she divorced that rotten husband of hers for good, and the kids would be better off without such a vicious man in their lives.

"Well," said Lena, "your dad inspired me, to be honest. I still can't quite believe everything that happened with *her.* But it made me realise I couldn't spend the next ten years with the wrong person."

Hans hummed, not wanting to get involved in local gossip too much on their opening day. But he couldn't help but feel just a little vindicated that Miriam's demise had been the talk of the town all year.

After their explosive family dinner, Hans had talked with

his dad and sister the morning after. Between the three of them, they had decided it was the right thing to do to go to the police and relay Miriam's confession. That way they knew they'd been as responsible as they could be, at least, and then it would be in the hands of the law. They'd expected the police to bring her in for questioning and for her to maybe have to do community service or something.

They didn't expect her to flee the country before she could even be brought in for questioning, let alone to spend the next year on the run from Interpol. The last Hans had heard, she'd been spotted in Berlin.

It gave him a wicked sense of joy knowing that she'd gone from a life of luxury at the expense of his family to out on her arse. He hoped she was bloody miserable. Terrible woman.

But Lena was right. Gingerbread had whole-heartedly supported Johan Jager in the wake of the truth being revealed, and they'd also welcomed the twins back with open arms. Even knowing that the village had never really blamed him and his sister, Hans had still been apprehensive about how he would be treated when he moved back. But he needn't have worried. In some ways, it was like he'd never left. In other ways, it was better than it had ever been.

Mostly because of Chester.

They shared a look across the shop floor and smiled at one another, making Hans blush. As much as he was revelling in the success of their relaunch, he also couldn't wait until it was just him and Chester, with the very special surprise that Hans had in store.

Nerves might have fluttered in his belly again if Greta hadn't snuck up behind him and whispered, "Boo!"

Hans rolled his eyes at her. "Halloween is over," he said with a sigh. "It's Christmas now. Hadn't you heard?"

"It will always be my job to torment you until the day I

die," said Greta with a grin, poking his side. "Then after I die, you can bet I'll still haunt your arse. You'll never be rid of me."

Hans shook his head at her, but secretly he knew he would be lost without his twin nearby. Which was why he had been equally surprised and thrilled when Greta had announced that she was *also* moving back to Gingerbread.

Hans hadn't been sure what she would want to do in this little town, but it turned out that her interest in the legal system went a little beyond courtroom dramas. She'd begun studying for a part-time law degree in September with the Open University, and in her spare time she was helping their dad on the council in PR-cum-office management capacity. She was very good at bossing people around, after all, and local council did need chasing to get through all that red tape.

She was the happiest she'd been in years. On their days off, the twins spent as much time as they could back at their childhood home, helping their dad refurbish it back to something much more to all their taste, much to Dodger's delight. They'd also rescued so many nostalgic keepsakes from the bunker and the attic, so their mum's wedding photos, riding medals, and snow globes were all back on display for the world to see.

Hans smiled over at his dad, who was currently outside the shop chatting with Miss Nancy. Jammie Dodger pulled on his lead, and Hans decided to go say hello before the naughty dog smashed his way through the window.

Or he would have if he hadn't just caught the tail end of what Chester was saying.

"We can't have run out of gingerbread people," he announced to Lena and her kids. "I know Hans made at least one more box. Let me go back out and check."

Panic rushed through Hans. Chester was already walking

behind the till to go through to the back room. Hans was near the front door with two dozen customers packed in the small space between them. If Hans hadn't been so tuned in to Chester's voice, he probably would never have heard him. But there was still no way he was going to stop Chester reaching the extra box of gingerbread in time.

"No!" he yelled, vaulting himself through the crowd, trying to stop the inevitable.

The whole shop stopped what they were doing to turn and look at him. Chester came out from the prep room with one of the regular cardboard boxes they used for all the pastries in the store in his hands, frowning at Hans in confusion. "Aren't these the last of the gingerbreads?"

Hans waved his hands, but it was too late. Chester was already opening up the lid. He tilted his head and looked at the box's contents, and Hans's heart dropped. He'd planned to put them in a proper Christmas box when they'd got home. He was going to wrap it up with ribbon. He'd even got a couple of bottles of the same red wine that his dad still kept stocked in the bunker. He'd made Elton a special bow to attach to his collar.

And now it was all ruined.

He continued pushing through the people, who were now all looking at Chester expectantly. Hans was hoping there was a slight chance that Chester didn't know what he was looking at yet. But then his mouth dropped open, and the cat was out of the bag.

Hans had said he'd been making a final batch of gingerbread people that morning, when in actual fact he'd sneakily made only two figures. One of them he'd carefully hand-cut down so it was smaller than the other, with blue eyes. The bigger one had a beard and brown eyes, along with the smiling faces and gumdrop buttons he'd iced on them both. Between the two gingerbread men was a gingerbread speech bubble, pointed towards the bigger, beardy gingerbread man as the one who was speaking.

On it were the words 'Will you marry me?'

Hans bit his lip and came to a stop at the end of the counter. Chester had placed the box down by the till, and those who had craned their necks to look inside were now gasping and looking up at Hans.

Chester blinked his beautiful blue eyes, his lashes wet with tears as he lifted his gaze to meet Hans's. "Is this for me?"

Hans held his breath. He hadn't wanted a public proposal, but…

…well, he did have the ring in his pocket, after all.

As he got down on one knee, a collective gasp rang through the shop, and the door bell tinkled. Hans wasn't sure if someone was coming or going, but he couldn't let this moment slide. He'd lost too much precious time with Chester. Much like their whole relationship, this might not be perfect timing, but it was still very much real and from the heart.

Chester squeaked and threw his hands over his mouth as Hans pulled the ring box from his back pocket and opened it for Chester to see what was inside. It was a gold band with a large ruby in the middle and two sparkling diamonds either side. A candy cane ring for the sweetest man Hans had ever known.

"I was saving the surprise for later," he said sheepishly as tears spilled down Chester's face. It was as if the whole store was holding their breath. "But you know what? I think we've waited long enough. Chester Wild, will you marry m-?"

"YES!" Chester blurted before Hans had even got the last word out of his mouth. He launched himself forward and flung his arms around Hans's neck, almost bowling him over.

The shop exploded into cheers, and a dog that had to be

Dodger began barking. He really shouldn't have been in the store, but Hans didn't mind just this once. If they had to have an audience, he was glad his dad had seen the moment where Hans had asked the love of his life to marry him.

Chester peppered kisses all over Hans's face as he cried. "Yes, teddy bear," he whispered into Hans's ear whilst the applause and cheering continued above them. "I'll be your naughty elf forever. I love you *so* much."

"I love you too, Santa Baby," Hans told him back. They broke apart enough for Hans to pull the ring from its box and slip it on Chester's left hand. It fit perfectly. Then they stood up so they could see everyone again, and their little audience went crazy once more.

As people yelled their congratulations and tried to get around the counter to hug them, Hans caught his sister's eye. She was standing with their dad, who had Dodger in his arms, and they were smiling as tears ran down their faces. Greta clapped so hard her hands were in danger of coming off, and then wolf-whistled loud enough it had to have been heard down in the village square. His dad made Dodger's paw give a little wave and nodded at him in approval.

Hans choked back a sob and waved at both of them like a total dork before his attention was torn away by all the well-wishers surrounding them. As Chester showed off his ring, Hans scooped up the box with their special gingerbread cookies to hide them out back. He still wanted to enjoy those later.

The only difference now would be that he'd be sharing them with his *fiancé*.

As he hugged Chester to his side and kissed his hair, Hans glanced upwards, hoping his mum was peeking in on him at that moment. He hoped she was proud of him. He knew for sure that she would approve of the man he was going to spend the rest of his life with.

He often thought back to that fateful night when his and Chester's paths had crossed again. They'd had to get lost in the woods to admit their true feelings for one another. In some ways, Hans had been lost since his mum had left him.

But for a time – the *best* time – he'd had Chester to guide him through those metaphorical woods. And then Hans had made it through the wilderness of his twenties alone, but in the end, he'd made it back to the person he loved like no other in this life.

Whether that life was sweet or sad, naughty or nice, Hans knew he'd never be alone again. He had someone to take care of him but also someone who he would love and cherish and protect for the rest of his days. They were the perfect flavour, the best pick 'n' mix.

Hans was lucky enough to be engaged to marry his best friend. What possible treat could be sweeter than that?

THANK you for reading Hans and Chester's story! If you enjoyed it, please take a moment to leave a review. For more contemporary MM fairy tale adaptations by Helen Juliet, please check out the links below for eBook, paperback, and audio!

Thorn in His Side – Beauty and the Beast

Hair Out of Place – Rapunzel

A Right Royal Affair – Cinderella

Rise and Shine – Sleeping Beauty (short story)

IF YOU'D LIKE to be the first to know what fairy tale I'll be working on next, make sure to join my Facebook group,

Helen's Jewels. We also have a lot of fun with games and giveaways, as well as ARC opportunities.

THANK YOU TO MY TEAM!
    Cover Design: Cate Ashwood
    Beta Reading: Amy Pittel
    Editing: Meg Cooper
    Proof Reading: Tanja Ongkiehong
    General Awesomeness: Cheesebags (Ed, Amelia, and Conrad), lovely Hubby, brilliant Mummy, and the magnificent fur babies, Arya and Tyrion.

The last thing beautiful, inexperienced Joshua Bellamy wants is an arranged marriage with the terrifying Darius Legrand. But if Joshua wants to save himself and his family from being thrown onto the streets by Darius's father, he has no choice. However, when Darius goes to extreme lengths to rescue Joshua from near-death, Joshua has to wonder if there's more to his beastly husband than he previously thought.

Former Captain Darius Legrand is used to being manipulated by his cruel father, but when Joshua is dragged into the feud between their families, he decides something has to change. Protecting Joshua is one thing, but Darius knows that falling in love can't be an option. Someone so young and beautiful could never give his heart to an older ill-tempered brute like Darius.

Joshua is determined to bring joy to Darius's life again, and Darius refuses to let Joshua hide his sweetness from the world any longer. Over time, it becomes clear that despite their differences, their hearts are drawing closer together. But can happiness ever be possible for a rose and a thorn when Darius's father will go to any lengths to see his deadly game through?

Thorn in His Side is a steamy, standalone MM romance novel featuring tender bubble baths, a stubborn but loyal horse, thunder storms, enough healing touches to mend any broken heart, and a guaranteed HEA with absolutely no cliffhanger.

Click here to get the Thorn in His Side eBook

Click here to get the Thorn in His Side audio

Hair Out of Place

Prince Raphael d'Oro's whole life has been trapped within the four walls of his London Penthouse. Nobody knows that he's royalty, not even his sexy yet grumpy new bodyguard. But when assassins attack, Raphie is forced out into the real world, and his crush on Griff is growing too hard to ignore. An experienced man like Griff would never want a fumbling young thing like Raphie, right?

Griff Thompson is a professional, even when he finds out that happy-go-lucky Raphie with his mesmerising long hair is a hidden prince. No, he has a race against time to return Raphie to his European home country to save the throne and Raphie's life. But there are only so many times they can share a bed before the pull between them is too strong to ignore.

No matter the draw, Griff knows his attraction to Raphie is pure fantasy. He'll do whatever it takes to keep the young prince safe, and that might have to include not breaking his heart. Can he truly walk away, or will true love conquer all?

Hair Out of Place is a steamy, standalone MM romance novel featuring inconvenient bed sharing, romantic home cooking, possibly the worst assassins in the world, really long hair, and one fierce kitty. This book has guaranteed HEA with absolutely no cheating and no cliffhanger.

Click here to get the Hair Out of Place eBook

Hair Out of Place audio – coming soon!

A Right Royal Affair

Theo Glass used to believe that love was just a fairy tale. Orphaned and disowned by his homophobic step-family, he and his grandma make ends meet as best they can. But when his grandma's tireless charity work is honoured, Theo makes sure he spends his last pennies to get her to the palace, hosted by none other than the gorgeous Prince James himself.

James is sixth in line to the throne of the United Kingdom and a disappointment to just about everyone. He never felt at home at school, on the rugby pitch, or even in the Army. Being royalty means he's been forced to keep a lid on his bisexuality. But when he meets Theo at the honours ceremony, he knows he's in serious trouble.

Needing to find purpose, James convinces Theo to use his charity event savvy to throw a fundraiser ball in a secluded castle. All James has to do is behave himself around the sassy twink. But soon the chemistry between them is too strong to resist.

Their lives are too different and there's no chance James can come out as the first Prince of the United Kingdom with a boyfriend. But James knows if he doesn't show Theo how much he means to him, he'll lose him forever. Can love conquer all? Or is that something just for fairy tales?

A Right Royal Affair is a steamy, standalone MM romance novel featuring a pack of unruly royal terriers, a romantic ball, feisty swans, a wicked step-father and a guaranteed HEA with absolutely no cliffhanger.

Click here to get the A Right Royal Affair eBook

Click here to get the A Right Royal Affair audio

featuring a match-making Labrador, too much pizza, just the right amount of sofa snuggles, and a guaranteed HEA with absolutely no cliffhanger.

Click here to get the Rise and Shine eBook

Click here to get the Rise and Shine audio

ABOUT THE AUTHOR

Helen Juliet is a contemporary MM romance author living in London with her husband and two balls of fluff that occasionally pretend to be cats. She began writing at an early age, later honing her craft online in the world of fanfiction on sites like Wattpad. Fifteen years and over a million words later, she sought out original MM novels to read. By the end of 2016 she had written her first book of her own, and in 2017 she achieved her lifelong dream of becoming a fulltime author.

Helen also writes contemporary American MM romance as HJ Welch.

You can contact Helen Juliet via social media:
Newsletter (with FREE original stories) – https://www.subscribepage.com/helenjuliet
Website – www.helenjuliet.com
Facebook Group – Helen's Jewels
Facebook Page – @helenjulietauthor
Instagram – @helenjwrites
Twitter – @helenjwrites